The Ticket

The Ticket

Cecilia Wichmann

Publisher: Wichmann & Co, LLC

Wills Point, TX, USA

hello@wichmannandco.com | www.wichmannandco.com

ISBN (paperback): 979-8-9934623-0-1

ISBN (ebook): 979-8-9934623-1-8

First edition, November 2025

Printed in the United States of America

For my late mother, **Pia Wichmann**, who taught me to play. *"If you do not play, you will not win."* Every page began with your voice.

I never pictured myself as an author, yet here we are. If you know me, my mind is a busy workshop of ideas and projects, a gift I carry from my mom. Her line kept me brave while I wrote: "If you don't play, you won't win." This story grew from the dare to try. It is also a little manifestation, a wink at the day a ticket might change everything, Powerball or Mega Millions, who knows.

To everyone who has steadied me, cheered for me, and asked with a smile, "What is she up to now?" Thank You! Your nudges made me better. I could fill a whole book with your names.

And to you holding this one right now, thank you! Readers turn dreams into work worth doing. I hope Rachel keeps you turning pages, and I hope her courage rubs off. Maybe one day we will trade stories about a very lucky ticket. Until then, keep playing in the best sense of the word. Happy reading!

Cecilia Wichmann

QT Morning

The alarm said six. Rusty said no.

He stretched across the clock and purred into the snooze button until the room went quiet again. When I finally sat up, his whiskers were in my face and the digital numbers had skipped past seven. His pupils were big saucers, very pleased with what he had done to the concept of punctuality.

"Conspiracy," I told him.

He rolled onto his back and presented a belly I had never once been allowed to touch. I took the usual bait, then withdrew my hand with my dignity intact and all my fingers. Coffee. Pants from the chair. The good blouse because it was clean and because hope is a habit. Rusty followed me to the kitchen and took his post on the counter like a foreman. I set his bowl down and he pretended not to care, then inhaled it as if I were late for his reservation.

"I am leaving five minutes earlier tomorrow," I said.

He yawned and blinked once, slow as honey.

Outside, the sky over Wills Point was that washed Texas blue that makes you think the day might behave. It did not. Two cars were half-hugging the shoulder near mile marker 503, hazard lights blinking like bored eyes. A trail of glass winked in the sun and popped under my tires. I turned the radio down, felt my jaw set, and promised myself I would not tell Maya the whole saga again about how if I left five minutes earlier none of this would happen. I would, and we both knew it.

The red Kia Soul had a new rattle, a little tin can percussion some-where under the dash. The gas light glowed a soft, accusing amber. I pulled off at the next exit and rolled into the QT in Terrell where the flags on the roof line never looked new or old, only tired. Two pumps were bagged with Out of Order signs. One of the air hoses coiled like a dead snake. I parked by the pump closest to the entrance and set the nozzle.

Fuel smell has a way of cutting straight through whatever thoughts you tell yourself to have. The numbers ticked. I watched the little black ants work at a crack in the concrete and wondered where they thought they were going in such a hurry. A breeze worked the prayer flyers on the bulletin board by the door. Missing cat, half-off auto detail with a Bible verse in the corner, casserole sale at the church on Saturday. And in the window, the red and blue lottery sign that changes by itself like a heart-beat: Powerball, estimated jackpot one point five billion dollars. Fourth largest in history.

I looked at the number. The number looked back.

Inside, the QT was cold in the particular way of a convenience store that keeps colder in summer because the cool feels like a product. The clerk was a broad-shouldered man with a tattoo of a sparrow on one knuckle, eyes kind, boredom professional. A teenager stood at the counter counting coins for an energy drink. A woman in scrubs stared into the coffee urn like it might answer for something.

I grabbed a large pineapple sweet tea and two taquitos to quiet my rumbling stomach. My feet did not take me to the lottery counter. They were very responsible feet. They took me to the register, to the small talk about heat and traffic and the wreck by mile marker 506. The clerk nod-ded like he had heard all of it twice already.

"Anything else?"

The sign glowed at my right shoulder. Almost two billion dollars... Numbers that sound like someone else's life.

I could hear Rusty's trill in my head, the sound he makes when he approves of a decision. I could also hear my father, half joke and half warning. Money only shows you more of yourself. Which would be fine if I knew exactly who that was.

"One Powerball with Power Play, please," I said, like it was a normal sentence I said all the time.

The clerk did not blink. "Quick Pick or your numbers?"

"Quick Pick."

He tapped the keys. The machine chirped. My cup left a cold ring on the counter. Behind me the door chimed and a sun-beaten man in a feed cap walked in and went straight for the jerky like he had been thinking about it since dawn. The clerk slid the ticket across the counter along with my receipt.

"Good luck," he said with the dry tone of a man who says good luck three hundred times a week. He might have meant it. He might have not. It landed either way.

The ticket was warm from the printer. Not heavy. Not special. It was just paper with ink and a string of numbers that had almost nothing to do with me. Almost.

Back at the pump, the handle clicked. I tucked the ticket behind my debit card in my wallet, then tucked the wallet into the zippered pocket of my purse, then zipped the purse and set it on the passenger seat where I could see it. I watched my own hand do all that as if it belonged to someone else. I told myself out loud that I was not that person who buys lottery tickets. I was a person who bought a lottery ticket once, on a Thursday, because the sign was bright and my Kia rattled and the world felt like it owed me a surprise that was not a dented bumper.

On I-20 the traffic stacked and unstacked in slow motion. I kept my eyes on the lane lines and my mind on the small things I could control. Lunch in the bag. A decent playlist. The way the sun on the crape myrtles along the access road made them look like they were lit from inside. The thought slipped in of Florida, the way it always did when the sky went big. Not just beaches. Land with live oaks and a fence line. A porch where I could hear my own breath.

By the time I pulled into MetroCare Support, the parking lot was already full. I slid into the back row by the dumpster and jogged inside with my badge held out like an apology.

"Morning," Maya said as I dropped into my chair. "You are glowing."

"That is speed sweat." I logged in and put on my headset. The first call of the day was a man who had been on hold for twelve minutes and had measured each of them with a stopwatch.

"Thank you for calling MetroCare Support. This is Rachel. How can I help you?"

He did not believe me at first. They rarely do. I pulled up his account and fixed the simple thing that had been making his life hard. When he exhaled, I felt my shoulders drop with him. It is a small power, but it is real.

By ten, the room smelled like burnt coffee and lemon cleaner. Brandi was telling anyone who would listen that she had eaten at the new barbecue place over the weekend and the sauce tasted like regret. On the far wall a television cycled weather, traffic, and headlines nobody read. The sound was off. The closed captions chased the anchors like they were a step behind on purpose. Every few minutes, the red and blue lottery logo bloomed in the corner of the screen and the caption caught up with the number. One point eight billion.

"You see that?" Maya said, following my eyes.

"I see it."

"What would you do with that kind of money?"

It was the kind of question people ask to shape the air. I said the kind of things people say. Pay off the house. Fix the Kia. Cover my parents for a while so they could breathe deep without watching the mailbox. Then I let the truth peek out, the one that sits under my ribs and hums.

"Florida," I said. "Land, not a condo. Trees that make their own shade. A porch big enough for Thanksgiving and a piano that does not have to live against a wall."

Maya smiled like she could see it too. "A better coffee maker for the break room. I would buy this place a coffee maker that does not sound like it is chewing gravel."

A call lit up my screen. The next caller had a problem with a payment portal that did not like his zip code. I smoothed it out and told him what would happen next so he would not have to guess. He said, Thank you, sincerely, and I felt the solid click in my chest that reminded me why I am good at this. I can make a stranger's day one notch easier. It is not glamorous. It is not nothing.

On my break I stepped outside to the thin strip of shade by the smokers and texted my parents in Houston a picture of Rusty sitting like a loaf on the windowsill. My mother sent a heart. My father sent a joke about how that cat had better pay rent. I typed, Someday he will, and surprised myself by believing it for a breath longer than a joke.

"Florida," I said out loud, just to taste it.

I opened TikTok and my feed turned into a lottery school. Numerology. Dream charts. People who swear by birthdays. People who swear by Quick Picks. People preach rules if you win: sign the ticket, take photos, call a lawyer, build a trust, tell no one. I took mental notes like a student and then reminded myself about the odds. They were a cliff. I shut the app and went back to work.

Back inside, I pulled open the bottom drawer of my desk and took a sip from the pineapple sweet tea I had brought in from QT. The ticket lived for the moment behind my debit card. I thought about moving it to my pocket, then thought about the way pockets betray you when you need them to be perfect. I left it where it was and closed the drawer like that would help. I wondered why I was so obsessed with this ticket. I never buy tickets, but this time was different.

At lunch, Maya and I ate in my car because the break room smelled like onions that had lost a fight. We watched people come and go, each with their own version of the day. A man in a suit and running shoes, late. A woman with a stroller who overshot the curb and laughed at herself. Brandi hurried to her car, keys already in her hand like they were a solution she could hold.

"Travis called me twice last night," I said, mostly to say it out loud. "I did not pick up."

"Does he know why?"

"He knows and he does not. He likes me right where I am."

Maya nodded in that way where she is not taking a side because she knows I already have.

"If you won," she said, and she meant it as an exercise, "what is the first thing you would buy that is not responsible?"

"A ticket to a Cody Rigsby show," I said, fast. "Front row. He would point at me during the chorus and I would believe he meant it."

She laughed. Then we sat with the idea, not touching it too hard. It was a warm stone that felt good in the hand and did not need to be thrown.

The afternoon slid into its usual rhythm, calls like beads on a string. A mother who could not get her app to add her child to the account. A man who forgot his password and his backup and the email he used to set both. An elderly woman who thought she was calling 911, and I stayed with her long enough to make sure she landed where she needed to land. When the line clicked over and the operator took her, I sat for a second with my hands flat on the desk.

On the wall, the television flashed the lottery logo again and a reporter with serious hair moved his mouth about the odds. The caption tried to capture the math. I did not read it.

At four thirty, the office buzz shifted as it always does when people start counting minutes. Brandi told the room that a big winner from years ago had lost it all on bad real estate and worse cousins. Someone else said a woman had hidden her ticket behind a loose brick in her kitchen and her contractor found it and there had been a lawsuit that ate half the money. People love the edges of other people's fortune.

I kept my eyes on my screen. I knew the odds in a way that was not factual. I knew them like you know the odds of rain in a sky that looks like a yes and behaves like a no. You take an umbrella. You also wear sandals.

When the day finally let go of us, I drove home without stopping. The sun hung low and mean in my rearview and I felt that particular kind of tiredness where your muscles remember the shape of your chair. I unlocked the door and Rusty greeted me with a chirp that sounded like a question and a greeting and a reprimand for being late.

"I brought home a moral dilemma," I told him.

He trotted ahead of me to the kitchen and jumped to his spot on the counter. I set my purse down where I could see it and took the pineapple sweet tea from the bag. The house had that quiet of late afternoon that makes you hear the refrigerator like it is a person in the next room. I opened the purse, opened my wallet, and looked at the ticket. There it was, exactly as printed, ink black and calm.

"Level with me, Rusty," I said. "Is this the kind of impulse that ruins people?"

Rusty blinked once, slow and deliberate. He wrapped his tail around his paws and sat like he was presiding.

"Right," I said. "Depends on the person."

I slid the ticket back into the wallet. Then I did a thing that would have made no sense to anyone who has never lived with my grandmother's rules. I took her old Bible from the china cabinet and opened it to the presentation page with my name written in her hand. I set the wallet on the counter and cut a piece of parchment paper to size. The ticket sat between the pages, not stuck, only held. It looked ridiculous. It looked right.

Rusty rose and touched the corner of the Bible with one paw like a notary seal.

"We are not telling anyone," I said. "Not Maya. Not Travis. Not anyone."

He was thrilled, and the verdict was delivered.

I pushed the Bible back on the shelf behind the glass. I stood there longer than I needed to, then closed the cabinet and checked the latch.

The evening folded itself into small chores. Leftovers warmed. A show that did not require attention hummed from the television. Rusty chased a fly with morose dignity and missed it every time. I showered the day off and put on the soft T-shirt from a music festival that had promised to change my life and had mostly changed my feet.

When I sat with a cup of tea at the table, the silence felt larger than usual. I let it be. The red Kia sat under the streetlight with bug dust on the windshield, a tired soldier who still showed up. My phone face down on the table stayed politely quiet. My mind did the math with itself, a tug of war between what I knew and what I wanted to be true. I pictured my parents sitting on the back porch in Houston, the way my mother tucked her feet under her when she talked about old friends, the way my father never let a bill sit untouched if he could help it. I pictured my own porch, not yet real, with a view of trees and a line of fence where nothing needed to be said.

"*If* it happened," I said to Rusty, because it felt safer than saying if I won, "we would keep our heads. We would do it right."

He hopped up and curled in the chair across from me like a small, polite person who had paid for his ticket to the show and did not plan to cause trouble.

"First thing, responsible," I said. "House, parents, tires. Second thing, something that is mine because I want it. A front row seat and a night where I am not worried about what comes next. Florida, but the quiet part. No jet skis. Not yet."

Rusty nodded off with his eyes half closed. I took that as assent.

At ten, I stood in front of the cabinet again. I checked the latch again. I told myself to let it go. I told myself I would sleep like I always do, the solid sleep of a person whose dreams are clear enough to see and far enough away that they do not wake you up.

"Tomorrow," I told Rusty. "I am leaving five minutes earlier."

He made the soft sound he makes when he is almost asleep and does not want to agree out loud.

I turned off the lights and the house went into its night shape. In bed, the air felt lighter than it had in a long while, like the ceiling had lifted half an inch. I did not pick up my phone. I did not look up odds or stories or advice. I did not think about how many tickets had already been printed that day, how many hands had held them and put them in pockets or glove boxes or junk drawers. I thought about the sign in the QT window, the way the number looked like it knew something about me I did not yet know about myself.

I thought about the way the clerk had said good luck like it was a blessing for people who needed it and a little joke for people who did not. I thought about Maya, Travis, and my parents. I thought about Florida, and trees that make their own shade.

Sleep came on like a tide. Rusty took the spot at my feet that is his by ancient right. The house settled and the refrigerator clicked and the distant sound of the highway ran like a river you do not have to cross yet.

In the morning, the number in the QT window would be the same.

For now, it was only a ticket in a book and a woman in a bed, and a cat who believed in rules when it suited him.

Kaufman County Morning

Rusty woke me before the alarm with a paw to the cheek and an opinion about breakfast. The phone on my nightstand lit the room in a hard white blink. A text from Travis sat on the lock screen, then another, and another.

TRAVIS: Why did you not answer the other day

TRAVIS: Are you ignoring me now?

TRAVIS: This is getting old Rachel

I stared at his name until it blurred. Rusty chirped and headbutted my chin like he was trying to knock the decision loose.

"We will write to him after coffee," I said. My voice did not sound convincing.

I told myself I would leave five minutes early. Then I lost seven minutes looking for the other shoe and five feeding Rusty twice because he convinced me I had not fed him the first time. The TV stayed dark. The little red light on the edge of the screen looked like an eye that could keep a secret.

The kitchen felt quiet, like a clean sheet on a hot night. I poured coffee, grabbed the lunch I had packed, and counted back from ten for no good reason. Rusty sat on the counter, hiding my keys until I scratched the right spot behind his ear.

The clock owned the room. I was late. Again.

In the Kia, the air conditioner coughed and then remembered its purpose. I pulled onto I-20 and braced for the usual crawl. It did not come. The highway moved like a river with somewhere good to be. I let the radio fill the car because I did not want to think about what to text Travis or what to do with a relationship that felt like a plant that would not bloom no matter how often you turned it toward the light.

The morning host bantered about school zones and a barbecue place that had run out of brisket by noon. Then the traffic guy with a calm voice came on and read the list of lanes to avoid. When he finished, the news reader took over.

"State lottery officials confirm the winning Powerball ticket was sold in Kaufman County. The store name has not yet been released."

I did not breathe for a count of three. The steering wheel under my palms went warmer. The road did its moving picture trick, trees, fence, sky, repeat.

Kaufman County. I lived in Van Zandt. I worked in Kaufman. I bought the ticket at QT in Terrell because the Kia had been thirsty and my stomach had said taquitos. I knew all of that. I also knew the ticket was at home, in the Bible, where I could not check it without turning the car around and making my life suspicious.

"We do not know anything yet," I told the empty passenger seat. Rusty would have answered. The seat only held my purse and the ghost of a pineapple sweet tea.

By the time I pulled into MetroCare Support, the parking lot buzzed like a hive. People walked faster than usual. Phones were up. The television inside was already tuned to the local morning show with the smiling anchors who could talk about anything and make it sound like a neighborly emergency.

Maya met me at my desk with both eyebrows raised. "Did you hear? Kaufman County."

"I heard." I put my bag down and pretended to look for my headset.

Brandi leaned over our divider like a plant that would not respect a fence. "My cousin says it was sold in Terrell. She knows a guy who knows a guy at a store."

"Your cousin also knew the end of that reality show before it aired because her neighbor's hairdresser had a dream," Maya said.

Brandi made a face and flounced away with her mug.

I logged in. The first caller had been locked out of his account because he fat-fingered his password and then guessed his recovery questions wrong. I talked him through the reset and listened for the moment when his breathing eased.

The TV on the wall flashed aerial footage of highways and shopping centers. The crawl at the bottom of the screen repeated itself like a mantra. Winning ticket. Kaufman County. Store not yet named. Someone would be calling a lawyer today. Someone would be standing in a kitchen holding a piece of paper that looked like nothing and everything.

My phone buzzed on the desk. I turned it face down. It buzzed again and I gave in.

MOM: Did you buy a ticket yesterday?

MOM: News says the winner is from your area. Your father is already talking about what we would do. I said we would tithe first.

DAD: If I win I am fixing the fence and the A/C and buying your mother a new recliner. Also we are going to Galveston for a week. Do not tell your brother I said that.

MOM: He would tell your brother.

I smiled and the smile surprised me. I typed back slowly so I would not say more than I meant to say.

ME: I did buy one. Lots of people did. We will see. Love you both. I'm working now.

I did not add that the ticket lived at home in a book behind glass. I did not add that my heart felt like a bird that had found a window.

The calls stacked. I handled them one by one. A woman cried because the system would not accept her card and I stayed with her until it did. A man told me he had been up all night with a sick kid and needed one thing to work and I made sure it worked. Small power. Real power. Under it, a humming wire I could not ignore.

At ten, a push alert lit my phone.

Breaking: Reporters gathering at a QT in Terrell after officials confirm the winning ticket was sold there.

Maya saw me go still. "What is it?"

I turned the screen so she could read it. She let out a low whistle. "That is your stop, right?"

"I mean, it is where I fuel up. Lots of people use that exit." My voice did not sound like mine. It sounded like a person trying to keep a balloon from floating to the ceiling.

Brandi appeared with her phone already playing a live stream. A reporter in a bright blazer stood with the QT in the background, red and white sign over her shoulder, a mop bucket gliding past like an extra who had not been told to hold.

"They say a single ticket hit it," Brandi said. "Can you imagine?"

I imagined a hundred ways to leave my chair and drive home. I imagined staying where I was and finishing my shift like a grown woman with a job. I chose the second picture and clicked back into a call.

Travis texted again while I was on hold with a vendor.

TRAVIS: So now you are not talking to me at all?

TRAVIS: I thought we were good

TRAVIS: Can you at least tell me what I did wrong?

I typed three messages and deleted them all. The truth was, not a single thing he did was wrong. It was a long series of not doing. It was the space between us that had become a fact. I put the phone in the drawer with the pineapple cup. I closed the drawer and stacked my hands on the desk like a person who knew her life.

By noon, the anchors had cycled through every way to say the same sentence. QT in Terrell. Kaufman County. The winner has not come forward. Odds of winning are one in something so large it does not fit in your mouth. The camera found the counter where I had stood with my cup ring and my ridiculous hope.

Maya slid a napkin onto my desk like a bartender in a movie. "Eat."

"I am fine." I answered.

"Eat anyway."

I bit a corner of my sandwich and tasted nothing. I told myself stories so I would not float off the chair. There had to be hundreds of tickets sold there. Thousands even. People on their way to Dallas. People who commute from Forney and Terrell and Crandall. People like me, people not like me. I added facts until they felt like sandbags.

At two, my mother again.

MOM: Your father says he would buy you a better car first thing. He is asking if you bought QT or Brookshire's.

ME: QT, but Mom, odds. I have to work. Love you.

MOM: Love you more.

DAD: Ford Expedition. White. With the big screen. Just saying.

The room hummed. The afternoon calls had that tired edge where the smallest problem feels like a personal insult. I took them one by one. I thanked people for their patience even when they had none. I listened more than I spoke and when I spoke I made sure every word did work.

By four, the live truck shot looked sunburned. The reporter's hair had lost the morning's fight with humidity. A little crowd had gathered at the edge of the frame, half curious and half hoping luck could rub off on them if they stood by the right door long enough. Someone held a sign that said Lucky Day in marker on a pizza box lid.

My supervisor asked if I could stay an extra thirty minutes to cover a late lunch break. I said yes because that is the woman I have always been. The choice felt small and it felt right.

When I finally clocked out, the sun had gone to the side of the building where it makes the lobby look like a fish tank. My phone pinged with a city alert about lane closures on eastbound I-20. Construction at the split, expect delays.

Of course.

The radio still talked about the winner like they knew them. They did not. The highway turned into a single slow breath. Orange barrels lined the shoulder like a parade nobody wanted. Brake lights stacked from the curve to the horizon. The Kia idled and the air conditioner tried and failed and tried again.

I counted exit signs like prayers. I let trucks merge. I let a woman with a dog the color of Rusty cut in front of me and I wanted to take that as a sign but I did not let myself. I stayed in my lane. My hands did not shake, not really. My thoughts moved in a circle. Store, county, ticket, Bible, door.

Travis called. I let it ring out. Then he called again and I let it ring again. The third time I turned the phone off and looked at the line of taillights and told myself I would give him an answer he could understand when I had one I could live with.

The sky deepened to a softer blue. Streetlights blinked to life one by one. When the worst of the jam broke and I rolled past the construction, I wanted to cheer for the men in vests with their slow signs and their patience. I wanted to pull into the shoulder and run. I did not.

Home smelled like air that had been sleeping. Rusty met me at the door with a trill and a look that said I had clearly missed dinner by a criminal margin.

"You would not believe the day," I told him. "Or you would because you believe everything I tell you."

He trotted to the kitchen and took his seat on the counter like a judge who had been waiting for court to resume.

I set my purse on the table where I could see it. I filled his bowl and he pretended not to care and then inhaled it. The house was quiet in the way it gets when the refrigerator is the loudest thing alive. I washed my hands. I dried them. I stood in front of the china cabinet.

The glass showed me a reflection I wanted to recognize. Tired eyes. A line at the corner of my mouth I had not noticed last week. Rusty's tail was like a question mark at my knee.

"We are going to open it," I said. My voice sounded steady.

I placed both palms on the cabinet doors and felt the cool of the glass. I thought about the live truck outside the QT. I thought about my mother's text and my father's list. I thought about Travis and the plant that would not bloom. I thought about Florida and the porch and the piano that did not have to live against a wall. I opened the cabinet.

Friday Honey & Saturday Night

The anchors on TV had said it enough times that the words floated through the house even with the set turned off. Powerball drawings are on Wednesday nights. By the time I closed the cabinet and washed my hands, Thursday had worn itself thin. The street outside was quiet. Rusty followed me to the kitchen and took his spot on the counter like a witness for the record.

"Moment of truth," I told him. "No speeches."

He trilled once and tucked his paws like a small judge.

I opened the china cabinet, lifted my grandmother's Bible, and slid out the ticket wrapped in parchment. The paper felt warm from my hands. My heart did what it does when a siren passes and you do not know if it is for someone you love.

I pulled up the winning numbers on my phone. Then I read the ticket like a recipe. First number. Second. Third. The fourth almost broke my breath. The fifth took the rest. The red ball matched.

The refrigerator hummed. The clock on the stove kept on being a clock. Rusty stretched and tapped the corner of the parchment with one neat paw.

"It is us," I said. The words came out soft and careful, like picking up glass.

I set the ticket on the counter and leaned my hips against the cabinet until my knees remembered what to do. Then I sat on the couch and let my hands learn stillness again. I did not run. I did not shout. I breathed until my breath came back.

The list from my late night TikTok schooling ran through my head in order. Photograph the front. Photograph the back. Sign only when ready. Add ID for your files. Selfie if you must. Save the files somewhere that does not live on the cloud.

"We are doing this by the book," I told Rusty. Trying to realize what just happened.

I signed the back in my neatest hand. I took a photo of the front. I took a photo of the back. I took one with my driver's license beside the ticket. One with my face because nerves wanted proof. I airdropped every photo to the old laptop that never goes anywhere. I copied them to a thumb drive that has lived in a drawer for years. I emailed nothing. I posted nothing. I breathed again.

Then I downloaded the Texas Lottery app because I wanted a machine to tell me what my eyes already knew. The app opened with a cheerful chime and a scan button. I held the bar-code over the little box on the screen. The phone buzzed in my hand.

Winner. The screen filled with numbers and words that did not all make sense to me. It told me to contact the Lottery Commission for claims. It showed an amount I could not hold in my head, then hid it behind instructions like it was trying not to scare anyone.

"Confirmed," I said to Rusty. "Twice."

He blinked, verdict noted.

I made tea for my shaking hands and forgot to drink it. I opened the calculator on my phone and started turning a mountain into smaller hills. The news called it one point eight billion dollars. If I took the cash option, the amount would be much lower. Call it nine hundred million to make the math honest and simple. Federal withholding would take twenty four percent right away. That's about two hundred and twenty million. The top rate at tax time would want more. Another hundred million or so. None of this would be real until a person with letters after their name wrote it on paper, but I needed round figures to put the floor under my feet.

Five hundred and sixty minus a hundred. Four sixty. Four sixty minus another fifty. About four hundred and ten. Give or take. Enough to build a life and not set it on fire.

"Rules," I said. "We write them down. We keep them."

I opened a fresh page in a small notebook. Real things first. Pay rent for six months so I could think straight. New tires for the Kia even if I replaced the Kia later. A cooling unit that did not cough before it worked. Quiet help for my parents disguised as something boring. A reserve before dreams. No cameras. No interviews. No boats.

Dreams could stand in the doorway and wait their turn. House in Florida. Not the tourist parts. Land and shade from trees that have seen things. A porch big enough for a long table. Music nights where no one has to shout. A fund I could use to fix one private problem a month. Someone's roof. Someone's bill. No speeches. My grandmother's name on scholarships for girls who work hard and vanish under the noise.

I opened a manila folder and wrote Florida Quiet Plan across the tab. I slid the first page of rules inside along with a list of names I might someday help. Then I made a matching folder on the old laptop called Florida Plan and left it empty on purpose. I put the manila folder in the locked drawer with the thumb drive and closed it.

Travis took his place in the line of thoughts. Not a villain. Not my future. Kind eyes and a way of avoiding decisions that made my days feel small. I opened our thread and typed what was true.

Can we talk? In person.

He answered quickly.

TRAVIS: Yes. Saturday evening?

ME: Seven at the park.

I turned the phone face down and felt a line of relief cut through the fog. Clarity is a kindness even when it stings.

Sleep did not visit much. I lay in the dark and watched the ceiling fan draw circles. When I closed my eyes, I saw the QT sign and the reporter's jacket and the string of numbers lined up like houses. I checked the cabinet once, then twice, then told myself out loud to stop because obsession is not the same thing as care.

Friday tried to look like any other day. I drove the Kia to MetroCare, swiped in, and put on my headset. I was a body in a chair and a brain in a cabinet at home. Twice I ended a ticket without the right note and had to backtrack while the caller breathed into my ear.

Maya watched me for one call, two calls, then slid a sticky note onto my keyboard.

You are not here.

I wrote back: Travis. She nodded, the way a friend gives you a little privacy without leaving you alone.

Brandi hovered with fresh gossip about the QT and who she thought the winner might be. On the lobby TV the live truck was still parked under that red and white sign, a reporter talking to people who had bought coffee and luck in the same place. I kept my face neutral and blamed the faraway look on "Travis and I need to talk this weekend." It was true enough to pass.

At lunch, I sat in my car with the air on low and stared at the dash clock until it meant nothing. My phone buzzed with three messages I did not open. My parents texted like they do when the news is loud.

MOM: You coming next weekend or the one after? Dad says he will grill if it is not one hundred degrees.

ME: Next weekend, I think. Love you both.

DAD: Bring Rusty. I want to see if he likes baseball.

I told myself to breathe, to do the next helpful thing, to sound like myself.

By mid-afternoon I had my rhythm back enough to be useful. I fixed a password. I calmed a man who was sure the system hated him. I thanked a grandmother for her patience and meant it. The QT segment looped again and I kept my eyes on the work in front of me.

When Friday finally gave up and evening came on, I did something I have not done in years. I turned all my alarms off. Saturday would not need me at a desk. Saturday could come in on its own feet.

I slept the kind of sleep that lives in layers. I woke once and checked the cabinet. I woke again because Rusty sat on my chest like a paperweight with whiskers and I owed him breakfast. The sky outside the blinds was soft and kind. Weekend air. No clock.

I made tea and sat on the couch and let the quiet tell me it was safe to think bigger than bills. Florida was a shape I could almost draw now. Not a mansion. Not a show. A place with live oaks and a fence line. A small barn that smells like clean hay. A piano that does not have to apologize. I let myself picture friends at a long table and the noise that good people make when they do not hurry.

I checked the Bible because that is who I am. The ticket was there. The page with my name looked like a promise I could keep.

I opened the old laptop and turned the Wi-Fi on just long enough to search two things, then turned it back off. Texas lottery lawyer anonymous claim. Fee-only fiduciary sudden wealth advisor Texas. I scrolled past the ads and the scare stories.

A short article caught my eye from an attorney in Dallas named Margaret Hall. It was plain talk about how to claim quietly, why you form a trust first, how to keep your name out of places where names like to live too long. The checklist matched the one in my head. I copied her number into the notebook and wrote, Ms. Hall, attorney, claims and trusts.

Then I found a small site with no confetti and no promises. Mr. Whitlow Wealth Counsel, Dallas. The page said fee-only fiduciary in the first line. No commissions. Credentials I could look up. CFP, CPA. It listed the work they do when money arrives all at once. Lottery winners. Oil and gas. Injury settlements. A few old press quotes about sudden wealth and how to make it boring on purpose. There was one sentence that felt like a handrail. Our job is to keep your money boring so your life can be free.

That sold me. I wrote his name under Ms. Hall's. Mr. Whitlow, fiduciary advisor, sudden wealth. I printed the contact page to a PDF, dropped it on the old laptop's desktop, and put the phone number in the notebook instead of my contacts. No email. No forms. A call on Monday from a quiet place would do.

By Saturday afternoon I had a short list and calm hands. Lawyer first on Monday. Mr. Whitlow next. No changes to my routine in public. No car shopping. No sudden generosity that teaches the wrong lesson. I put the list in the drawer with the thumb drive and the Florida folder and closed the drawer.

I put on clean sneakers and a shirt that makes me feel like I know what I am doing. I locked the door and drove to the park.

I parked by the oak with the bench and watched Travis walk toward me from the lot. He looked the same as yesterday and last month and the day we met. Kind eyes. Good hands. A way of smiling that had always felt like a safe place and a locked door.

"Hey," he said.

"Hey."

We sat. The air smelled like cut grass and a little rain somewhere else. A kid rolled past on a bike with a baseball card clipped to the spokes and it made a sound like an old motor trying to start. We had not seen each other in weeks without meaning to make it that long. The space had grown on its own like a thing that thrives without water.

Travis rubbed his jaw and looked at the pond.

"I am sorry about the other night. I have been a mess with shifts. The gas station keeps cutting hours. Then they call me in and I go. I know it looks like I am not trying. I am trying."

"I know you are trying," I said. "I also know I cannot be the only engine running all the time."

He nodded like he had rehearsed that agreement with himself. His phone lit up in his pocket. He silenced it without looking. I watched the small move and filed it away.

"I do want to talk to you about something," he said. He took a breath like a swimmer about to push off the wall. "I would not ask if it was not serious. I am in a bind. It is temporary. I can pay you back in a month or two."

There it was. The story walked in wearing a clean shirt.

"What kind of bind?"

"My truck needs a transmission. I am behind on rent. They moved the due date up without telling me and I am short. I can pick up more shifts if I get the truck back on the road. I just need to bridge it. I am embarrassed to ask."

It was almost believable because parts of it were true. The truck had coughed through September. The station had cut hours. The rent story had the sound of something borrowed.

"How much?"

He gave me a number that could fix a truck or keep a door open for a month. Not small. Not enormous. The kind of number that fits in a glove box and a story.

I let the silence sit between us so I could hear it. My gut made its quiet case. I thought of the shampoo that was not mine in his bathroom last month and the bobby pin that had no history with my hair. I thought of the way he had started to keep his phone face down. I thought of the woman at the register the last time I stopped by his station who had called him Trav in a way that felt older than small talk.

"I cannot help right now," I said. "I am sorry you are in a tight spot. My own budget is not in a place where I can float anything."

He nodded like he had prepared for no and hoped for yes. "I get it. I just thought I would ask. I will figure it out."

We let the conversation change lanes by agreement. We walked the loop. He told me about a kid who comes into the station for a fountain drink and calls every flavor by a different city. He told the story well and I let myself laugh because the picture was good. The light went soft and the cicadas tuned up and the park felt like the kind of place where people turned back toward each other.

At the edge of the lot he touched my hand. It was not dramatic. It was steady and familiar and I felt the years in it. We stood there a moment and the quiet did the rest. When he asked if I wanted to come over for a little while, I said yes. I did not owe him that yes. I gave it to myself.

His apartment smelled like laundry soap and a cologne he wears when he tries. The living room was picked up but not clean. A glass sat on the coffee table with a ring under it. A hair tie rested on the arm of the couch. The kind with the little metal clasp. Not mine. I let the detail pass through me and did not give it a home.

We talked for a while about nothing that mattered. The game. A neighbor who feeds stray cats. A story about a customer who brought him a pie and called him sweetheart. He kept looking at me like I had stepped out of a picture and into his room and he was not sure how long I planned to stay.

When he kissed me, I let the thoughts move to the edges of the room and I stood in the center with the part of me that had been quiet too long. The kiss was slow at first, a question. It warmed. It was memorable. My hands found his shoulders and he pulled me closer and the old rhythm woke up.

He is not the man I will build a life with. He is the man whose hands know my back. There is a difference. I let the difference be.

We did not hurry. We did not talk much. He held my face like it mattered what I was thinking and I held his shirt like I had wanted to feel something that was not worrying. Laughter came once when we bumped the coffee table and nearly lost the glass. Then the kind of quiet that lives inside a room when the world forgets it is there. Warm skin. Breath against my ear. The old map between two people who have walked it before and found the parts that are still beautiful.

I will not write it like a checklist. It was not that kind of night. It was a return to color after a long stretch of gray. It was a song where the chorus lands in your ribs and stays. It was the kind of touch that makes the ceiling higher and the clock kind.

We found our way to the bed. The window was cracked and a draft lifted the curtain like a slow breath. He traced my hair behind my ear and whispered that he had missed me and for a moment I let myself be only a woman who is wanted and not a woman with a secret that could change the temperature of a room.

When it was over, we lay quiet and the quiet did not crowd me. I felt alive and bright at the edges. The feeling did not fix anything. It did not need to. It reminded me I still carry a light that belongs to me.

Next to me Travis had drifted fully asleep. I lifted his hand gently from my hip and tucked the sheet to his shoulder, then found my keys on the dresser. His phone lit again with the same name and a heart. I turned away and let the room keep its secrets.

I sat on the edge of the bed and tied my second shoe. In the bathroom I washed my face and found a mascara I had never seen on the counter. I did not move it. I did not need proof. My gut had already delivered the verdict.

I stood at the door for a second and listened to the night sounds. Distant traffic. Someone walking a dog who refused to hurry. A neighbor's laugh through a wall. I felt proud of myself for the things I had not said and the things I had not done. I had not told him about the ticket. I had not solved his problem with a promise that would only grow a new problem.

I drove home with the windows cracked to let the air cool my face. The highway was almost empty. The world felt possible and mine. Rusty met me at the door with a trill that sounded like welcome and judgment in equal parts.

"I know," I told him. "I know."

He followed me to the cabinet and watched while I checked the latch without opening it. I poured water and drank the whole glass. Then I turned out the kitchen light and the house found its night shape again.

I could still feel the good part of the night in my skin. I kept that part. I let the rest float away. Tomorrow would come and I would keep my circle small and my mouth closed and my rules on the page. I pulled the sheet up and Rusty settled at my feet like a warm stone.

The phone stayed dark on the nightstand. The ticket slept in the book. I slept next to the life I was building and not the one I had left in a quiet apartment with a man who would not be coming with me.

Sunday Clue, Monday Storm

Rusty kneaded the blanket at my feet and purred like a small engine that never quits. The house had the soft sound of a weekend with no alarms. I checked the cabinet because that is who I am. The Bible sat where I left it. The ticket sat where it should. The page with my name in my grandmother's hand looked like a promise I intended to keep.

I made tea and let it go cold while I walked the rooms for no reason. I opened the notebook where I had written my rules and copied them again. I added one more. Small circle. No changes in public. I kept my phone face down until curiosity lifted it.

A text from Travis waited at the top.

TRAVIS: Last night felt good. Thank you for coming by.

ME: You are welcome. I hope you sort things out this week.

He did not answer right away. A minute later I opened TikTok out of habit and closed it when the noise felt like sand in my ears. I set the phone down and lasted ten whole minutes. Then I opened Venmo because I am human and because sometimes people forget everyone can see things there if they do not change the setting.

Travis's feed was public. The last few payments were pizza slices and gas money and one to a woman I did not know. Bex J. with a lightning emoji. The note said utilities. The same name again three days earlier with rent and a smile I did not recognize. Another small line of writing said thanks baby on her side. I stared until the letters felt like ink on my own hand.

I did not take a screenshot. I did not call him. I did not change the story I had chosen for us. My gut had delivered its verdict already. This was a supporting exhibit, not the case itself.

I called my parents after their online church was over. Dad talked about changing the oil on the Buick, a porch light that keeps flickering, and how Mr. Alvarez down the block is home from surgery. Mom told me the church is organizing a school supply drive next weekend and asked if I could bring notebooks and crayons. She said Cousin Erica's shower is on the calendar and Aunt Linda wants me to sing harmony if I come. I promised next weekend and felt the promise settle in the good part of my chest.

I sat at the kitchen table with my notebook and wrote a question at the top. If no one had an opinion about my choices and money was not a limit, what would I do?

I answered like no one was watching. I want land with shade, a porch with a long table, work that feels honest. I want time to take care of my parents when they need it. I want to help people one at a time without making a speech. I want music in my week. I want to sleep at night because I am tired from the right things.

I listed work ideas without judging them. A small events barn on the future property called Porch-Light where Friday nights are for songs and stories. A tiny consulting shop that teaches local businesses how to answer the phone like a human and set up simple help desks. A weekend market on the land with vendors from town and a stage for new writers. A fund that fixes one quiet problem a month. Foster cats until they find homes. None of it flashy. All of it steady.

I wrote a second list called Standards. Keep promises. Pay people on time. Close on Sundays. No debts I don't understand. No partners I don't trust. Start small and build slow. Protect the quiet.

I wrote what I will not do. I will not brag. I will not rush. I will not apologize for wanting a big life that looks simple from the road.

When the lists were done, I dated the page and closed the notebook. I checked the cabinet one more time because that is who I am and then told myself to stop. The ticket was safe. The plan could wait its turn.

The sun went down. I packed my lunch for Monday out of habit. I placed my badge by the door. I slept with the kind of rest that comes when you have decided one true thing and let it stand.

Monday looked normal if you didn't know where to look. I left five minutes earlier and still arrived right on time because the highway had decided to gift me that. The parking lot at MetroCare was its usual full. The crepe myrtles along the front walk looked like they could not agree on a season. I swiped in and took my seat.

Maya gave me a long look that ended in a small nod. I nodded back. We understood each other without putting anything on the floor.

The morning calls stacked. People had weekends and weekends make systems forget their manners. I was halfway through an address change when the room changed temperature. A current went through the cubes. Heads popped up.

"He is here," Brandi whispered like we were in a library. "Tornado Tom."

Tom Rigsby owns MetroCare. No one calls him Mr. Rigsby. They call him Tornado Tom because he arrives with new rules, standards and procedures that he thinks up on the drive and expects by lunch. He does not always send the email. He trusts the air to carry his thoughts and the rest of us to catch them.

He came through the double doors with his tie loose and a brand new binder under his arm. He clapped twice like a coach calling a time out.

"Morning, team. New identity verification starts right now. Three-step confirmation on every password reset, no exceptions. New call time targets on the board. Two minutes shaved. We will post the script later."

There was no later. There was only the next call and the new line items no one had read yet. The first woman I helped did not have her backup email and I had to bounce her to a secondary queue that did not exist until five minutes ago. She was kind about it. The second caller was not. The third hung up when I had to ask the new security question in a tone of voice that sounded like I did not believe in it.

Across the room, Tom stood at Kendra's desk. Kendra answers to no one and yet somehow answers to him. He leaned on the edge of her cube and smiled in a way that did not belong in a workplace. Everyone calls it a secret. No one is fooled. He touched her elbow and she laughed without laughing. I kept my eyes on my screen and minded my business while the entire floor did the math.

By ten, the new call time target was a joke and an ache. The white board by the break room said Two minutes off average handle, effective today. No one had the new script. Someone had taped a sticky note under the target that said Sure Jan in a handwriting I recognized as Maya's.

At lunch I took my phone and my sandwich to the small strip of shade by the smokers and called the number on the index card under the Florida magnet. It rang twice.

"Mr. Whitlow," a calm voice said.

"Mr. Whitlow, my name is Rachel Mercer. I found your firm last night while searching for a fee only fiduciary who handles sudden wealth. Your site said your job is to keep the money boring so life can be free. I would like your advice about something important and sensitive."

He did not breathe heavily into the line. He did not fill the silence with words that would make the moment about him.

"I am listening." He said

I told him only what I was ready to say. I did not say the numbers. I did not say my name a second time. I said I had a ticket that needed careful handling and a plan before any next step.

"All right," he said. "You are not in a hurry. Everyone else will try to make you feel like you are. That is often the first trap."

I let the words sit.

"Do not tell anyone else," he said. "No purchases that look like a change. Photograph, which you did. Copies, which you did. Put them in two places. Good. Keep the ticket where you have it for now. Lock the doors. If anyone calls you with advice you did not ask for, hang up."

"What about the claim?" I said. My heart started its little drum again just saying the word.

"We will not claim until you have counsel and a trust, if a trust is possible. I can recommend an attorney who has seen this before. You will talk to her first, not to me. I am only a bridge and a list maker. She is the wall and the lock. We will also talk about a CPA and a security consult. For today, you go back to your life and act like you do on any Monday. You call me after work and tell me if you feel safe."

"I am not sure I can trust you," I said. Honesty felt like the only currency that mattered.

"Good," he said without insult. "You should not. Trust is earned. Do three checks before we go any further. Look up Mr. Whitlow Wealth Counsel on the SEC adviser site and read our Form ADV. Call the community credit union where I consult and ask the branch manager to confirm my standing. If you prefer, have an attorney request my fiduciary oath and E and O insurance certificate. Until then, give me no numbers and no last names."

I did not expect to like that answer. But I did. I did not expect it to make me more nervous. It did that too.

"If you want a neutral place, I can reserve a small conference room at a local credit union branch so no one asks questions. Or we can meet at your attorney's office once you choose counsel. Tomorrow, late morning works. Or we can wait."

I watched a truck back past the dumpster and wondered what it would feel like to be a person who moves through a day without the sense that the air is watching.

"Tomorrow is fine," I said. "Late morning." My voice did not shake and I counted that as a victory.

"I will text you an address," he said. "Paper first. Feelings later."

We hung up. I stood there with my phone and my sandwich and the feeling that I had stepped onto the first plank of a new bridge. The old ground was still under my feet and I did not know which way felt safer.

Back inside, Tornado Tom clapped again.

"Heads up," he said. "New wording on the identity question. Ask for the favorite teacher, not the street you grew up on. Legal says teachers are less exposed online. Effective immediately."

No one said that the list of favorite teachers is often shorter than the list of streets and easier to guess. We all thought it together and kept typing. Kendra brought him a coffee with too much sugar and he thanked her like a secret that is not a secret. The white board target did not change and neither did the time it takes to be kind to a person who is struggling with a website.

The room had the hum of controlled panic that call centers know like a weather pattern. Maya passed me a piece of chocolate like a communion. I ate it and felt human again for three bites.

Travis texted a new version of the same story. 'Any chance you could spot me something small. I hate to ask. I am in a bind.' The number he named had grown by a little. I typed and deleted, typed and deleted. I settled on 'I cannot' and sent it without a second sentence. He read it. He did not reply.

My phone buzzed with an unknown number and I let it go to voicemail. A woman's voice said she was from a financial concern and had an opportunity for me to grow my wealth. She used my first name and a tone that suggested she thought she knew me. I deleted the message and blocked the number. I made a note to ask Mr. Whitlow about getting my name off the lists that breed like summer bugs.

At five, the day let go with reluctance. The white board still said two minutes off and the sticky note still said Sure Jan. Tom had left ten minutes earlier with his binder and Kendra's laugh in the hall behind him. I packed my bag and waved at Maya and promised the cake story from my mother when I had the recipe. I walked out into the parking lot and watched the sky try for pink.

The drive home was slow for no reason. People driving their usual stupid way. I didn't turn on the radio. I let the road be noisy enough.

I fed Rusty and checked the cabinet and then closed the cabinet with a hand that did not shake. I took the Florida folder out and slid in a new index card with Mr. Whitlow's name and the address he had texted. I wrote the appointment time and the word bridge because it helped to put the thought on paper.

I stood at the sink and watched the last light leave the street. I felt torn in a way I did not have a word for. Trust no one, the loud videos had said. Trust someone, the quiet ones had whispered. I did not know which voice to give the chair.

Rusty hopped to the counter and sat like a magistrate.

"We start small," I told him. "Paper first. Feelings later."

He blinked once, slowly, and that was the verdict for now.

Paper First, Left Hook

I slept in pieces with the sense that the dark was listening. Rusty stretched at my feet, unimpressed. He did his long-cat routine, spine like a fishing rod, toes spread. I fed him, checked the cabinet out of habit, then told myself to stop. Habit is not safety. Safety is the plan you make and the plan you keep.

Belt pouch. Plain envelope. Two zip-lock bags with taped edges. The ticket, still wrapped in parchment, went against my ribs where my heartbeat could keep me honest. Jacket with no logos. Hair pulled back. Phone set to low power. Notebook and a pen that does not leak.

By ten, I was on I 20 west with the sun on the passenger side and a list in my head that did not try to live beyond three lines. Open the box. Hear the lawyer. Write one next step that can be done today. Trucks moved like large animals who know the route by heart. A billboard promised a roof for less money than the roof cost. I kept the radio off and let the tires hum.

At ten forty, I parked in front of a credit union that looks exactly like a credit union should. Brick that looks the same in every season. Flag quiet on a short pole. Inside, a receptionist with soft hands and a cardigan led me to a small conference room with a table, four chairs, and a framed print of a heron standing in water that looked colder than it had any right to be.

Mr. Whitlow stood when I came in. He looked like his website had promised he might. Early seventies. Clear eyes. Tie knotted like he meant it. A yellow legal pad and a pen that looked used. He did not reach for my hand. He nodded once.

"Rachel," he said. "Thank you for coming."

I sat. My back found the chair. My breath found a steady pace.

"We will do three things," he said. "Open a safe deposit box. Call Attorney Hall so you can hear her voice and decide if you want her. Set a short list for the next two days."

I liked that there were only three. I liked that he did not pretend the list was everything.

He rang the tiny room phone and asked the receptionist to call the vault manager. The manager arrived with the calm of a person who has seen people carry all kinds of paper and jewelry and grief into drawers built into walls. Dual control. Two keys. A small cart with blue felt on top. She did not ask what we would store. She showed me where to sign. She checked my ID like a person who respects their own job.

In the vault, cool air hugged the edges of the metal. The manager inserted her key, I inserted mine, and together we opened a drawer that slid out with a sound that belonged to good hinges. Inside was a plain metal box. Mr. Whitlow set my plain envelope inside with a second plain folder. He wrote today's date on a sticky note and stuck it to the folder's inside lip as if dates are how sanity keeps a calendar.

We closed the box. The manager slid the drawer back. The lock found itself again, and the small heavy sound it made had more comfort in it than I expected. My shoulders lowered when the door shut and the world stayed where it should.

Back in the small room, Mr. Whitlow dialed a number and put the phone on speaker. He did not give the number to me. He did not say the name into the air.

"Ms. Hall, this is Rachel," he said. "The line is clean. We are at the credit union."

The attorney's voice was clear without being loud. "Good morning, Rachel. I will not ask for details on this line. Here is what I need today. Your comfort level, your questions, and your sense of timeline."

"Comfort level is cautious," I said. "Questions are about privacy and pace. Timeline is soon, but not frantic."

"That tells me enough to begin," she said. "If you work with me, first I will draft a simple trust with a name that does not point to you. We will confirm what Texas allows for privacy in claims, and we will plan for the parts the law makes public whether we like it or not. I coordinate directly with the Commission for scheduling and document checks. We will keep your name out of places where names like to live too long."

"What would you need from me now?" I asked.

"Only the name you want on the trust and a list of two people you would trust to sign something if you could not sign it yourself," she said. "No account numbers by phone. We meet in person for anything that could be used to bother you. My fee is a flat number. It covers the trust, claim coordination, a first financial plan draft, and the first ninety days of questions." She told me the number without flinching and what I would get for it. "Paper first. Feelings later."

I liked her voice. I liked that she did not sell me confetti. "I will tell you by five," I said.

"That is fine," she said. "If you say yes, I will bring the draft tomorrow. If you say no, I will give Mr. Whitlow two other names and step back."

When we hung up, Mr. Whitlow pushed his legal pad across the table. Three lines were written in a small, neat hand.

No purchases. No changes. No confessions.

"You go back to your life this afternoon," he said. "If anyone asks for something large, you say you cannot. If anyone offers you anything, you say you are not buying. We will add the next three lines tomorrow. Phones. Mail. Cover story." He smiled like a man who has watched storms pass and knows they do, eventually. "I will call you at five. If you want Ms. Hall, we will set the papers tomorrow. If not, you will have two names and I will step back until you find someone you like."

He walked me to the front like any customer and nodded at the heron on the wall like it had said something wise.

The sky had cleared to a pale blue that felt undecided. I stepped out into the brightness and did the small check the day had taught me to do. Parking lot. Two cars I recognized from earlier. A white Camry with a baby seat. A gray work truck with a ladder rack. No one watching that did not have a reason to watch.

I pulled onto the frontage road and let the car find its way back toward Forney. The plan was to go straight there, slide into my shift, and pretend the day did not have a vault in it. At the Forney exit I tapped the turn signal and saw the brown paper sack on the passenger seat. It was empty. Lunch was still in my refrigerator in Wills Point, where my refrigerator lives and does not follow me.

I sat at the top of the ramp with my blinker ticking a metronome and pictured the break room onions. I pictured the tin of soup in my bottom drawer that tastes like punishment. I also pictured my cabinet at home and the feeling that had not left my ribs since yesterday. The ticket was safe in a drawer across town. My hands did not know that. They shook anyway.

I turned the wheel east and said out loud, "We are going home."

Back on I-20, the westbound traffic drifted away in the mirror. Terrell announced itself with its brick and its water tower. The Buc-Ee's billboard grinned at me from a distance and promised a thousand snacks and a fuel price that makes men have opinions. I did not stop. I wanted my own kitchen. I wanted Rusty's tail flick in my periphery while I opened the fridge.

Wills Point lifted up like a small boat at a good dock. I took the exit and slid through downtown where the stoplights understand mornings and do not rush them. My little street held its shade. The neighbor's crepe myrtle threw purple the way a generous person throws compliments.

That is when I saw the white paper folded under my doorknob.

The side gate stood ajar even though I latched it by habit. I do not leave it open. On the back step a single blue shoe cover sat flipped on its side like a shed skin. The air had a faint tang of citrus and something sharp.

I stood on the porch and let the room behind the door tell me what it wanted to tell me. The feeling moved up my arms until my mouth went dry. I turned the knob and went in.

Rusty scolded me for being late for a schedule he invents each day. He circled my ankles in a figure eight and then jumped onto the counter like a magistrate who planned to hear my case after lunch.

SERVICE RECORD. Quarterly exterior perimeter treatment. Time logged: 11:58 am. Technician and helper printed on the hanger with a number I did not recognize.

Through the kitchen window the side gate still hung open. A faint muddy zigzag print near the mat did not match my shoe. The china cabinet door sat shy of closed by a breath. Not open. Not right. The ribbon in my grandmother's Bible hung an inch lower than it had when I left.

I knew the ticket was safe in a drawer across town. My hands did not know. They shook anyway.

I crossed the room and closed the cabinet properly. I touched the ribbon and set it where it belongs, then took my hand away like a person leaving a sleeping child alone for her own good.

I took photos because photos do not argue. The door hanger front and back. The gate from inside and then from the yard. The blue shoe cover, flipped and then righted. The muddy print with a quarter next to it for scale because a cop once said to do that on a TV show. The cabinet before and after I put it right. I did not post. I did not text. I filed the photos into the old laptop when I had the chance.

The number on the hanger went to a receptionist whose voice said she had said this sentence twenty times today. "Routine sweep," she said. "We had reports on that block. Your address is on the list. We only treated the exterior. We do not enter the interior unless it is scheduled."

"Do you log names," I asked. "Do you log plate numbers?"

"Technician names are on the hanger," she said. "Plates, no ma'am."

"What about service orders for this address," I said. "Who requested it?"

She paused and then said, "We had a neighborhood request. I can mark your house as no service unless you call."

"Please do," I said. It was not her job to make me feel safe.

I hung up and stood still until the room felt like mine again. It took a minute. I opened the fridge and pulled out my lunch and the small container of fruit I had cut last night. I put them in the brown sack that had been empty in Forney. I locked the back door. I fixed the side gate and pushed the latch until it said I am closed. I checked the knob twice.

At the corner by the stop sign, a silver sedan idled with its lights off. It could have been nothing. It could have been everything. A woman sat in the passenger seat with a clipboard. A man in a cap stared at nothing in particular. I turned my wheel without making a show of it. I lifted my phone and took a photo through the open window. The corner of the plate and the dent near the taillight. Not enough, but something.

Back on I 20, I headed west again. The clock on the dash did its small math. I would be late. I would be later because the county had decided to stitch the highway one lane at a time and the line of brake lights ahead of me looked like a holiday someone forgot to cancel. I used the time to breathe. The steering wheel is a good place to learn how to breathe if you do not want anyone to notice.

I pulled into MetroCare with nine minutes gone. Tornado Tom had added a new sticky note to the white board near the bullpen. The new greeting line goes live tomorrow. No exceptions. He draws exclamation points like he is paying per exclamation and wants his money's worth. Kendra's laugh floated from his office like a radio someone forgot to turn down.

"Sorry," I said to Maya as I slid into my chair.

She slid a granola bar onto my desk like a bartender with a quiet pour. "You good?" she said.

"I am here," I said. It was the truest sentence I had.

I put on my headset and made the afternoon small. One call at a time. No purchases. No changes. No confessions.

The first caller was a man who believed the system hated him. He had locked his account by accident and then yelled at the machine like it could hear guilt. I let him talk until the boil settled. I walked him through the steps with the voice I use when someone is teaching themselves to drive a stick. We reset his password. He tested it. He said, "I am not stupid, I just get mad." I told him that was a sentence I believed.

The second caller was a grandmother who had written her password on a piece of paper and then washed the paper in her pants and then hung the pants on the line because she does not trust dryers. I told her how to answer her own security questions without sharing her mother's maiden name with anyone who did not deserve it. She thanked me for listening to the story about her grandson's spelling bee because sometimes people want to tell you what matters about their day even if they called for something else.

In the gap between calls I let my eyes slide to Tom's office. The wall of monitors showed the lobby, the hallway, the exterior door, and a feed that no one has admitted exists that shows the parking lot. Tom talks about safety. Tom enjoys watching things. Those can both be true.

"A truck ran the light on the service road again," Brandi said near my shoulder. She carries news the way other people carry perfume. "Did you see the QT on TV again? They keep asking if anyone knows the winner. My cousin says it is probably some guy in Rowlett with a lucky birthday."

"I did not see," I said. I kept my face calm and let the headset be a mask.

I went out to my car and ate the sandwich I had driven twice across the county to rescue. It tasted like bread and meat and a woman who keeps her promises to herself even if the promises are small. I looked at the photo of the silver sedan and the corner of the plate. I zoomed in and learned nothing new. I thought about the gate latch and the blue shoe cover, and then I put the thoughts into a box in my head and told the box it could not open until seven o'clock.

Back inside, Maya held up a sticky note. New greeting line script. She rolled her eyes like a person who has watched a man reinvent the wheel and then call it leadership. I put the script next to my keyboard and read it once out loud without letting the words become mine. I would say hello the way I say hello. I would not pretend a sentence written by a man who does not answer his own phone had found a new way to make humans comfortable.

At four forty two, a caller cried. She cried the way people cry when their day is already hard and then a small thing becomes the reason they cannot carry the pile. I stayed with her until the reset email arrived and then I stayed twenty seconds longer so she could hear a voice that was not a machine. When she said thank you, she meant it all the way to the bottom of the word.

At five on the dot, my phone buzzed.

"Mr. Whitlow," he said. "We keep this brief. Do you want Ms. Hall."

"Yes," I said.

"Good. Nine tomorrow. Same room. Bring only a notebook. Two copies of a name for the trust if you have one. Do not tell anyone you are going to the credit union. If a person knocks while you are home tonight, you do not open the door unless you have ordered something and something says its name through the door."

"Okay," I said.

"And Rachel," he added. "If your door has a chain, use it. If it does not, a chair works fine."

I laughed, a small honest sound that felt like the first step onto a bridge. "Already done."

"Good," he said, and hung up like a man who believes sentences should end when they are done.

Before I left the lot, my phone lit again.

TRAVIS: Any chance you can help me today? It is urgent. Rent. Please.

The message turned the air in the car a degree colder. I let the screen glow. I typed We are done, then deleted it. I typed I know about Bex, then deleted that too. Not in a parking lot, not by text.

I opened my notebook and wrote a small plan instead. Breakup, in public, late afternoon, no nighttime talk. One friend on standby to call if voices rise. Return his mug and the sweatshirt. No money. No long explanations. One sentence I can keep. I wrote the sentence and then put a box around it. We are not good for each other. I am saying no.

I put the phone face down and sat very still until my hands were steady again. Boundaries are not speeches. They are sentences you keep.

Traffic on I-20 east was a little kinder on the way home. The sky had found a color I like. The silver sedan was not at the corner when I turned onto my street, which means nothing and also something. The notice still hung under my knob like a flag I did not pick. Inside, Rusty circled my ankles and then took his post on the counter like a magistrate who had seen it all.

I opened Amazon and searched Ring doorbell, wired versus battery, and indoor cameras that store to a card instead of a cloud. A doorbell would be obvious. Neighbors may notice new hardware. A small camera in the front room could tell me if anyone crosses the line again. I added a doorbell, two small indoor cameras, and a pack of microSD cards to the cart. Then I remembered Mr. Whitlow's list. No purchases. No changes. No confessions. I moved everything to a private wish list named Porch and wrote questions for tomorrow. Best way to buy quietly. Power or battery. Local storage. Where to point them so no one feels watched.

I walked the fence line with a flashlight even though the sun had not left us yet. The latch held. The shoe cover was gone because I had thrown it away. I checked the windows and the back door stick and the tiny gap under the kitchen door that lets summer ants pretend they are invited. I did not make the house into a bunker. I made it into a place that could rest.

"Paper first," I told Rusty. "Feelings later." He blinked once, slowly, and that was the verdict for now.

Before I turned in, I took the notebook to the table and copied the three lines again because sometimes writing something a second time is how you convince your own bones.

No purchases. No changes. No confessions.

I added a fourth line for the morning.

Not forgetting lunch!

Rusty thumped onto the foot of the bed and pretended he had never in his life considered sleeping anywhere else. I turned off the lamp and let the night be what it is. The dark listened. I listened back. The drawer in a vault across town did its job without needing to be thanked. The blue shoe cover was only plastic. The muddy print was only mud. I held both truths until sleep finally decided to try its small rescue.

Walls & Locks

Wednesday carried the kind of sky that makes you believe in fresh starts. It looked clean from the window until I remembered the side gate and the blue shoe cover. Rusty watched me tie my shoes like I might forget a step. I checked the cabinet out of habit and then told myself to stop. The ticket lived in a drawer at the credit union where the walls were brick and the keys lived on wrist chains.

I brewed coffee and made a list while the kettle muttered. My handwriting looked steadier than I felt.

1. Meet Mr. Whitlow and Ms. Hall. Trust name. Claim plan.
2. Ask about surveillance purchases. Doorbell and small indoor cameras. Cash or card? How to keep it quiet.
3. UPS mailbox with street address. Package acceptance from all carriers.
4. Call landlord about the gate and the hanger. Keep voice calm.
5. Work like a person who has not rearranged her life.
6. Quiet exit plan from MetroCare. Health insurance bridge. No big goodbye.

Rusty blinked at the list and made a small sound that could mean anything. I fed him and he pretended he had never eaten.

At nine I parked in the same spot at the credit union. Mr. Whitlow met me in the lobby and led me to the small room with the heron print.

Ms. Hall was already there. Mid forties. Navy suit. Hair back. A pen that clicked once and then stayed still.

"Good morning, Rachel," she said. "You have done the hardest part. You waited."

I sat and let the chair carry more of me than I usually allow.

"We are going to keep this simple," she said. "Simple is fast. Simple is quiet. We will form a revocable trust with a neutral name, a corporate trustee for appearance only, and a private manager who answers to you. We will claim at the Dallas claim center under the trust. You will not be the person in the frame. Texas gives us some privacy at this level if we do the paperwork cleanly. I will be your mouth when a mouth is required."

"What kind of name?" I asked.

"Names that do not sound like a shell," she said. "No numbers. No initials. No Sunshine. I brought a few. We can also build from yours. Tell me three words you want to live under."

I looked at the heron and thought of the porch I could almost see. "Shade. Oaks. Porch-Light."

She wrote as I spoke. "Porch-Light Oaks Trust," she said. Then she wrote two more and slid the paper to me. "Briar Shade Foundation. North Fence Holding. The trust can own a holding company later if we need distance for purchases. No rush."

"Porch-Light Oaks Trust," I said, and felt the words click into a place in my chest like a well set nail.

Ms. Hall turned a page on her pad. "Cash option versus annuity. I will not argue religion with you here. You told Mr. Whitlow you want the cash option. That is fine. We will plan for federal withholding at twenty four percent at claim, with more due at tax time. You will hate how big the number is and then you will breathe because the money left is still a mountain. I will have a CPA on the line this afternoon to forecast the first year plan."

Mr. Whitlow slid a single sheet across to me. Three lines in his neat hand.

No purchases. No changes. No confessions.

He tapped the second line. "Ms. Hall and I agree safety purchases can be treated like repairs. We want you safe. Cameras and a doorbell are not a Mercedes. We still buy on a quiet path."

Ms. Hall nodded. "This is what I want you to do. Get a P.O. box today. Use cash. Ask the clerk if your box can accept packages from all carriers. Then go to a big store outside your usual circle. Cash purchases. Doorbell and two indoor cameras with local storage. Save the boxes in case you want to return them if it feels like a mistake. Install nothing until you feel calm enough to do it slow. There is no trophy for speed."

"Can I say porch pirates if anyone asks?" I said.

"Yes," she said. "It is boring and true enough. Also freeze your credit. Place a port out PIN on your phone line so no one can steal your number. I will send instructions. If you get calls from advisors you did not ask for, hang up. Scams bloom after big jackpots like mushrooms after rain."

I told them about the side gate and the shoe cover. Ms. Hall listened the way doctors used to, not waiting to speak. "The hanger reads the exterior only," she said. "We will not assume the worst or the best. You will call your landlord. Ask if he scheduled service. Don't mention fear. You will ask him to have the technician text you next time before they come inside the fence. If he pushes back, you thank him and say you will be home more the next two weeks."

Mr. Whitlow checked his watch like the kind of man who never misses a bus. "We will set the claim appointment for next week," he said. "You will keep working this week. You will keep your rhythm. You will meet me here again tomorrow to sign trust papers if you like Ms. Hall's terms. If not, I will step aside and give you two other names."

Ms. Hall slid a small packet toward me. It had a list titled Quiet Moves.

1.   P.O. box today. Cash.
2.   Credit freeze at three bureaus. Port out PIN with phone carrier.

3.   New email with a name that looks like an old aunt. Use it only for lawyers, banks, CPA.

4.   Data broker opt out list. This will be annoying. We will do it anyway.

5.   One friend for logistics if needed, not for company. She or he will sign an NDA I will provide. They will be the person who sits with Rusty on claim day or drives you to the bank.

I did not know which name to place in that last blank. Maya would ask clear questions I did not want to answer. My mother would feel the shift through the line before I could protect her from it. I thought of Ruthie from the church. A woman who knows how to carry water without spilling it on anyone.

"Ruthie," I said. "If she says yes."

"Ask her in person," Ms. Hall said. "Do not text. Give her the chance to say no without having to type it."

We stood. The meeting had lasted less than an hour and felt like a pillar had been set into wet concrete. I could build on it when it healed. For now, I walked back through the lobby and watched a toddler in a red shirt throw his snack and then gnaw on the container like victory.

I turned toward work and pulled into the UPS Store across the highway from MetroCare. The clerk at the counter said they had one mailbox left. Street address with a suite number. Package acceptance from all carriers. I paid six months in cash and walked out with two keys and a form that looked official. Easy, quiet, useful.

On the way there, I called my landlord. Mr. Beasley answers his phone like he is still surprised it rings.

"Morning, Mr. Beasley. Quick question about pest control. I had a door hanger yesterday. The gate was open when I got home and there was a shoe cover on the back step. Did you schedule an exterior service at my place?"

He made a sound that could mean yes or maybe his dog had jumped off the couch. "They do a sweep on that side of town once a quarter. Exterior only unless folks call in. You want me to have them text you first."

"That would be good. I work odd hours some days."

"I will tell them," he said. Then he added, "The side gate swings on that latch. Wind will do it. I will send my nephew to tune it up."

It was the right level of practicality and it let my shoulders drop an inch. I thanked him and promised I would leave the gate unlocked on Saturday morning so the nephew could check it.

The mailbox took fifteen minutes. The clerk wrote the suite number under the street address so delivery drivers would not guess it was a mailbox. She did not ask why I paid in cash. She handed me a small card with the store phone number and told me to text if I needed an after hours pickup. I liked her for making it feel ordinary.

I created a new email that sounds like a person who bakes pies and paired it with the UPS mailbox address for anything official. Then I drove to Mesquite to a box store that will sell you a sofa and a gallon of milk on the same receipt. Cash for a doorbell and two small indoor cameras that save to cards. Batteries because my house is older than both of us and I do not want to guess at wiring. I put the bag in the trunk and covered it with a blanket that used to live at picnics.

Back at MetroCare the floor was vibrating. Tornado Tom had discovered a way to load a custom greeting into our system without testing it. Calls had been dropping at the one minute mark for half an hour. Maya caught my eye and pantomimed a swan dive. I laughed because the alternative was a kind of crying that leaks sideways.

"Heads up," Tom called, clapping from his doorway. "Short outage. We are back online. The new script is live."

The screen told another story. The new script inserted the wrong account number in the verify prompt and sent two callers to their neighbor's mailboxes. Kendra appeared with a printout that did not match what I was seeing. I did not envy her life.

I started each call with a human voice and overrode the script in my head. It cost me seconds. It saved the room. Brandi whispered a thank you from the next chair over because her headset had already met one caller who did not see the humor.

At lunch I walked to the small strip of shade and called Ruthie. She answered on the second ring like a person who always does.

"I need a show up friend for an errand next week," I said. "It is boring, and I cannot talk about it, and it matters. If that is too strange, tell me no."

"I can sit on a chair and keep a secret," she said. "Tell me when to be ready."

I thanked her and felt the ground under my feet get wider.

The afternoon brought a call from a man who wanted me to fix a problem with a portal that had eaten his payment. He came in hot and then calmed when I told him where the money had gone and what would happen next. When he thanked me, I felt the old click in my chest that meant I still knew how to be useful.

I sat in my car on my last break and filled out the credit freeze forms on my phone. It took longer than it should have and the instructions looked like they had been written by a committee with three pens and no coffee. I set the port out PIN with my carrier and wrote it in the back of my notebook in pencil. I ticked off the data broker list until my eyes crossed and then decided to do the rest after dinner.

When the day let go, the sky had found its blue again. I drove the long way home to see if the silver sedan had a habit. The corner by the stop sign was empty. The side gate hung right. The shoe cover was gone. My trash can sat two inches off where I left it which could mean nothing or that the world was still watching.

I fed Rusty and set the doorbell box on the table like a question. The instructions told me it could be installed by a distracted person in fifteen minutes. I am a focused person and it took me forty. The indoor cameras were easier. One watched the front room. One watched the back door. Both stored to cards I could touch.

I started to write the cover story in my head and then realized I did not need one. The number of porch pirate videos on Nextdoor is high enough to explain a small hardware change. I still told myself to keep the boxes in the closet for a while.

My phone lit. A text from Travis.

TRAVIS: I am sorry about asking again. I am trying. I hate this month. Can we talk later? Not about money.

I let the screen glow, then dim. I did not answer. I placed a small sticky note on the first blank page of my notebook that said only: One clear sentence. Public place. Daylight. Return his things. No money. I will choose when after the trust papers are signed. The truth about Bex can live in my pocket for now.

I slid the notebook into the drawer under the catch all bowl by the fridge. Under the Florida magnet I tucked the sticky note that said keep it simple. The word Florida gave me a small clean hope without lighting a flare I could not control.

I walked the fence line with a flashlight to make sure the latch had found its groove. I met my neighbor on the sidewalk. Mrs. Keene is seventy and carries her keys in her palm like a set of brass knuckles.

"You see the bug truck yesterday," she asked.

"I saw the hanger," I said. "They left my gate open."

"Two fellas came through here with a clipboard and a smile," she said. "I always ask them who sent them. They like to say a name. I tell them I sent me."

I laughed and meant it. "Did you notice a silver sedan on the corner last night?"

"That car sat a bit after supper," she said. "Lights off. Could be a kid on a phone. Could be a man on a break. I am putting numbers on the block watch text this week. You want in."

"I do," I said. She typed my number with one finger and told me if anyone tries a door in the night her dog will inform the county.

Back in the kitchen I opened the laptop and answered Ms. Hall's email with my new address and thanked her for the list. She had sent exact steps for the data broker sites and a note that said I could hire a service to do it but that doing it once by hand would teach me what the services cost. I respected the lesson.

Mr. Whitlow called at five on the dot, because of course he did.

"How do you feel," he asked.

"Like the room has walls and locks," I said.

"Good," he said. "We will aim to sign trust papers tomorrow at ten. Ms. Hall will bring a draft. If anything unusual happens tonight, text me first, then call the non emergency line if there is a real concern. You do not need to be brave. You need to be steady."

"Why this level of vigilance?" I asked. "Who else could possibly know. I told no one."

He did not pause to build drama. "You are doing the right amount. Here is why. Retail staff sometimes talk. A clerk at the store may have seen the timestamp and started a rumor. Stores have cameras over the counter. News crews ask questions in ways that make people feel important. Maintenance outfits and pest crews move through yards and notice things without meaning to. Data brokers sell more about you than you think. Phone numbers travel. When jackpots get loud, cold callers guess and cast a wide net. Some bad actors watch parking lots at the winning store for a day or two. None of this means you are seen. It means you act like the paper is cash and you move with margins."

"So trust no one," I said.

"Trust a few," he said. "You, Ms. Hall, me for as long as I carry the work well. One friend for logistics. Everyone else can wait. Caution is not fear. It is planning."

"Copy," I said.

"One more thing," he added. "If you are thinking about leaving MetroCare, do not say it out loud yet. Give yourself a quiet plan. Health insurance, pay cycles, tax timing. We will thread that needle after the claim."

"I was already making that list," I said.

"Good," he said. "Text if anything feels off."

After we hung up I sat on the floor and let Rusty head butt my arm until I laughed. I put the cameras on test mode and walked out the front door and back in to make sure the little light blinked when it should. It did. The video is stored. The face in the frame looked like a woman who had decided things and was doing them in order.

I cooked something simple and ate half. I sent my mother a photo of Rusty asleep on his back with his belly in the sun and she sent a heart and a request for the full story of Mrs. Keene one day. I said Next weekend and meant it.

When the house went into its night shape, I stood at the cabinet and touched the glass. The drawer at the bank was a better home for that paper than any shelf in this kitchen. I thanked myself for letting go of the idea that I had to do this alone.

I sat on the couch and wrote one more list. Three places I wanted to visit before the year turned. Cedar Key for the quiet. A tiny town outside Ocala where the live oaks keep secrets. The stretch of beach on the Forgotten Coast where the pelicans fish like old gentlemen. Not to buy. To see. To remember what I want if the world gets loud.

The cameras did not blink at anything but me and a moth. The phone did not chirp with numbers I did not recognize. The gate clicked once in the wind and held.

At ten I turned the lock and slid the chain. I fed Rusty a second dinner because he had convinced me I had not fed him the first. I told him we would be boring for one more day. He looked pleased. The house breathed. The heron on the wall of the small room at the credit union came to mind and I let it be the last picture I saw before sleep.

The last thought I kept was the trust name. Porch-Light Oaks. It felt like a place where my grandmother might have sat with a glass of tea and told me to keep my head. I planned to try.

Rain, Paperwork & Nerves

The morning woke the house with a Texas kind of rain. None of the polite kind. A full body drench from a sky that had opinions. Lightning stitched the horizon and the thunder rolled over Wills Point like a train that forgot to slow for town. Rusty sat on the windowsill with his tail wrapped tight, eyes big, tracking every flash like a referee.

I checked the cameras on my phone. The front room showed a gray morning and the back door showed the fence holding. Ordinary. The ordinary felt like a blessing so I let it count.

I had trust papers at ten with Ms. Hall and Mr. Whitlow. I needed to get to MetroCare first so no one would read me like a postcard. I packed lunch, grabbed the UPS mailbox keys, and told myself today would be small moves and good posture. On the way out, I touched the china cabinet glass because the habit made me calm. Then I locked up twice.

The road out of town threw water in sheets. My wipers beat time and lost. I stayed in the slow lane and still felt fast. People passed me like they had been promised immunity. A pickup with flags on the back window cut across two lanes and sprayed my windshield blind. When the view cleared I was drifting toward the rumble strip and my heart thumped hard enough to make me say a word I do not say in front of my mother.

I needed gas and I needed a steady breath. I signaled early and took the Terrell exit out of habit. The QT lot looked like a shallow lake. The red and white sign glowed brave against the rain.

Inside, the cold air wrapped me like a refrigerator. The floor held a slick shine where people had tracked the storm. I went straight for the fountain wall. Pineapple sweet tea first. The ice sounded like relief. Beside it, a new row of taps for the iced coffees. I pulled a small cup of caramel to try. I could hear the employees moving on the other side of the counter and the chime of the door kept time with the thunder.

That is when the feeling pressed in. The sense that everyone was watching me. No one was. A man in a cameo cap was fighting a plastic lid. A woman in scrubs was counting change with her lips. A teenager was buying a bag of chips like it might save his life. I knew all of that and my neck still prickled. Two days of strange cars and door hangers and a Bible askew had taught my body a new language.

I paid in cash. The clerk gave me a receipt and said good luck that he says to everyone when the lottery logo blooms on the screen. The words landed wrong today. I felt like I had painted a sign across my chest that said Look here.

Back at the pump, the wind shoved against my umbrella like it had a grudge. The nozzle clicked and I watched the rain ripple in the puddles and thought about how habits are comfortable until they are not. QT has been my stop since the Kia was newer and my mornings were boring in a way that felt like mercy. Now the sign felt like a stage light. I told myself I could love pineapple tea and still break up with a place for a while.

On I-20 the rain turned mean again. Brake lights bloomed back to front and a little white sedan twitched across lanes like it wanted to sit in my lap. I eased back, breathed out, and let the space widen. In the mirror I watched a pickup spin two lanes over. It skidded, caught, and kept going. The sound it made in my head was worse than the sound it made on the road.

For a half mile I forgot the cameras and the trust and everything but the thin painted line that said this is your lane, keep it. Then the radio cut in with a lightning alert and my whole body remembered how exhausting it was being on high watch.

At MetroCare the parking lot churned with umbrellas and bad decisions. Inside, the floor smelled like wet carpet and burnt coffee. Maya handed me a paper towel like a priest with a blessing.

"You look like you swam here," she said.

"It sure feels like it," I said. "Storm is all elbows."

She looked at me a second longer than usual. I gave her the cover she needed. "Travis and I are talking tonight," I said. "My brain is made of bees."

She touched my elbow and let it go. The kindness of not asking is a gift in a place like this.

Tornado Tom was already on one. He had printed a new greeting in a font that looked like it came from a history lesson. He wanted it read word for word and he wanted the call times down by thirty seconds because the storm meant more outages and he had thoughts about volume. Kendra carried his binder like it contained the commandments. Brandi whispered that she would take the smiting over another script change any day and then she smiled so he would not hear it.

I took the first call and did the work I know how to do. I said the new greeting and then said the human version because the person on the line sounded scared. The system hiccuped and I smoothed it. My brain tried to float back to the credit union and I pulled it into the chair like a dog that wants the porch. At nine thirty I told Maya I had a quick errand at ten and would be back by lunch. She nodded and slid me a granola bar like a bartender.

The rain did not let up on the drive to the credit union. The lot was a shallow lake there too. Mr. Mr. Whitlow met me in the lobby with a small umbrella and the look of a man who has never once been surprised by weather. Ms. Hall was already in the heron room with a short stack of papers and a pen that did not click because grown women know how to hold still.

"Ready?" she said.

We reviewed the trust. Porch-Light Oaks Trust. Neutral and simple. I read every line even when it sounded like it had been written by a committee of very cautious owls. Ms. Hall walked me through the parts that mattered. Who can sign, who cannot. What the trust can own and how it can hide my name without breaking any rules. We created a new email for the trust using a plain alias that did not point to me, something like porchlightoaks.office@gmail.com. We wrote it in pencil on a single card. Mr. Whitlow tucked the card into a small envelope and slid it into the folder with the trust papers like a man packing a lunch.

We signed. The attorney notarized. I felt the paper turn from idea to a thin, real thing that could carry weight. Ms. Hall handed me a laminated sheet with three lines that sounded like Mr. Mr. Whitlow had written them in his own style.

Do not rush. Do not talk. Do not spend to feel.

"I booked a claim window for next Wednesday morning," she said. "Dallas claim center. It can be moved. The trust is the claimant. I will be the voice. You will be a person in a chair. We will coordinate bank wires and an immediate home for the funds so you are not sitting on a giant check like a parade. The CPA will join us by phone this afternoon to map the first thirty days. T-bills or a money market sweep for parking while we build the scaffolding."

"How long from the claim meeting until the money sits in the trust account?" I asked. "I am not in a hurry. I want to plan like an adult."

"If every form is clean and the bank officer is ready, the Lottery can initiate the wire the same day," Ms. Hall said. "Most land within twenty four to seventy two hours. Sometimes a bank shows a same day credit and posts final the next morning. We do not count money until your banker confirms receipt and availability. You will not spend to feel better. You will take the win like a pilot lands a plane."

Mr. Whitlow rested his pen and looked at me, not at the papers.

"What do you want your life to look like when you do not have to clock in?" he asked. "What is the Monday you would keep if no one had an opinion?"

The question hit me in the ribs. I had been walking around the edge of it for days. It opened in my chest like a clean window. I saw the porch with the long table. I saw trees that make their own shade. I saw a small barn with lights strung for music nights, and a piano that did not have to live against a wall. I saw my parents on a Sunday with plates in their hands and no worry behind their eyes. I saw the work I chose. I felt a happy spur kick inside and I put my hand on the table because my eyes had gone bright.

Ms. Hall slid a small box of tissues toward me without a word. I took one and laughed once because joy can make a fool out of you and that is fine.

"You do not have to work if you do not want to," she said. "You will work if you have a purpose. Both are allowed. The trust will give you time to decide."

"That is the point," I said. "Time without fear. A farm that pays its own bills. A porch that fills with people I love."

Mr. Whitlow nodded like a man who had seen good plans grow. "Now ask your next practical question," he said. "Then we will put one foot in front of the other."

"What about work," I asked.

"You keep it for the week," Ms. Hall said. "You leave when it serves your plan, not your mood. Health insurance, final paycheck timings, tax timing. We will talk about a quiet notice period and a reason that sounds like the kind of life you live even without this paper. Family care helps. Back on the market helps. Tired helps. Choose one truth."

We covered phone security. She had me set a port out PIN while she watched and had me show Mr. Whitlow the number so two brains knew it. We put the UPS mailbox on the file and the new email to the trust. She gave me a list of bank officers who did not ask the wrong kind of questions at the wrong time. She put a star next to one in Rockwall and another in Dallas that would open accounts for the trust and walk slowly.

"Last thing," she said. "Between now and Wednesday, you might feel the urge to test people. That urge comes from fear. If you feel it, take a walk. If it does not leave in ten minutes, call me and we will give the feeling a job that keeps it out of the driver's seat."

I wanted to laugh and cry and do neither. "Copy," I said.

I was back in the car at eleven with rain beating the roof like talkative knuckles. I texted Maya that I was grabbing lunch nearby. I picked up two tacos from a drive thru and ate them in the parking lot while the storm ran lines down the glass.

That is when the old habit called to me again. QT was in the rearview and pineapple tea is a small joy. I told myself I had already been there once and that was enough. I told myself I could pour tea into a cup in my own kitchen. They did not listen. I turned the key and drove back toward work and did not turn in. Sometimes victory is as small as letting a light pass and staying in your lane.

Back at MetroCare the storm had knocked a dozen customers off their portals and the phones were a string of small emergencies. I did the hours. I did the work. I blamed my quiet on Travis when Brandi asked who had tied my tongue. I said, "Tonight we are going to talk," and let the words be a bridge that kept her from crossing into rooms I could not host right now.

By four my nerves felt like they had been grated. I couldn't see if the rain had stopped from inside the building. I checked the cameras on my phone again. The front room saw nothing but a moth. The back door saw the fence. I breathed and stood up straight like my grandmother had taught me.

When my shift ended, I sat in the car and typed a message I had already rehearsed.

ME: Can we meet tomorrow at 5 at Ben Gill Park? I want to talk in person. Not about money.

He replied in seconds.

TRAVIS: Yes. I will be there.

I put the phone face down on the seat. One step. One door at a time.

On the way home, the highway performed its favorite trick where all the cars speed up at once like the state had changed its mind. A truck in front of me hit a puddle and sent a sheet of water over my windshield. For a breath I could not see the world. It came back in a hurry and so did I. I gripped the wheel and stopped letting my brain rehearse the talk with Travis and the claim day and the list of data broker sites I still had to climb through. My life needed two hands and both eyes. I gave it just that.

At the house the cameras blinked their quiet green. The side gate was closed and latched. No shoe covers. No door hangers. Rusty greeted me with a trill that sounded like he had notes.

I fed him and opened the UPS mailbox app to check the box. One flyer. Nothing else. Good. I closed it and took the doorbell test videos again because I liked watching the little light blink on command. I made dinner that tasted like food and read Ms. Hall's email with the first draft of the claim day schedule. Arrive early. Quiet room. Two forms of ID even though the trust is the claimant. Wire instructions with a second secure confirmation. Leave by a side exit. I could see the day like a diagram.

The storm eased around ten and left the kind of quiet that lives after a loud thing goes to bed. I took a shower and felt the muscles in my neck release an inch. In the mirror I saw the face of a woman who is keeping a secret and keeping her head.

I laid in bed and listened to the rain's last fingers tap the window. I let the trust name roll in my mouth once. Porch-Light Oaks. It sounded like a place where you could be steady. I told myself I would be the woman who is steady tomorrow. I would get through the day without being interesting. I would meet Travis and say one clear sentence that leaves both of us free.

Rusty settled at my feet like a warm punctuation mark. The house was held. The cameras did not blink at anything but me and a moth that had survived the storm. I turned the ringer low and put the phone face down. I closed my eyes and saw a porch with a long table and a piano that did not have to apologize. Then I let the picture float and I followed it into sleep.

The Park & The Line

The new day carried a hangover sky, washed clean from the storm but still heavy in the corners. I left work at four thirty with my stomach tight and my plan small. Public place. Daylight. One clear sentence. No money. Return his mug and the gray sweatshirt in a grocery sack. I had my keys in my right pocket, my phone in my left, and a calm I was not sure I believed in.

The park smelled like wet grass and summer trying to hang on. A little league team had the far diamond, parents on bleachers with folding chairs and big cups of ice. I parked under an oak and watched three minutes tick by because sometimes it helps to arrive and then arrive again.

Travis pulled in close to five and took the space two cars down. He walked toward me with the same shoulders I knew and a face I did not read well anymore. I stood by the bench near the pond. Ducks did serious laps like they had deadlines.

"Hey," he said.

"Hey."

We sat. The grocery sack with his things waited between us like a polite witness.

"Before we start," I said, "I need to be clear. We are not borrowing, we are not lending, we are not solving bills together. I care about you. I am not your bank."

He stared at the pond. "So that is it."

"There is more," I said. I kept my voice even. "I know about Bex. Utilities, rent, dinner. I do not want a postmortem. I want us to walk away with the truth in both hands."

It landed like a thrown thing. His jaw tightened. He laughed once without humor. "You're spying on me now?"

"Public feed," I said. "Two taps."

He stood, then sat, then stood again like his legs did not know where the ground was. "It is not what you think."

"It is exactly what I think," I said. "And even if it was not, this is not our future."

The air shifted. Heat came off him like a road in July. He stepped in, too close. The grocery sack bumped his knee and fell. The mug slid out and cracked against the concrete with a sound that made two ducks lift their heads. He did not look down.

"You are going to do this to me now?" he said. "Right now. After the month I have had? After everything?"

I stood because sitting makes you small. I kept the bench between us and wrapped my fingers around my keys to feel something solid. "I am going to do this because the truth is always going to happen. It is not a punishment. It is the end."

He planted a hand on the back of the bench hard enough to make it creak. His other hand opened and closed like it had lost its orders. The look on his face was something I had never met. He took another step and shadowed my path to the sidewalk.

"You think you are better than me," he said. "You think you can walk away and leave me holding the bill. You owe me for the time I gave you."

"I do not owe you money or a future," I said. "We are done."

He leaned in close enough that I could smell coffee and rain. "You are not done until I say we are done."

My body went cold in the hands and hot in the neck. I kept my voice level. "Step back, Travis."

He did not step back. He lifted his hand like he might point or he might grab and then he stopped it in the air. His jaw worked like he was chewing words and spitting out the parts I would not recognize. He kicked the cracked mug and it skittered under the bench and broke again.

He leaned in, voice low. "Maybe I will swing by later. We should finish this without an audience." His eyes slid past me toward the lot like he was already mapping it. He lifted a hand like he might point toward the car or the road or me and held it there.

A Terrell Police Department SUV rolled slowly down the lane by the tennis-court. The window was down. The officer inside looked like a person who knows how to read a field at a glance. He pulled up, parked a car length away, and stepped out. Late thirties. Calm face. Rain still dried on his boots.

"Afternoon," he said, neutral, not loud. "Everything okay here?"

Travis turned to him fast. "We are fine. We are talking. You can move along."

He stood two feet in front of me. From where he was, he could not see me shake my head no. I did it once, small, then again so there was no mistake. The officer saw it. He shifted the angle of his body so he was facing Travis and still seeing me.

"Mind telling me your names," he asked. "And why you are here?"

Travis's shoulders rose like a cat. "You do not need our names. We are having a conversation."

"I would like your names," the officer said, in the same tone, nothing sharp. "And I need to make sure no one is in danger."

Travis took a step toward him. "We are fine. Leave us alone."

The officer's hand moved to his radio, not his belt. "I am Officer Morales," he said, and he looked at me for the first time like he was asking me and not the air. "Ma'am, are you okay?"

"I am not," I said, and I was proud of my voice for staying inside my mouth.

Travis spun. "Rachel, what are you doing?"

Officer Morales raised his left palm without drama. "Sir, I want you to step back and keep your hands where I can see them. We are going to separate and talk." He pressed the radio button. "Morales. 10-97 at Ben Gill Park, next to the tennis-court. Start me a second unit. Possible disturbance."

"This is ridiculous," Travis said, louder. The little league game paused on an outfield fly and started again when the ball dropped. A man on the next bench stood up and then sat back down. The world kept moving and also narrowed.

"Sir," Morales said, still in that steady tone that does not give you anything to push against. "Hands where I can see them. Step back to the end of the bench."

Travis paced one step right, one left. "We were just talking. She is making this something it is not."

"It is something," I said, and my hands were shaking and I let them.

I heard tires on gravel and another unit pulled up. A younger officer stepped out, eyes already reading the scene. Morales nodded to him without taking his eyes off Travis.

"Sir," Morales said, with a little more command now, "turn around for me. Hands behind your back. You are being detained while we figure this out."

"Detained for what," Travis snapped.

"For the safety of everyone here," Morales said. "You are not under arrest at this moment. You are not free to go."

Travis looked at me like we were on a stage and I had forgotten my lines. He did not fight. He let the cuffs go on, red blooming in his cheeks. Morales guided him to the back of the SUV and seated him without bumping his head because he is the kind of officer who has done this a hundred times and still remembers people are people.

The younger officer, name plate reading E. Soto, walked me a few steps away where the ducks could not overhear. "Can you tell me what happened," he asked.

I told him. Daylight. Public place. Ending a relationship. A month of asking for money. A second woman I had discovered on a public feed.

The step toward me. The voice. The way my body had answered a question I did not want to be asked.

"Did he put hands on you," Soto asked.

"No," I said. "He stepped close. He raised his voice. I felt unsafe."

He wrote without making faces at the paper. Morales walked over. "We are going to keep him back there while we sort this out," he said. "Do you want to call someone?"

"No," I said. "I am okay to drive. I would like to leave when you say I can."

Morales nodded. "We can also stand by while you go, if you prefer. Do you feel safe going home."

"I will not be going home right away," I said, which was true enough.

He weighed his next words and chose the right ones. "In Texas, what you probably want is a protective order, not just a restraining order. You qualify as dating partners. You can apply through the county. If there is an immediate threat or an assault, a magistrate can issue an emergency protective order after an arrest, but we are not at arrest tonight. What we can do is document this, give you a case number, and if you want, we can give you the victim services contact who will walk you through filing. We can also trespass him from your residence if you want to make that request through your landlord."

The words felt like a bridge and a burden. I took them anyway. "I would like to start the paperwork for a protective order," I said. "And I would like the victim services number."

He handed me a card with two numbers and the case number written in neat block letters. Morales returned and asked if I had any property to return. I handed him the grocery sack with the mug and the sweatshirt and he passed it to Travis in the back seat, who stared at it like it had betrayed him personally.

"Here is what will happen now," Morales said. "We are going to release him after we speak with him and advise him to leave the park. You can leave when you are ready. If he follows you, call 911. If he contacts you against your wishes, keep the texts and tell us. Do you understand."

"I do," I said.

Morales looked at me one more time, making sure he was reading the whole picture and not just the frame. "Do you want an escort to your car?"

"Yes," I said, and the word felt like a strong choice, not a weak one. He walked me to the Kia and waited while I got in and started the engine. I pulled away slowly, heart beating like a drum line, hands steady enough.

I did not drive home. I crossed town to the Buc-Ee's off I-20 and sat in the far corner of that sea of red beaver logos and gas pumps. Terrell is proud of that place. The constant traffic felt like cover, the safest kind of crowd, and I let my breath find a normal pace. When my hands were steady I looped the access road once to make sure no one followed, then headed for home.

When I finally got home, I did the check. Cameras. Latch. Lights. Rusty met me with a look that said he approved of neither cops nor lateness. I fed him and sat on the kitchen floor and let the fear unspool in a way that would not scare the cat.

I texted Mr. Whitlow, short. Met with police at the park after an escalation. Safe at home. Will call in the morning. He answered with three words that did not tell me who he is and still told me who he is. Standing by, steady. Ms. Hall would get the facts tomorrow. Tonight I needed to be quiet inside my own house.

At 10:47 my phone chimed once. Front Door: Motion. The clip showed a dark sedan roll past my curb slowly, brake lights feather, then creep again. It looped the block once, came back, paused near my gate for the length of a breath, then moved on. Headlights off for three heartbeats, then back on. The plate smeared in the wet.

I saved the clip, wrote the time, date, and case number on a sticky note, and dropped a copy on the thumb drive. I texted Mr. Whitlow again: Motion alert. Slow roll. 10:47. Clip saved. He replied: Save only. Share with Ms. Hall. Lights on. Inside.

I called the non-emergency line to Wills Point Police Department, told the dispatcher about the earlier encounter at the park and Terrell Police and a clean description. She said a unit would cruise the block. I watched the next fifteen minutes live. Nothing. Rusty made a perfect loaf on the back of the couch like a small orange guard. I let my breath come back.

I slept in pieces and woke up with a plan that belonged to me in the morning.

The following morning, I called my landlord at nine. Mr. Beasley answers the phone like a man who has a list and does not resent it.

"Morning, Mr. Beasley. I wanted to let you know I ended things with the man I have been seeing. I have a safety concern and would like to have the locks changed. I will cover the cost. Is that okay?"

He cleared his throat. "That is fine. I prefer a locksmith I know. I will text you his number. Tell him I sent you. If you want me there while he works, I can be there."

"Thank you," I said, and meant all of it.

He texted the number. I called. The locksmith said he could be there by noon. He arrived in a van with magnetic signs and the air of a man who notices hinges for sport. He re-keyed the front, the back, and the side gate latch while I stood by with Rusty peering through the screen like a foreman.

When he finished, he handed me three new keys and a small zip bag for a neighbor. "Do you want me to put a no reentry note on the file under your address," he asked. "So if anyone calls pretending to be you, we ask for a password."

"Yes," I said. I chose a word my grandmother would have liked. He wrote it on a card and handed it to me and then crossed it out on his copy because that is what a careful person does.

After he left, I sat on the porch and let the quiet take the shape of a morning after a storm. The park felt a mile behind me and also a turn I had needed to take for months. I thought of the porch that is not mine yet and the trees that will someday throw their own shade. I thought of the trust paper that now exists in a drawer across town with my name removed so my life can widen.

I didn't feel brave. I felt like a woman who keeps her word to herself. That was enough for a Saturday.

The Open Door

Monday morning felt like glass. Too clear. Too breakable. I stood in the kitchen and listened to the house hold its quiet and knew I was not equal to a day at MetroCare. I have never called in sick when I was not sick. Today I did.

I texted Maya first. I will not be in today. Taking two mental health days. Will burn PTO. Then I called the main line, left a message for HR, and sent the email Tornado Tom always pretends he reads. I did not add any details. I owed no one a diary.

Rusty watched me zip his travel carrier like a judge who approves of escape. I filled his bag with food and the toy mouse that has never once looked like a mouse. I set the house lights to random on the plug schedule and checked the cameras. Front room. Back door. Green. Normal.

My parents answered the speaker phone. Mom first. "Morning, baby."

"I am going to come down for a couple of days," I said. "I will bring Rusty. I need sleep and your pancakes."

Dad's voice drifted in from a room away. "Thought of you last night. News said the winner is somewhere local. Have they found them yet? You live on one side of Terrell and work on the other. You stop at that gas station every week. Maybe it is someone you know?"

"No idea," I said, which was true in the way I needed it to be.

Mom's tone turned practical. "Drive in daylight. Text me every hour." She does not ask for explanations. She builds bridges made of casseroles and strict instructions.

I left a note for Mrs. Keene with my new locksmith password and tucked it under her mat. I set the metal latch on the gate and tugged twice. The road out of Wills Point looked like a ribbon that knew where it was going. Houston felt like an answer my body had written before my brain agreed to it.

I took US 80 toward the big roads, past fields that remember work, past a water tower that insists on being the tallest thing in a small sky. Terrell slipped by on my right with brick and pride and the beaver billboards that make even serious people smile. I thought about stopping there, then kept going. Four hours is a kind of prayer. Let the miles come to me.

Rusty sang the first ten minutes like a tenor who wants everyone to know he is alive. Then he settled, nose tucked, one paw through the door of the carrier like a hand on mine. The radio stayed off. I wanted the sound of tires and the soft thrum that tells you the car is doing its job without needing applause.

When the highway widened and the signs turned their faces toward Houston, the billboards began to count my trip for me. Fireworks, furniture, a lawyer who can fix anything, a burger that can fix anything, a mattress that can fix anything. I let the jokes pass without catching them. I watched the right lane where the trucks pull their duty. I watched the mirrors the way Ms. Hall taught me, two breaths, then back to the glass in front of me.

An hour in, the beaver showed up again, this time with a promise that always delivers. Buc-Ee's in Ennis. I did not argue. I needed fuel. I needed a clean restroom. I needed the small invention that is a wall of ice and drinks that sparkle like permission.

The lot was a small city. Rows of pumps, rows of pickups, whole families walking like they had been assigned a mission and chose snacks instead. I pulled to a pump near the outer edge, set the nozzle, and stood in the shade of my door with my phone dark and my eyes doing the quiet sweep I have learned. No Tahoe with a dent. No silver sedan with a clipboard. Just travel and the ordinary happiness of people who like snacks.

Inside, the air was a bright slap of cold and cinnamon sugar. The smell of brisket leaned over the aisles and said hello without being pushy. I used the restroom that could have taught a lesson about how to run the world. Then I walked past displays that could outfit a small ranch and a large Christmas. I took a large iced tea that tasted like a clean day. I added a kolache because bread with something warm inside is the kind of comfort that does not need a permission slip. For my dad I grabbed a bag of Beaver Nuggets because tradition and sugar sometimes share a name. I paid cash and smiled at a cashier who called me hon and meant it in the way we mean it here.

Back outside, the wind nudged the flags overhead. I gave Rusty a few drops of water from his travel bowl and a scratch between the ears. He blinked as if to say the world is big but the carrier is safe. I agreed. I set the drink in the cup holder, checked my mirrors, and eased back onto I 45 with the kind of patience that keeps paint where it belongs.

South of Ennis the land begins to roll a little, small hills that remember rivers. The traffic stretched into a ribbon of red and white lights, steady without being slow. I drove under a sky that found its blue again and let my thoughts stretch into a shape I could carry. Family. The word has its own temperature. Mom with her careful questions that never dig. Dad with his stories that start with weather and end with baseball. Both of them wanted me to rest. Neither of them knew the real reason I could not breathe in my own house last night.

Near Corsicana, sunlight hit a field of rolled hay like coins in a story about saving. I let the sight fill me up for a minute. I let it sit next to the worry that has learned my address. A hawk tilted a wing and moved air with the confidence I wanted in my shoulders. I copied him and rolled mine back so the tension could fall away for a while.

Huntsville announced itself with pines that stand like a chorus and the white figure of a man who has been greeting travelers longer than any of us have had tires. I always look, even when I tell myself I will not. I looked. I said hello to the big general like he was a cousin I do not see often. Rusty shifted and sighed. The carrier hummed with the road. I ate the kolache one careful bite at a time and let the tea do its bright work.

Clouds gathered near the horizon the way people gather before church. A few drops hit the windshield and clicked like coins. Wipers did their slow dance twice and the road dried as if someone had changed their mind about the weather. I passed a trooper writing a ticket and eased my foot off the gas because respect is free. A long train paralleled the highway for a stretch, black cars like a line of thoughts that needed time.

Two and a half hours in, the road settled into the long middle. That part of a trip where you have already left and have not yet arrived and your mind is a porch swing moving because you pushed it once and now it will finish on its own. I let myself rehearse the story I would tell. Breakup with Travis. Work stress. Needed Mom's kitchen and Dad's long talk about nothing that turns into something. All true. Not all.

I checked my mirrors again. The same white truck I had seen near the last exit pulled off toward a feed store. A dark SUV with a roof rack passed me and kept going. No one sat in my lane for more than a minute. My breath found a steady pace. I reminded myself that distance is part of safety and routine does the rest.

The miles peeled back. Billboards began to shout about Houston barbecue and Houston furniture and Houston sports as if the city was warming up its voice. I felt the pull I always feel when the lanes stack and the signs announce loops and exits that argue with each other. I kept to my line. I stayed in the right lane because the right lane is a loyal friend when you are not in a hurry.

Rusty woke and watched the world through the small windows of his crate. I told him what we would do. Stop at the house. Say hello. Put him in the quiet room where the laundry hum covers new sounds. Let Mom pet him for ten seconds because that is how he likes it. Let Dad pretend he does not love cats and then make him a liar by sneaking him a treat.

The skyline did its first soft trick, then the second. I stayed with the signs I know. The city is a large animal. You do not surprise it. You let it notice you and then you do the thing you came to do.

The tires hummed. The tea was almost gone. My hands were steady on the wheel. The sun slid a little and I slid with it. Four hours is a prayer. I said mine without words.

Mom met me at the door with a towel for the cat and a kiss for me. Rusty explored two rooms and adopted the guest bed like he had paid rent. Dad put coffee in my hand and then started in again.

"Have you heard any more?" he asked. "I keep thinking about that QT. We saw the camera crews there on the news Saturday. They say the winner might be in Kaufman County. Imagine that. One point eight billion dollars! If it was me, I would fix the fence, then buy your mother a recliner that will catapult her to the kitchen if she falls asleep during Jeopardy. I would get an RV with a horn that plays a song. I would give some to the church, not a big show, a quiet gift. I would take us to Galveston and pretend it was Paris."

Mom set a plate in front of me and tapped his arm with the back of her hand. "Let her rest. Let her eat. And for the love of mercy, stop telling horn stories."

He grinned and did not stop talking right away but he softened it to memories. He told the one about the summer the A/C gave out in the middle of July and the cat lived in the sink for a week. He told the one where we drove all the way to San Antonio for a concert that was canceled and still had the best night because the hotel had a piano in the lobby and a woman in a green dress who knew four chords on anything.

I let the noise wrap me like a quilt. We napped in the afternoon. Then went out for dinner at a grocery store cafe where the fried chicken is always better than it looks. Mom and I split a slice of pecan pie that tasted like a childhood I wish I could lend to strangers. For a few hours, the room inside my head went quiet.

We let the evening stay ordinary on purpose. Mom and I did dishes shoulder to shoulder. Dad told two more stories and fell asleep in his chair with the TV low. I took the guest room, closed the door, and slept the kind of sleep that has weight.

Morning brought coffee and pancakes and the brief mercy of forgetting. At seven minutes past nine my phone rang. Mr. Beasley.

"Morning, Mr. Beasley," I said, already standing.

He sounded out of breath. "Rachel, are you okay? Where are you?"

"I am in Houston with my parents. Why?"

He took a beat. "Wills Point Police called me this morning. Your front door was found open. Obvious burglary. They secured it for the night and asked me to notify you. Are you safe?"

I set my fork down. "I am safe. How bad did it look?"

"I have not seen inside. The officer said drawers tossed, signs of forced entry. Do you want me to meet you there?"

"Yes. I am leaving now. It is a four hour drive. Please ask them to keep it secured and I will call their non-emergency line."

I turned to Mom and Dad. "I have to go home. Can Rusty stay here for a couple of days until I know how bad it is?"

Mom was already nodding, carrier in hand. "He is ours until you say something different."

Dad reached for his keys. "I will drive you."

"I need to talk to the officers and find an attorney on the way," I said. "I will call when I get there."

He did not love it. He let me go anyway. Mom pressed a bottle of water in my hand and a bag of pecans in my purse like a talisman.

Once down the road I called the Wills Point Police non emergency line. A woman with a radio voice took my name and address and patched me to the officer who had answered the call. He sounded calm and alert.

"We will have a unit return when you arrive," he said. "Do not enter until we get there if you can help it. The door has been secured for the night but I would rather you walk through with us the first time."

"Thank you," I said. I meant it so much it stuck in my throat.

I called Ms. Hall next. She answered by the second ring and did not say hello in a way that made me feel like I was not the first person to bring bad news to a calm room.

"Someone broke into my house," I said. "Wills Point Police called my landlord. I am on the way back."

"Do not go in alone," she said. "You did the right thing by calling the police. When they clear you to enter, take wide photos. Do not touch drawers or handles if you can help it. If any of your cameras are missing, note it and tell the officer. If the SD cards are gone, tell him. Ask for the case number and the property receipt list. Text me the officer's name. Call me when you have air again."

"What am I supposed to do tonight?" I asked. It came out smaller than I meant.

"Sleep somewhere else if the house does not feel like a house," she said. "We will not solve safety in one night. We take the next right step. If anything looks like a targeted search for the ticket, say so. Do not speculate about names. That is for later and for me."

Her steadiness worked on me like a sedative without the fog. I hung up and drove the miles back like a person who has a job and the job is not to cry.

The streets around my block were still. No patrol in sight when I pulled up. Mr. Beasley's truck sat at the curb. He climbed out and met me on the walk with the posture of a man who wants to shield a thing he cannot shield.

"An officer is on the way," he said. "I checked the back gate without touching the latch. It is closed. The front door has a tape seal."

We waited on the porch without talking. The cicadas tried for loud and missed, the temperature finally remembering it was fall. A patrol car turned the corner slowly. The officer stepped out and introduced himself. Peña. He lifted the tape and unlocked the door after taking two photos of the seal.

"Let us walk the main path first," he said. "Hands in your pockets if you can."

We stepped inside and I felt something stand up in my chest and howl without sound. The living room looked like a postcard from a storm. Cushions on the floor. Books off the shelves. A drawer pulled and left like a mouth mid sentence. The lamp that was my grandmother's sat on its side without breaking because mercy sometimes shows up.

In the hall, every drawer in the small desk had been yanked and dumped. In the bedroom, the mattress had been lifted at one corner and dropped again. My jewelry box lay open, the parts and pieces worth more to me than any buyer spilled like beads of a story that did not tie.

In the kitchen, cabinets gaped. The china cabinet doors were open, just enough to turn my skin cold. On the floor beneath, my grandmother's Bible lay open, face down, wide, unhurt. I set my hands on the back of a chair to keep them from disobeying every good instruction.

Peña turned and looked at me without saying the thing he did not need to say. Someone had been searching for a specific paper.

"We will document everything," he said, and his voice carried a small weight that made the room hold still.

Then I saw the living room table. A sheet of notebook paper sat in the center, torn from a spiral so the edge had that fringe of frail teeth. Thick black marker. The handwriting is angry and hasty. Four words that froze the house.

Where is the ticket?

The blood went out of my hands. I heard Mr. Beasley say a short word that did not echo. Peña leaned in without touching the paper.

"All right," he said. "We are going to collect this. We are going to dust for prints on the obvious places. You will give me the names of anyone who has been in here in the last two weeks and the names of any service companies who have worked near your doors. You will also give me the camera model numbers and where the cards live."

I nodded. The front room camera was still in the corner where I had set it. The back door camera was on the shelf where I had left it. Both were powered on. Both had the tiny covers slid shut where the cards should be.

"They took the cards," I said.

"Sometimes they do," he said. "Sometimes they take the whole unit. Sometimes they forget the side yard camera. Do you have a side yard camera."

"No," I said. The answer burned. "I will by Thursday."

He didn't smile. He didn't make me feel small. He asked for the app. We pulled up the timeline. The front room camera showed motion at 7:13 pm. The clip ended early. The back door camera had nothing at that time. The cards were gone by then. The feed had blipped like a blink and never came back.

Peña wrote the times. He asked about new locks. I told him the date and the locksmith's name and the password on the file. He nodded and wrote it all down without saying that a password does not keep men out who force a door.

Mr. Beasley found the end of his voice and used it. "What can I do tonight?"

"Board the back door if the frame does not catch," Peña said. "I will request extra patrol. You can request a trespass warning against a named person if you choose. Victim services will call you in the morning with the protective order process."

I gave him the case number from Terrell. I told him about Officer Morales and the park and the dark sedan at 10:47 captured by my camera. He took it all in like a man stacking firewood just right.

"We will cross reference," he said. "Do not assume connection. Do not assume none."

I stood in the middle of what had been my living room and felt two things at once. Fury. Relief. Fury that someone had touched my grandmother's book and stood in my kitchen and pulled my drawers like they had rights. Relief that the ticket was not here, that the drawer at the credit union had done its job, that Ms. Hall had said paper first and I had listened.

"I cannot sleep here," I said.

Peña nodded. "No reason you should."

Mr. Beasley cleared his throat. "I will get a board and screws. My nephew can be here in twenty minutes."

"Thank you," I said, and meant it with a gratitude that had weight.

When the prints had been dusted, the photos taken and the paper collected into a bag that said evidence, Peña handed me a card with the case number and the time. "If you think of anything before morning, call that line. If anyone contacts you, keep it. Save every clip. If you need to breathe, sit on your parents' couch and breathe."

I looked at the empty camera slots and thought about how fear learns your floor plan before you do. Who did this I asked myself. For some reason I did not think Travis was behind this. How could he know about the ticket? It's impossible.

I stepped outside while Mr. Beasley called his nephew and the house aired its shock. I texted Ms. Hall the case number and the four words from the table. She replied with a short message that was a promise. I am on the line with Mr. Whitlow. We will set immediate next steps in the morning. Tonight you go to Houston. Do not spend the night there.

The porch light made a soft circle on the steps. I stood in it like a woman in a photograph who looked braver than she felt. I thought of the porch that is not mine yet and the long table and the piano and the fence line. I thought of the trust paper that exists so I can get from this door to that one.

Mr. Beasley's nephew pulled up with a drill and a board cut to a size that told me he had measured twice. They worked in the calm language of men who fix what can be fixed tonight and leave the rest for daylight. I put the plate of pecans on the kitchen counter because that is who I am and because I needed to do one ordinary thing in a room that had been made strange.

When the door was braced and the lights were off and the tape was fresh, I locked the front, checked the side gate, and got in the car. I sent my parents a short text. On my way back. House secure. Love you. I added a note to Mr. Whitlow. Four words on the table. We will talk at eight.

The highway held me like a long, careful hand. I drove toward Houston and the quiet bed and the cat who thinks he is in charge and the parents who will talk about recliners and horn songs and then let me sleep. Behind me, the house stood with a board on the door and a cabinet closed tight. In front of me, a life I had chosen waited its turn. The note on the table was a question from a person who did not know that the answer lived in a different room across town and had a lock that did not talk.

The question would not be the last. It would not be the loudest. It would be the one I remember when I sign my name under Porch-Light Oaks and walk out a side door and put the keys of this house on a ring that will someday sit on a table under an oak that makes its own shade.

Market Day & Measures

I left Houston before the streetlights surrendered. The guest room smelled like coffee and cedar from the closet. Mom set a travel mug on the dresser and kissed my hair, the way she has done since I was small enough to argue with bows. Dad loaded Rusty's carrier into the back seat and tested the latch twice. He pretended not to be worried and failed in the gentlest way a father can fail.

"Text when you hit the loop," he said.

"I will," I said.

Rusty protested for five minutes like a tenor who demands to be heard, then settled with one paw through the carrier door like a hand on mine. I kept the radio off. Tires on concrete sounded like prayer beads. The dark thinned to gray over the fields, then the gray slid into light with the steady manners of a weekday. I thought about the credit union vault and the small metal drawer that did not care about anyone's nerves. I let that comfort sit in the passenger seat with the coffee.

At the county line I called the non-emergency number for Wills Point Police and gave the case number. Dispatch said Officer Peña could meet me mid-morning for a slow walk through if I was free. I said I was. When I hung up, I called Ms. Hall because some days are better when you begin with a voice that has seen storms and still trusts umbrellas.

"Today is bricks," she said. "You shouldn't sleep there. Do the inventory slowly with the officer. Two locksmith follow ups next week. Side yard camera added. Motion lights with bulbs, not apps. I asked Mr. Whitlow to prepare a short list of banks that will open a trust account without theater. We are pushing the claim window back a week to give space after the burglary. Dallas accommodated."

"Peña wants names for everyone near doors in the last two weeks," I said. "Landlord. Pest crew. Gate repair. The nephew who braced the back door."

"Give him all of it," she said. "Morales in Terrell is coordinating the 10:47 clip with Peña. Plate fragment in progress. Cross county teamwork is slow by habit, but both are practical. Small and steady. That is your job."

I wrote three lines in the small spiral. Locks. Side camera. Bulbs by the back step. Then I added a fourth. A soft day soon because I felt older than my license.

By seven forty the crepe myrtle on my street was throwing color like it did not know fear. Peña's cruiser waited at the curb. He stood under the eave with a clipboard and a paper cup and greeted me with a nod that felt like a blessing from a neighbor, not a speech from a badge.

"We will take this slow," he said. "You tell me what feels off. I will tell you what is off. Those are cousins, not twins."

Inside, the air still held that strange mix of lemon cleaner and dust and the echo a house keeps when a stranger has breathed in it. We started in the kitchen and moved clockwise like a good clock. He set the evidence bag with the marker note on the table so we would not pretend it belonged to a drawer. The words were the same. My stomach did the small hard pull it did yesterday, like a rope tied to my ribs had been jerked once.

"The lab will try prints on the smooth side and fibers," he said. "Marker bled through and ruined the best surface. We will take what the paper is willing to give."

Mr. Beasley's nephew had braced the back door frame with a square cut board and a line of neat screws that looked like soldiers at attention. The latch plate told a rougher story. One screw did not match. Peña leaned close and used a small ruler that appeared from nowhere.

"Different thread," he said. "It might be nothing. It might be a thumbprint with a sense of humor."

In the hallway a baseboard near the floor vent wore a scuff the color of old pennies. The shape looked like the corner of a boot. We both saw it at the same time. He photographed it and I added it to the list in my head where I file reasons to move.

At the china cabinet the glass had a second arc of polish that did not belong to me. My lemon track ran straight. The second one curved and dropped near the latch. He did not touch it.

"Glove or sleeve," he said. "Either way, hands were here."

In the bedroom a drawer sat more open than I left it. Shirts stacked neatly enough to pass a fast look. The picture of my grandmother at the church piano was not in its fold. I kept my mouth closed for two breaths because truth is steadier when it wears shoes. Then I told him.

"They moved more than the kitchen," I said. "A photo is missing from this drawer."

He wrote that without rolling his eyes at the value. Not worth anything to anyone else is not the same thing as nothing. He added time. Weather. Latch condition. He writes like a man who respects his own pen.

"Officer," I said when we made the second circle. "Can I start cleaning? I want to take my rooms back. But I don't want to erase help."

He weighed the room for a beat, then nodded. "You can clean," he said. "Vacuum and wipe. Do not touch the baseboard scuff. Leave the strike plate alone. The marker note stays in our custody. Photograph before you return anything. Email me the shots. Here is my address."

He printed the email in block letters on my notepad and underlined it once.

"Thank you," I said. Permission felt like air.

He walked the exterior while I opened windows and let the morning in. I put on gloves and pulled the vacuum out of the closet. I lit two incense sticks Mom had tucked into a drawer last spring because she thinks rooms need smoke sometimes. Cedar and orange shouldered the chemical smell into the corners, then out the screens.

Peña came back to the kitchen and set his card on the table. "I will loop the block before lunch," he said. "If you see that silver sedan, call. We have a partial. It may grow up to be a plate."

"I will," I said.

He left me with the sound of his tires moving away like a courtesy. I stood very still until I could feel my house again and not just its shell. Then I went to work.

Top to bottom. Left to right. Books off the shelf, wipe, then back in better order. Light switches. Knobs. Drawer pulls. The face of the oven, which does not ask to be touched and sometimes is. I vacuumed under the couch and found a sock and a movie stub from a year I do not miss. I shook the rugs outside and watched a small cloud of dust lift and fall like a curtain call that knows when to end. A car rolled past slowly. I noticed the plate but didn't memorize it. I finished the rug and went back inside.

Mrs. Keene tapped the door frame with one fingernail and held a glass dish under foil like a nurse holds a vaccine.

"Food," she said. "Don't argue."

"I won't," I said, and meant it. We stood under the eave and talked about roses and sun and her trick with ice in buckets. She promised to watch the porch tonight from her kitchen sink. I told her I would be here instead of Houston. She nodded. That was all.

I ran vacuum lines into calm stripes like a lawn tended by a woman who wants order without scolding anyone. I stripped the bed and washed the sheets even though I couldn't tell if anyone had sat there. The pillowcases got a second wash because there are rituals you do not skip if you want your mind to sit down. I hung the duvet in the sun and let the sun do the old work it knows how to do. I took pictures of every surface I had put right and sent them to Peña with three short notes. Boot scuff still there. The strike plate is still mismatched. Photo of Grandma missing from the top drawer. He answered with two lines that said he had them and thank you.

I replaced two bulbs over the back step with bright LEDs. No apps. No cloud. I tested the motion and watched cones of light find the grass and the edge of the step and the latch. I printed a small sign that said No service without appointment and taped it inside the glass near the knob. I swept the back porch because a porch looks like a promise when it is clean.

My body remembered lunch. I stood at the sink and ate the sandwich Mom had packed, then gave Rusty a treat for surviving my morning mood. He stretched on the windowsill like a union man on break.

The clock said noon and the air said get out for an hour. Heritage Market day in Terrell would remind me that small things still run. I locked the doors, set the timers, and drove toward Terrell under a sky that had finally decided on blue.

Moore Street wore its best face. Booths lined the sidewalks like bright sentences in a story that tells itself. The British Flying School mural watched the lot with its calm blue plane. Tents flapped. A child rode in a wagon under a hat that could have fit a pumpkin and looked proud of the problem.

Sweetie Pies drew me like gravity. Lattice tops winked behind clear lids. Signs promised peach, pecan, and a lemon icebox that ought to require a permission slip. The owner smiled with her whole face and used my name like we had a little history, which we do. I bought a hand pie and slipped it into my tote like a small sun.

Mizell Farms had loaves that made the air smell like patience. The sourdough came with a card about feeding your starter and a story about a grandmother who talked to bread like it was a child with a good future. I bought one and thought about my grandmother's Bible in the cabinet and felt the clean click of a circle that keeps its shape.

Original Visuals had a rack of mugs and prints that turned the stall into a tiny gallery. Terrell's water tower leaned a millimeter the way it always does in their line art. I ran a hand over a matte black mug with a white oak leaf and decided I would come back for it when life was less fragile to carry. Then I changed my mind and bought it now. Sometimes you do not make the future do all the work.

Be The Light Wax Trade turned the air around their table into clean linen and orange. Whitney stood behind the candles the way a captain stands at a wheel. I picked one that smells like strong coffee and pecans and the first cold snap, because I plan for the weather I want. Whitney said, "You look like someone who needs a good scent on the counter." She was not wrong.

The Heart of Avon pulled me in with light. The window glowed and the colors answered. Erin rang up a small lotion for my mother and told me their shipment had arrived all at once, which is how life behaves when you try to live it in order. We laughed and called it timing and not chaos, because some days you have to pick the word that helps.

Terrell Coffee Co poured a cup that tasted like punctuation. I took a bag of beans for my kitchen and sat by the window for four minutes that did not ask me to be brave. People did the small talk that keeps towns going. Kids. Knees. Tires. A joke that lands without hurting anyone.

Whisked Away Bake House worked like a hymn. Kristy waved with flour on her wrist and slid me a chocolate chip cookie the size of my palm.

"You look like you could use something steady," she said.

"You nailed it," I said. "Thank you."

She studied my face the way bakers test a loaf, by ear and by feel, not by recipes. "You are good," she said, not quite a question.

"Good enough," I said. We nodded because we had said everything that needed saying.

I did a full loop of the market, not to shop, to remember. A guitarist tuned an open G that settled the air. A couple argued about a dog bed and then bought it and laughed at themselves for arguing about a dog bed. A kid chose a rock with stripes like a planet and would tell a story about it for a week. The ordinary did its work.

I bought light bulbs from a hardware table because the universe had placed a coupon on my kitchen counter this morning and it felt like good manners to say yes. I thanked the volunteers at the crosswalk for being the kind of people who stand in the sun so strangers do not bump into each other.

On the way out of town I stopped at Hickory Roots BBQ. The line snaked and no one minded. I ordered ribs and a baked potato the size of a small planet. The man at the counter asked if I wanted extra napkins and I said yes because that is the kind of question you always answer yes.

Home felt closer than it was. The porch light clicked on as I pulled in, which should not have made my throat tight, but it did. Inside, rooms held their lines. Nothing out of place. Rusty greeted me like a man who keeps office hours and had been waiting politely for mine to begin.

I did small work for the next two hours. The kind that tells a house it has a future. A dab of spackle in the dent near the hallway light switch. A felt pad under the wobbly chair. A drawer divider in the kitchen so spoons would stop arguing with one another. I put a bright bulb over the sink. I tightened two hinge screws until they stopped telling their tired story.

I made three boxes and wrote on their sides with a thick black marker. Keep. Give. Florida. The third one was new. It felt like writing my name on a door I had not opened yet.

From the bookshelf I chose two novels I will read again and one I will not. The one I will not go into Give. A city map from a trip I want to repeat went into Keep. The spare set of measuring cups went into Florida because no one tells you how comforting it is to know you will be able to bake the first week you move. I pulled the top drawer of the buffet and found three white candles, a pack of napkins with blue stripes, and a corkscrew shaped like a fish. The fish went into Give because jokes have their seasons. The napkins went into Keep because meals do not impress me unless they let me wipe my hands. The candles went into Florida because evenings need a way to glow.

I stood in the bedroom doorway and pictured a flat plan of a new house. Live oaks. A screened lanai. A pool that looks like water more than design. A small barn that smells like clean hay, even if what I keep in it is a bicycle and two rakes. Marion County sits in my head like a word I already know how to spell. Not the coast. Drive to the beach when I want the horizon to argue with me. Quiet enough to hear frogs. Far enough from storms to sleep.

I wrote a line in the spiral while chewing on the delicious ribs from Hickory Roots BBQ. Porch-Light Oaks Trust buys, not Rachel. Florida addresses wait until the claim clears. Then another. The cover story for work must be simple and kind. No confessions. The pen moved like it had found the path.

At five my phone buzzed. A two line text from Ms. Hall. Bank list in your inbox. Pick the top two. Open on paper, checks only. I answered with the one that still treats tellers like professionals and the national that does not turn a lobby into a theater. Ten minutes later Mr. Whitlow sent models for motion lights that use bulbs and answer to switches. Boring on purpose. Bless that man.

I stepped onto the porch and watched the light cones touch the grass and the gate latch. Mrs. Keene raised a hand from her kitchen window as if we were part of a code. I lifted mine back. A patrol car rolled slowly and politely at the corner. Peña lifted two fingers without making it a production. It is a small thing when a man does his job where you can see it.

Dessert was the hand pie and a little fruit because my body wanted steady, not fancy. I put the new mug from Original Visuals on the counter by the stove and looked at it like people look at a small piece of proof. Water tower a fraction off. White leaf on black. Imperfect on purpose. Alive.

I did the dishes and packed one box clean to its edges. Books and the mug and the extra measuring cups and the lotion for my mother, which I will not ship but had to place somewhere. I taped it and wrote Florida 1 on the top. The number looked like a beginning.

I walked the fence line with a flashlight even though the sun had not fully left. The latch held. The gate sat square. The shoe cover memory had gone to the land where city trash lives and is not missed. I checked the windows, the back door stick, the tiny gap under the kitchen door where summer ants hold their meetings. I didn't turn the house into a bunker. I gave it back its purpose.

Rusty and I sat on the floor in the living room for a minute with my back against the couch and let the day talk. This town had woken up on my side. My neighbors had done their jobs. The market had cooked and sung and sold and smiled. The officer had carried a clipboard that mattered. The lawyer and the advisor had moved paper without making it a parade. I had pushed a vacuum and a pen where they needed to go. Rusty climbed into my lap and turned into a heavy loaf with whiskers. I told him what I tell myself when I can remember to be kind. We keep it small and steady. We make rooms that remember who lives here. We plan a life that can be lived without explaining it to strangers.

Florida will happen in its hour. The trust will sign with a name that does not tip its hat. The bank will open without music. I will leave one day with boxes and a cat and a car that knows how to point east without losing its nerve. But tonight I will sleep in a room that smells like cedar and soap and the first tug of a fresh future.

I turned off the kitchen light and left the porch on its timer. I set the chair under the knob because old habits earn their keep. I put the small spiral on the counter with the pen on top.

One more line before bed. Small and steady, then Florida.

The Order

Monday started with a courthouse kind of sky. Bright in a flat way. I drove in early and parked two blocks from the doors so I could watch the steps fill. Ms. Hall had told me to bring only what

The hall smelled like coffee and copy paper. The docket board clicked from one set of names to the next. A bailiff with a voice like a church usher told everyone where to stand and where not to. I sat beside Ms. Hall on a wooden bench and held my hands together like I was keeping a small bird still.

"You will answer only what is asked," she said. "No speeches. Yes and no when you can. Details when they help. If you do not know, say you do not know."

"Copy," I said. My voice sounded normal. My stomach did not.

Officer Morales arrived in uniform and nodded once like a person who sees a room settle. Officer Peña came in plain clothes with a folder under his arm. They greeted each other in a way that told me they had already compared notes. Mr. Whitlow texted a small thumbs up and then left me alone. That is his talent. He knows when to be a wall and when to be a window.

Across the hall, Travis stood with a man who looked like a public defender on a tight schedule. Travis wore a clean shirt and a look I did not recognize. Not the boyish grin. Not the sharp heat from the park. Something in between. He kept glancing at the door like he might practice leaving.

The clerk called our case. The courtroom was all light wood and straight lines. The judge read the file for a minute that felt longer than a minute. Then she looked up.

"Ms. Mercer, you are petitioning for a protective order based on two incidents, a confrontation at the Terrell city park and a subsequent burglary at your residence in Wills Point," she said. "We will proceed. Counsel."

Ms. Hall stood like she does. Confidently and centered, not loud. "Your Honor, we have sworn statements, video from the park, an officer who witnessed the escalation, and a report and photographs from the burglary. The respondent and my client were in a dating relationship. She seeks no contact, a stay away distance, and surrender conditions that are standard. We are not asking the court to find responsibility for the burglary, only to consider it as part of the safety context."

The judge nodded once. "Understood."

Morales was first. He told the story of the park the way good officers testify. Time. Place. His arrival. The head shake I gave him. The way Travis spoke to him and to me. The detention for scene control. No arrests. No injury. His words had weight without wearing boots.

Peña followed. He described the call to my landlord, the secured door, the walk through. The open drawers. The Bible on the floor. The note on the table that asked a question no house should have to answer. The missing SD cards. He did not speculate. He said what he had seen and what he had logged. The judge asked one question about the timing of the clips. Peña answered without looking at his notes.

My turn. I stood and told the truth like a list. Yes, we had dated. Yes, he had asked for money more than once. Yes, I told him we were done at the park. No, he did not touch me. Yes, he moved close and spoke in a way that made me feel unsafe. Yes, he said he might swing by later. Yes, I called the non-emergency line that night when my camera captured a slow roll. No, I do not know who broke into my house. Yes, I am afraid of contact now.

Travis watched me with a face that tried to be still and failed at the corners. His attorney stood. "Your Honor, my client denies any intent to harm. He admits to being upset. He admits to words he should not have said. He has not contacted Ms. Mercer since that evening. He understands no contact is wise. He seeks to move on."

The judge looked at Travis. "Do you wish to speak?"

He lifted his chin like the world had put a string on it. "I do not want trouble," he said. "I was mad. I should not have been. I had people in my ear. A guy asked me if I knew her stops, and said folks were saying things online. I told him to get lost. I did not go to her house. I did not touch her. I am sorry for the park."

Ms. Hall leaned very slightly toward me and wrote two words on the yellow pad. Do not react.

The judge turned back to Morales. "Officer, did the respondent comply when you detained him."

"After verbal commands," he said. "Yes."

"And Officer Peña, have you found any evidence that ties the respondent to the burglary."

"No, Your Honor," he said. "Investigation is ongoing in multiple directions."

The judge set her pen down. "I find family violence is likely to occur again if not restrained. The court grants a two year protective order. No contact by any means. No third party contact. Stay at least two hundred yards from Ms. Mercer, her residence in Wills Point, and her workplace in Forney. Violation will result in arrest. Ms. Mercer, your address will be omitted from the public copy under the confidentiality provisions. Victim services will assist you with safety planning and with service."

She stamped the order. The sound felt final and kind. The bailiff handed copies to counsel. Ms. Hall checked both pages like a person counting keys.

Travis looked at me over his attorney's shoulder with a small flare of something that could be pride or anger or habit. I kept my eyes on Ms. Hall's pen.

"Next steps," Ms. Hall said quietly. "We walk this to the clerk for certified copies. One goes to Wills Point PD and one to Terrell PD. One to your landlord. One to HR at MetroCare. I will coordinate service. You will keep a copy in your car and one in your bag. You do not engage. If he reaches out, you call."

Morales stopped by and gave me a short nod. "You did fine," he said. "We will add the order to our system today. If you need a drive by tonight, call the non-emergency line."

Peña said, "I will fold this into your case file. If anything comes in on the burglary, I will let you know."

At the clerk's window we signed twice, watched three stamps land, and walked back to the car under a sky that had learned how to be blue again.

I let my hands shake for thirty seconds and then I put them on the wheel like a person who knows where she is going. Ms. Hall texted a summary in case my brain needed paper. Mr. Whitlow texted the same small thumbs up. I let both messages sit.

I drove to MetroCare and went straight to HR. The manager, a woman with kind eyes who always smells like peppermint gum, made a copy of the order and walked it to security. She thanked me for telling her and told me to let her know if I wanted to park closer for a few weeks. Kindness is a door that opens after a long hallway.

Maya met me at my desk with a look that was fifty percent questions and fifty percent restraint. I tapped the side of my bag where the copy sat. "Paperwork," I said. "All quiet."

"Good," she said. She slid a chocolate into my hand like communion. "I have been saving this."

The afternoon was ordinary on purpose. Tornado Tom shouted a new greeting from his doorway and we ignored it until someone found the email that said we did not have to. I watched the clock and did not move it forward. When five came, I packed slowly and walked out into air that smelled like the tail end of summer.

At home I lit Whitney's coffee and pecan candle and set the certified copy on the fridge with a magnet that says Florida. I texted my parents a safe and short update. Order granted. No contact. I told Mrs. Keene that a patrol might roll by and that I would bring her a slice of sourdough if she promised not to give it to the dog.

The house felt like it had corners again. I made toast from the Mizell loaf and ate it with butter that knew what to do. I opened my notebook and wrote three lines.

Order in place. Keep the circle small. Build what lasts.

Then I let the pen keep going because the room was quiet and the candle was kind. What do I want my life to look like when no one is telling me what Monday must be? Is Florida the place? I saw the same picture I have carried since Sunday. Oaks that make their own shade. A porch with a table long enough for the people I love. Friday nights with songs and stories. A small barn that earns its keep. I saw the Gulf in the distance like a promise you do not say out loud.

Should I stay in Texas? Houston would put me near my parents and closer to the doctors my mother trusts. That matters. But the pull is east. A new start where no one knows the shape of my old days. Country, not city. Enough acres that quiet sounds like water. Near a small town that minds its own and shows up when asked.

When do I leave MetroCare? After the claim is clean and the funds are parked and the first taxes are planned. I can give two weeks or I can give less? Ms. Hall will have an opinion and I will listen. A quiet exit with a final paycheck and health insurance bridged. No big goodbye. A kind hug for Maya in the lot and a plant left on her desk.

What should I tell my parents? They deserve truth and they deserve peace. I can give them both in order. After the claim, after the house is steady, I can tell them I have a Florida opportunity and that it gives me time to be useful. I do not have to say amounts. I can say standards. Promises kept. Bills paid. Sundays are closed. Come visit when the porch is built.

People will notice if I move to a farm and change everything at once. So I will not. I will rent first under the trust, small and quiet. I will buy later when the right land shows itself. No trucks with signs. No photos online. No talking about square footage. The trust will buy and I will live and the porch will be for people, not for pictures.

Logistics. Pack a little each night. Room by room. A storage unit near the highway for two months. A moving company that takes cashiers checks from a trust. The UPS mailbox becomes my mail. Change of address after the move, not before. Utilities are staged so the house breathes without me. New bank in Florida for day to day and the trust account kept boring. Driver license in time. Voter registration when I have an address. Rusty's vet records in a folder I can carry.

The work I want is simple. Two Porch-Light nights each month for music and community. A small customer care consulting practice to keep my skills sharp and be useful. A fund that fixes one quiet problem a month without a speech. Church on Sundays where the hymns are old and the coffee is strong.

I chose Florida. Not because Texas is unkind, but because the pull is real. I wrote a heading on a clean page. Quiet Exit. Under it I listed dates. Claim day next week. Notice to HR two weeks after funds post. Lease search in month one. Move target in month two. Buy only when the land answers yes.

Official story. I will rehearse it until it sits in my mouth without wobble. I am taking a Florida opportunity that fits my skills and gives me time to help my family and build something small. If someone wants more, they get less. "Not ready to share details yet, thanks for understanding." I will carry three versions. One sentence for the hallway. Thirty seconds for a coworker who cares. Two minutes for HR. No numbers. No hints. No timelines that invite follow up. The story must match for my parents, neighbors, and church without feeling like a lie. Truth first, detail later.

Questions I will practice and the lines I will keep: Why so fast? "The start date is soon and the fit is right." Where in Florida? "Near the coast, still sorting housing." Are you coming back? "I do not know yet." What will you do there? "Customer care and community work." Every line ends the talk and keeps the peace.

Digital. I will update LinkedIn after I land, not before. No Facebook hints. Photos of cats and bread only. The trust stays silent while I practice quietly.

When the night settled, I walked the fence line once, more for routine than fear. The cameras blinked. The latch caught. Rusty did his patrol of the windows and returned to his spot with the air of a guard who approved. I slept like a person who had put a strong hinge on a door. The morning would bring lists. The week would bring the claim. The end of this would bring a porch and a table and a new map of my days. For now, the stamp on the paper was enough.

Lines At MetroCare

Tuesday looked like it had been ironed flat. I parked early, walked in with coffee, and told myself small moves, no speeches. The protective order copy sat in my bag. The official story sat in my mouth, practiced until it felt like a stone I could carry without chewing it.

I had barely logged in when an email flashed red from Tornado Tom. Attendance Review Immediate. No greeting. No context. Just a demand for me to report to his office.

Maya mouthed, "You good?" I touched the side of my bag and nodded. "Personal matters" is a door that shuts. It would shut today.

Tom's office looked like a storm closet. Binders stacked. A whiteboard crowded with ideas that had never met a test plan. One wall was a bank of big screens cycling through every camera in the building. Break room, lobby, copy room, back door, like he was running air traffic control for a call center. Kendra sat in the spare chair with a legal pad and a look that oscillated between sympathetic and superior. Tom did not invite me to sit.

"You have missed three days in two weeks," he said, voice already at the setting he uses when he wants the whole floor to hear. "You leave for long lunches. You disappear for errands. This is not how we do things here."

"Personal matters," I said. "I put in PTO. I cleared the slots with Maya. The team met their numbers."

He slapped a hand on the desk. "That is not the point. You think the building runs around you. It does not. We have standards. We have scripts. We have people depending on call times. We cannot operate if folks go rogue."

Kendra lifted her pen like she was the court reporter in a play. Tom's face went red at the edges. He liked this part. He liked the sound of his own anger.

"You have been late three mornings," he said, louder. "You have not explained. You have not apologized. You think you can phone it in and let other people carry the load."

I kept my voice level. "I have explained. Personal matters. I do not owe details. I have not asked anyone to cover me. I have covered others. Including Kendra's queue twice last week while she was off the floor." I let the sentence sit.

Kendra looked at me like I had stepped on her shoe. Tom pushed his chair back, stood, and used volume like a tool.

"Do not try to be cute," he said. "Do not bring Kendra into this."

"She is already in it," I said, softly, not looking at either of them.

He moved closer to the door and I thought of the park for a bright second and shut the memory in its box. This was different. This was a man who believes yelling is leadership. I chose a smaller thing. I chose to tell the truth I could say out loud.

"Tom," I said, still even. "I am doing my job. I am doing more than my job. I am handling escalations and taking angry callers after your script changes break the system. I am covering Kendra's work when she is in your office. I am not your problem. I am your solution. And I am getting tired of pretending that this is normal."

The color rose another shade. "Excuse me?"

"You heard me," I said. "You have turned this floor into a guessing game. New standards with no emails. New greetings with bad account numbers. You make rules in the hallway and punish people who did not hear you say them. And yes, I am doing Kendra's job when she is un-available because she is in here with you a lot. People talk. You should know what they are saying."

Silence bent the air. Kendra set her pen down like it was hot. Tom's jaw moved like it was trying to find the right word and the word was not available.

"You do not get to accuse people," he said finally. "This is a workplace."

"Correct," I said. "Which is why I am saying this in your office. I am not asking you what you do with your time. I am telling you what I will not do with mine. I will not carry the weight of a broken process and a broken tone. And I will not be shouted at for doing the work."

He stepped around the desk and put both hands on the edge like he wanted to flip it. "If you do not like it here, you can go."

"I will," I said. "Soon. I am already looking for other employment. This is simply bullshit and you are one of the worst bosses I have ever had."

The room did not break. It held. Kendra looked at the floor. Tom blinked like anger had dried his eyes.

"Get out," he said.

I turned, opened the door, and found Maya three steps away pretending to need the stapler. She raised her eyebrows as we walked back to our row.

"You standing up or you quitting," she whispered.

"Both," I said. "In that order."

I sat and did the work. I took calls. I fixed things. I wrote the real greeting on a sticky note and passed it down the line. I covered Maya's queue for twenty minutes when she had to run the kind of errand you cannot schedule. I told the team leader we were caught up and that I was available for escalations. Kendra did not come back to the floor for another hour.

At lunch Maya and I ate in the corner where the plant has survived three reorgs. She watched my face like a nurse.

"You okay," she said.

"Yes," I said. "More okay than I expected."

"You know he is going to try to make an example," she said.

"Probably," I said. "I will be gone soon. Probably after next week. I have a plan. I am not telling him anything. Personal matters are enough."

She nodded. "If he comes at you in the afternoon, I will sit down at your station and throw the first call to myself."

"You don't have to," I said.

"I want to," she said. "You cover me. I cover you. That is how we do things here."

We went back to the floor. The day did its usual tricks. The wrong recording played in the IVR for twenty minutes. The portal ate a payment. Tom sent an all caps message about call times and then disappeared. I watched the clock and watched my mouth. No speeches. No extra words. No confessions.

At four fifteen he sent another summons. I walked in and closed the door because privacy can protect you too.

"I spoke to HR," he said. "Your attendance will be formally reviewed. You need to provide documentation for all future time off."

"I will follow policy," I said. "Which does not require me to give you details about my personal life."

He leaned back like he had scored a point. "You are on notice."

"So are you," I said. "On tone. In process. On the way you use people like parts. The team is tired, Tom. You do not have to like that sentence. You should hear it."

He opened his mouth like he was going to shout again and then remembered the wall between his office and the floor. He lowered his voice to a hard whisper.

"If you spread rumors about me and Kendra, I will terminate you."

"Do not worry," I said. "I am not spreading anything. I am leaving. And I am taking my work ethic with me."

I walked out. Kendra was at her desk, cheeks bright. She did not look up. I felt a flicker of something that might have been pity and let it pass. Grown people make choices. I was making mine.

Before I left for the day I stopped by HR to confirm everything was in place from yesterday's order. The manager pulled up my file, nodded that the protective order and security note were already logged, and offered closer parking and a direct line if anything was feeling off. I told her I would follow the policy for documentation and time off. She thanked me and said the right words about safety and process. I believed her. She feels like a hinge that will hold even if the door shakes.

I sat for a minute in the car and let the adrenaline run out. Then I pulled onto highway 80 and met brake lights stacked for a mile. Another wreck. We sat nearly ten minutes while sirens threaded past and a wrecker eased into place. I counted the reflectors and wondered why this stretch had carried so many crashes lately. There was nothing to rush toward. The house would be there and so would the lists. I let the quiet hold me and thought about my little secret in the kind of loneliness that feels like a room. When the lane opened, I drove steadily home and put water on for pasta because that is what you do when you need to remind your body that the world still knows how to boil.

I sat down at the table and opened my notebook to the "Quiet Exit" page and added dates in ink. Claim day next week. Resignation letter drafted now, delivered two days after funds post. Last day ten business days after notice. Health insurance bridge set before I hand in the badge. UPS mailbox active. Florida rentals bookmarked under the trust. Movers researched. A short list of banks in Florida starred.

I wrote my official story three times. One sentence. Thirty seconds. Two minutes. I said each one out loud until it fit. Then I practiced answers to the questions that come fast in hallways. Why so fast? Where in Florida? Will you be back? I kept them short. I kept them true without inviting the wrong kind of curiosity.

I texted Ms. Hall: Heated day with boss. I intentionally stayed vague. Exit timeline set for post-claim. She replied in four lines that straightened my spine. Good. No details. Draft resignation tonight, keep it in your drafts. I will review it if you want. Walk calm.

Mr. Whitlow texted at five on the dot. Steady?

Steady, I wrote back. Angry. But steady.

Rusty watched me from the counter like a supervisor who approves of comfort food. I ate, washed the plate, and sat with the candle Whitney poured that smells like coffee and pecan and the first cold snap. The house felt like a place that could carry me through a few more days without asking for secrets I could not give.

I opened the laptop and wrote the resignation letter. Two paragraphs. Grateful for the opportunity. Accepting another role that fits my next season. Final day set. HR copied. Badge and equipment to be returned. No heat. No history. I saved it and closed the lid like I had put a piece of glass in a safe place.

Before bed I walked the fence line again. The latch held. The camera blinked at a moth. I stood under the porch light and told myself the sentence I needed: soon. Not because I am running. Because I am choosing. I went inside and slept with Rusty at my feet and the order on the fridge and the plan in my pocket.

Boxes & Boundaries

The phone rang before I finished the first coffee. Mom first, then Dad from the other room, a duet I know by heart.

"Come down this weekend," Mom said. "Sleep, eat, sit in the good chair. Your father will grill. We will not ask questions."

Dad forgot the last part. "We miss you. You should be here. We have pecans and a fresh pie from the lady at church. Drive down today and stay until Monday."

I closed my eyes and let the love sit where it belongs. "I want to," I said. "I cannot. Not this time. I have things I need to do here. It is a lot. I promise I will come soon."

Mom did not argue. She knows the difference between no and not yet. "Then tell me what you need," she said.

"You are already doing it," I said. "Keep Rusty's extra carrier handy. Save me a slice of that pie for next time. Pray that next week is boring."

Dad sighed in the way that means he is accepting my answer and also reserving the right to repeat the invitation tomorrow. "Fine," he said. "We love you. Call tonight."

I stood in the kitchen and looked at the cabinets like they were a mountain. Moving had always been a picture I kept far away. Now it had a grocery list. I opened the laptop and typed in the words that make it real. Amazon. Bubble wrap. Moving boxes. Tape gun. Sharpies. Dish sleeves. Wardrobe boxes. Labels that do not peel off in the heat.

The screen filled with options that all looked both identical and urgent. I chose heavy duty boxes in two sizes because that is what the calm blogs say. I added a twelve pack of tape with one of those dispensers that sound like you are tearing fabric in a quiet theater. I added a hundred feet of bubble wrap even though I suspect I will need another hundred. A dish sleeve that promises to keep plates from learning how to break. A roll of fragile stickers for the boxes that hold glass and keys and the parts of a life that cannot be replaced with a gift card. Prime promised tomorrow. I clicked Place Order and watched the little confetti check mark that means cardboard is on its way.

I looked around the room and felt the size of it. A whole house, even a small rented one, is not just walls. It is objects that have learned your hands. Every drawer is a story. Every shelf has an argument for why it still belongs in your life. I set the timer on the stove for forty minutes and told myself I would not overthink. Keep. Donate. Trash. That is all I have to do today.

I started in the kitchen because there are rules there. I opened the cabinet with the mismatched mugs and pulled them all down. Three I kept. The yellow one with the chip, my mother's extra from a set that did not survive college apartments. The heavy white one that feels like a diner and holds both coffee and bad news. The matte gray one with the oak leaf I bought from Original Visuals at the market because it felt like a plan. The rest I set in a box labeled donate in a hand that would never win a penmanship award.

Next drawer. Towels that are more hole than cloth. Trash. A whisk that tangles itself. Donate. The good knife, keep. The cheap peeler that always judges me. Donate without mercy. I moved faster once I accepted that deciding is a muscle and mine had been underused.

When the timer dinged I closed the box and taped it. The sound of the tape gun satisfied something I cannot name. I made a keep stack for the things that know my kitchen and a donate stack near the door. I tied the trash bag and set it by the back steps for later. I set the timer again and worked the other side of the room.

By late morning I had four boxes marked in red. Keep. Donate. Keep. Keep. The keep stacks looked like a life, not a museum. I wiped the counters and let the room be better than I had found it.

The living room is trickier. Memory hides there. I made three piles on the rug. The books I will read again. The books that should go to someone else. The books that I will pretend I have not already read. The music pile. The piano books that I keep in the secret hope I will have a wall that deserves them. The stack of concert programs that should have felt lighter than they did.

I set my grandmother's Bible back in the china cabinet the way I have since the night the house was opened and read without me. I put cotton gloves on like a museum keeper because respect does not make you fragile, it makes you careful. I whispered thank you to a woman who learned how to stretch a dollar and a Sunday without complaint.

I paused for lunch and ate a leftover rib from Hickory Roots with my fingers because forks sometimes get in the way of mercy. Then I opened the laptop again and typed Zillow. The world is a map until it is a house. I typed Marion County, Florida, and watched the page fill with dots that represent lives I do not yet know.

Ocala. Dunnellon. Belleview. Ocklawaha. Silver Springs. Names that sound like water and horses and oak trees that do not ask for permission to grow. I checked the filter because this is the first time in my life the price does not have to be the first thing. It felt wrong not to slide the budget bar down to the low end. I slid it to one million and let the number sit like a quiet animal in the room. I will not spend to feel different. I will buy what fits the life I want. One million is a ceiling that gives me space to breathe and buy trees.

Pool. That filter clicked without shame. I need water to swim laps at night and forgive the day. Land. I checked five acres and up. I do not need a ranch. I need enough room for a porch and a fence line and a place to put a long table. House size. Modest. I do not want a mansion that eats weekends. I want a place that works hard and rests well.

The photos showed tile floors and screened lanais and kitchens that look like they understand supper. I saved ten that called my name. One with a live oak bent like a sentence you want to read twice. One with a small barn with lights already strung. One with a piano in the listing photo, out of tune in a way that made me smile. The descriptions were the same kind of brag. New roof. Updated HVAC. Saltwater pool. Three car garage. I do not need three cars. I need one good reason to invite people over and a place to set their plates.

I clicked over to Realtor.Com and repeated the ritual because sometimes you need two maps to believe in a place. The same houses with a different order. A few rentals. I saved a small house with a pool that does not look like it belongs to anyone on a magazine cover. Three bedrooms so my parents can come without sleeping in a room that smells like boxes. A lawn a person could mow without hating Saturday. I made a list of rents and set it beside the list of purchase prices. Numbers do not scare me when they are honest. I will rent first under the trust for a few months so my feet can learn the grocery store and the way the rain sounds on the roof. Then I will buy when the right place raises its hand.

I moved the map around and let the towns show me their patterns. Ocala near the center, horse farms and people who know how to build fences straight. Marion County. That is not the coast, which takes some vulnerability out of the weather. The beach is still reachable in a drive that feels like vacation. The areas near Silver Springs look like they keep their shade. Dunnellon has a river that makes the air softer. Nothing felt wrong. That surprised me. I wrote in the notebook. Marion County. East of Ocala. Under one million. Pool. One to five acres. Trees that know their job. Close to church and a grocery that sells pecans.

The phone buzzed with a shipping notification. The boxes and bubble wrap were already on a truck somewhere between here and a warehouse that does not need to sleep. Tomorrow my porch will be made of cardboard and decisions.

I closed the laptop and started another forty minute timer. Hall closet. Jackets that do not know how to be useful in Texas. Hats that never fit right. Gloves that belong to a woman who thought she might learn to shovel snow. Donate. Keep. Trash. I taped two more boxes. The sound filled the house with something like progress.

I pulled the plastic bin of old photos down from the top shelf and set it on the floor. I didn't open it. Not today. There are boxes you cannot open without a friend sitting next to you and a glass of tea for both of you. I labeled it with a heart because I needed a joke that was not a joke. I wrote a plan to scan on the lid. I will buy a scanner that can eat them slowly and deliver them to a folder that does not get lost in water or fire or a drawer someone can open when I am not home.

I locked the back door and stepped onto the front porch. The side yard camera blinked once to say it was awake and paying attention. The latch held. The sky thought about rain and did not commit. I breathed and felt the way my body keeps score. Fear has been a sound in the house. Today it was not first in line. Being busy is a kind of blessing when you are trying not to live inside your own head for too long at a time.

On the way back in I checked the mailbox. Bills that will be paid and canceled soon. A flyer for a place that thinks I need gutters. A white envelope from the United States Postal Service with my name printed wrong by one letter. I did not like the way that felt. I opened it right there by the street like the houses were witnesses.

Inside was a Move Validation Letter. It thanked me for submitting a change of address request and said the carrier would begin forwarding soon unless I did not authorize the change, in which case I should call a number in bold print immediately.

I read it twice. I had not requested a change. My mail is not being forwarded. My life is not being forwarded without me. I held the paper by the edges the way you hold a thing you plan to keep clean for finger-prints. I looked up and down the street. Nothing moved but the dog that barks every day and is still surprised I exist.

I went inside and set my phone on speaker. Menus. A song from ten summers ago. No person. After ten minutes I hung up, grabbed my keys, and drove to the post office.

A poster of holiday stamps. A line that moved like a patient animal. When it was my turn, I slid the letter across the counter. "Someone filed a change of address in my name. It is not mine. I need it canceled."

The clerk nodded like this happens more than people think. "ID, please." I handed over my driver's license. She checked my name and address on the screen, asked me to confirm the last four of my phone, and turned the monitor so I could see it. Dallas apartment number I have never had. Submitted online yesterday morning.

"We will cancel it now and add an extra validation flag on your address for sixty days," she said. "Future changes must be in person with ID. Here is a receipt with the case number. Watch for a confirmation letter. If anything else shows up, bring it in."

She printed the receipt and stapled it to a copy of the letter. I thanked her with the kind of gratitude you feel in your shoulders.

I took photos of the letter and the receipt and texted them to Ms. Hall and Officer Peña. Did not request this. Canceled in person. ID verified. Address flagged. I have a receipt.

Ms. Hall replied in less than a minute. Good. Save the envelope and the USPS receipt. We will add both to the file. Create an online USPS account if you have not and turn on Informed Delivery. Two factors on. New password.

I had already created the account two weeks ago when Mr. Whitlow made a list of common sense steps. I logged in and checked the settings anyway. Two factors on. Email alerts set. Package tracking tied to my phone. I changed the password to one the dictionary would not recognize, which is the kind of victory adults keep to themselves.

Peña replied after his next call. Thank you for logging. Bring the letter and the USPS receipt when you come by to pick up your copy of the report at the station. We are looking at attempted change of address cases in the area this month.

I set the letter and the receipt in a clear folder labeled with the case number and put it in the top drawer of the china cabinet where the Bible sits like a heartbeat. I closed the drawer and pressed both palms flat against the wood. It felt like closing a book to keep the page.

For one hour I stopped packing and sat in the quiet. I let the fear be a person who wanted a chair and did not get one. I wrote down what I had done and what I still need to do if anyone tries again. Freeze credit at the bureaus. I had already done that. Security alerts on my bank accounts. Done. Remove my name from data brokers the way the list tells you to. I had started and would finish. Put a lock on my credit and a lock on the way I talk. I circled the phrase. Do not talk to men who ask about your stops.

By the time the shadows moved across the living room rug, the feeling had stretched thin enough for me to pick up the tape again. I filled one wardrobe box with the dresses that knows how to show up at church. I filled another with the shirts that have endured call center air conditioning. I filled a bag with the clothes that will not be invited to Florida. Donate. Somewhere there is a woman who will be glad I finally let go of a jacket that fits her and not me.

Mrs. Keene suddenly knocked the neighbor's way, three short and friendly. She peered past my shoulder at the stacks. "Moving party?" she said, smiling the soft smile of a woman who has seen a few.

"Packing practice," I said. "Trying to get ahead of the chaos."

She handed me a small loaf in plastic wrap. "Zucchini bread. And I saw a car I did not know ease past twice during the lunch hour. Dark sedan, no front plate. Could be nothing. I wrote the time on this," she said, passing me a folded index card. The time was neat. The handwriting steady.

"Thank you," I said. "I put the patrol number on the fridge. I will log it."

"I will keep an eye out," she said. "You do the same. Holler if you need me to sit with boxes while you run to the store."

I promised I would. She waved at Rusty through the window. He blinked like a monarch blessing a subject and she laughed.

I checked Zillow again because hope is a habit I am allowed to practice. A new listing had appeared with a gray roof and a lanai that looks like it keeps the bugs on the outside of the screen where they belong. The pool is a blue rectangle that looks like a sentence with a period. The trees are live oaks that make their own decisions. The price sits right under the number I set and does not scare me in the way it might have before. I saved it and wrote a small note in the margin of the notebook. Call Ms. Hall this week about how the trust rents before it buys. Ask Mr. Whitlow which bank officer in Marion County understands quiet.

The porch light clicked on behind me as the timer on the plug remembered its job. The side camera blinked at a moth. The street was quiet enough to hear the dog two houses down snore through his shift.

At eight thirty there was a soft knock that did not belong to anyone I know. Not the neighbor knock that carries your name. Not the delivery knock that announces itself with a photo. I checked the doorbell app. A man in a vest with no company logo. A clipboard. He leaned in close to the door as if trying to read the wood grain. He stuck a rectangular notice on the glass by the handle and walked away fast enough to make my neck notice.

I waited until he turned the corner and the side camera saw nothing. I opened the door and used a paper towel to pull the notice down. No logo. No phone number. Just a QR code and the words Delivery Attempt and a line for a signature. The handwriting on the line was mine because it was not. It was a sloppy attempt at my name with the wrong tilt.

I held the paper the way I had held the USPS letter. I did not scan the code. I set the notice on the kitchen counter and took photos front and back. I texted Peña. Unmarked door tag just left by unknown male. No logo. QR code. Wrong signature. I attached the two photos and a third of the man from the doorbell camera. Baseball cap. Plain vest. Sneakers that looked new and bored.

He replied. Do not scan. Thank you. If you can print the photo, do. I will come by tomorrow with a bag for collection or you can drop it at the station.

I put the tag in a zip lock bag and wrote tonight's date across the top. I put the bag with the letter and the receipt in the drawer because the drawer understood the assignment.

Ms. Hall called instead of texting. "How are you?" she said. No flinch.

"Annoyed," I said. "Not scared."

"Good," she said. "Your job is to keep a record and keep your routines boring. The police will chase the QR code. You will not."

"Copy," I said. "I ordered moving supplies. I started boxes. I set up a search in Marion County. I wrote down a budget that made me laugh and then made me cry and then made me breathe again. One million and a pool. Trees. One to five acres."

I could hear her smiling. "That sounds like a woman who knows what she wants. I will send the rental checklist in the morning. We will put the first month under the trust and put utilities in a name that belongs to the trust. Your parents will be told you have a job that fits your schedule and lets you visit. All of that will be true."

"Thank you," I said. There are two kinds of thank you and she always earns both.

After we hung up I did one more pass in the bedroom and filled a box with photographs that I will not look at until the new porch exists. I put a sticky note on top that said open when Florida feels like home. I promised myself I would honor the note.

The night had the kind of quiet that is not a gift, it is a decision. I locked the back door and watched the side camera blink. I stood at the window long enough to recognize the shapes of the cars that belong on my street and the way the trees move when they are only trees.

At ten the phone chimed with one new email. Amazon. Your order is ten stops away. I pictured a driver who is tired and doing the job well anyway. I set a cooler with a bottle of water on the porch and a note that said thank you because gratitude is a practice that works even when you are keeping secrets.

When the boxes arrived I didn't open them. Not tonight. I stacked them by the wall and let the sight of them count as work. Tomorrow will be a day for sorting pans and wrapping picture frames and deciding which towels have earned their retirement. Tonight is for lists and a candle and the feeling in my ribs that I am electing a life instead of being chased into it.

I sat on the couch and scrolled the saved houses again. The blue pool. The oak that bends like a blessing. The kitchen that looks like it forgives mess. The idea that my parents could drive over and sit at a table I picked and eat a pie my mother did not bake in a kitchen that still tastes like hers. The spurs of happiness ran through me like a low current that makes your fingers tingle. I did not try to calm it. Joy has been waiting. It can have the room for a minute.

I set the phone down and let the candle burn low. I wrote the next three steps on the notebook page. Call Peña to drop off the letter, the receipt, and the tag. Call Ms. Hall about the rental setup. Freeze the last data broker that still has me listed under ten old addresses. Then I wrote the sentence that keeps me pointed in the right direction when the noise of other people's plans gets loud.

I will leave because I choose, not because I am chased.

Rusty jumped onto the cushion and pressed his warm side into my hip like a statement of fact. I scratched his neck and told him about the house with the pool and the way the screen will make the air smell after rain. He blinked slowly and authorized the purchase.

When the house was dark and the porch light had gone off and the neighborhood had settled into its late clock, I checked the door one more time. I looked at the stack of boxes and felt the size of the project and did not let it scare me. I blew the candle out and went to bed with the kind of tiredness that makes sleep quick. The camera blinked at a moth. The new lock caught. The old Bible sat where it should. The night did not reach for me.

In the morning, the house will look like a warehouse and I will look like a woman who knows how to pack. The market will open in Ocala whether I move there or not, and I will show up when I am ready. The UPS mailbox will hold a key I have not yet used. The porch I want already exists in my mind. I am walking toward it. One box at a time. One list at a time. One quiet, chosen step at a time.

Digital Locks

Morning started with a list and a login. Coffee. Notebook open. Cursor blinking. I told myself out loud: today I lock down the parts of my life that live in the air. I wrote a title across the top of the page so I could not forget what this was.

Digital Locks.

I drew three columns under it. Phone. Accounts. House. The plan would live there in ink before it lived anywhere else.

First search: How do I keep my phone number from being stolen? The results read like a foreign language for five minutes, so I did what I have been doing since the world tilted. I opened ChatGPT and asked like I was asking a neighbor over a fence.

How do I stop a SIM swap and keep my number safe? Give me plain steps.

The answer came back steady.

1. Call your carrier and set a port out PIN on the line.
2. Ask for a port freeze or number lock if they offer it.
3. Add a verbal passphrase on the account.
4. Turn on two factors for the carrier app and email.
5. Put a lock code on the SIM in your phone settings.
6. Remove your phone number as the only recovery option on banks and email. Use an authenticator app.

7.	Watch for any "we are moving your number" texts and call the fraud line immediately if you get one.

I called my carrier and asked for all of it. The rep sounded surprised in a kind way.

"We can do a port out PIN and a 72 hour no port freeze," she said. "I will add a verbal passphrase too."

"Make it a long one," I said, and chose a sentence that would make no sense to a stranger. I wrote it down on a sticky note I would destroy after I memorized it.

I opened the phone settings and set a SIM lock. The phone warned me that if I forgot the code I would make a mess I could not fix with coffee. I wrote the new code in my notebook in a place only I would look, then I practiced it twice and closed the page.

Back in ChatGPT I asked the second question.

How do I move my banks off text messages to an authenticator without getting locked out?

Add the authenticator as a second factor while you are already logged in on a trusted device. Scan the code. Save the backup codes. Confirm the code work before you turn off text. Update recovery email and remove phone as a recovery method where possible. Do this one account at a time. Don't rush.

I moved one plate at a time. Bank one. Authenticator set. Backup codes stored. Text turned off. Bank two. The brokerage that only ever emails me quarterly statements. The credit card I use for gas and groceries. I signed out of each one on my other devices so the system would ask for the new code and I could be sure the new lock was actually locked.

Mr. Whitlow texted when the sun got higher. Carrier locked?

Locked, I wrote. PIN, passphrase, SIM code. The app is 2FA now.

He replied with a check mark that felt like a hand on my shoulder.

Next on the list: tighten the mailbox setup I opened the day I met Mr. Whitlow. I already have a UPS street address. It is a thirty minute drive from my house in Wills Point to the store in Forney, so I planned it for the end of the workday instead of evening.

Work passed by smoothly for once. I stopped at the UPS store across from MetroCare on my way home to make sure it worked the way I needed. The clerk pulled up my box, added text alerts for packages, a second authorized recipient name, and a note to require ID on pick up. I bought an extra key and asked for my suite number on a small card for my wallet.

Back in the car I opened ChatGPT again.

What should I move to the UPS street address right away, and what should wait? I want less mail at my house.

Move: new utilities for the Florida rental when ready, bank statements you do not need daily, packages, subscription boxes, business correspondence, and any vendor that will sell your info.

Wait: driver license and voter registration until you truly move. Leave tax records where your CPA can reach you securely. Never move official court or protective order documents by mail. Pick those up in person.

I made a column for now and a column for later. Then I emailed two companies that still print statements and asked them to stop. Quiet is a choice you make more than once.

Back at the house the doorbell app pinged a motion alert while I was labeling a box of kitchen things I will want in week one. A moth tested the lens and left. I laughed at myself for flinching at a moth and got back to work.

Half an hour later a text from my carrier lit the screen. Request received to port your number to another carrier. If this was not you, reply NO.

My heart did the small drop, then caught. I typed NO with both thumbs and hit the call on the fraud number like the message told me to. The rep had my file up.

"Your port out PIN blocked it," she said. "We see the attempt. It came from an online request. We are keeping your 72 hour no port freeze active and adding a longer note to your account. You might see a few more texts like this today. Keep replying NO and call if anything changes."

I sat still for a full minute and let my body process the adrenaline without deciding it needed to be fearful. Then I opened ChatGPT again.

SIM swap attempt blocked. What else should I check right now?

1.   Email: review recent logins, revoke any unfamiliar sessions, and change passwords.
2.   Banks and brokerage: verify contact info and alerts.
3.   Cloud storage: turn on alerts for new devices.
4.   Social media: audit recovery settings and turn on login approvals.
5.   Voicemail: set a strong PIN and disable "skip PIN" from your own number.
6.   Router: change admin password, update firmware, and turn off WPS.

I moved down the list like a person washing dishes. One plate at a time. Email, clean. Bank, clean. Cloud, clean. Socials, quiet with cats and bread. Voicemail, now a code a stranger cannot guess. Router, updated and locked. I split my Wi-Fi into two networks, one for the cameras and one for me, because ChatGPT said that is how you keep the toys from touching the wallet.

Then another question because I could feel a blind spot trying to stay blind.

Should I rename my Wi-Fi and hide it?

Rename it to something boring. Do not include your name or address. Hiding the SSID does not add real security. The real wins are a strong router password, up to date firmware, and separate networks for smart devices and personal devices.

I renamed the network to something so dull it made me laugh. I turned off WPS. I changed the admin name off the factory default because I did not need a stranger guessing that part for free.

After lunch I tackled the part that feels like trying to drain a lake: data brokers. I asked a plain question.

Which people search sites should I opt out of first? Give me the top ten and how to do it.

Start with Whitepages, Spokeo, BeenVerified, TruthFinder, Intelius, Radaris, MyLife, FastPeopleSearch, PeopleFinders, and Number. Each has a form or email. Use a new, dedicated email alias for opt outs. Save confirmation pages as PDFs. Repeat every few months.

I made a new email just for this chore and started clicking. Each site wanted me to prove I was me and that I did not want to be listed. I found three entries with my house, two old rentals, and a version of my name that belonged to a girl who kept too many magazine subscriptions. I removed them one by one and saved every confirmation in a folder named after the chore. When a site insisted I upload an ID, I backed out and chose a cousin site that accepted text confirmation instead. I do not feed copies of my license to machines I do not control.

I asked another question because it sits next to this one and nobody ever tells you that until it is too late.

Besides the big credit bureaus, who else can I freeze so new accounts are harder to open in my name?

Freeze ChexSystems and NCTUE for telecom and utilities. Freeze Innovis and request a security freeze at LexisNexis. Consider a fraud alert at the main bureaus if you want lenders to call you before opening accounts. Keep copies of all confirmations.

I checked my file. Equifax, Experian, TransUnion, and ChexSystems were already locked. I added freezes at Innovis and NCTUE and printed the confirmations. I submitted the LexisNexis request and set a reminder to check for the letter. I slipped each page into a page protector and added it to the drawer that is turning into a small fortress of paper.

Mrs. Keene texted at two thirty. Clipboard man again. Noon today. Took a photo toward your side yard, then walked on. Blue cap. She attached a grainy photo from her porch camera. I sent it to Peña with the time. He replied with a thumbs up and the two words that let me breathe. Logged, patrol.

I put the kettle on and stood by the window with a mug that knew my hand. The block looked normal. A truck that belongs on this street. The boy across the way skateboarding with a helmet his mother finally convinced him to wear. The ordinary keeps me honest about what is dangerous and what is just Tuesday. But never could I have imagined that I had to do all this work for my own safety.

In the afternoon I turned to passwords because I could feel a lecture from Ms. Hall building in the air. I asked Chat GPT again.

Best practices for passwords for a normal person. I do not want to be a hacker. I want to be boring and safe.

Use a password manager. Let it make long, unique passwords. Turn on two factors for anything that pays a bill or holds a photo. Use passkeys where offered. Make three security questions that are not real answers. Example: Mother's maiden name: CountryPie1979. Do not reuse that pattern. Back up your manager with a printed recovery code stored in a safe place.

I chose a manager, let it build the long strings, and printed the recovery sheet. I put the paper in the china cabinet drawer with the other papers that matter because the drawer has earned the right to hold things.

Then I looked at the list of devices that can touch my accounts. Laptop. Phone. The old tablet I had not charged in two years. I signed the tablet out of everything and put it in the donation pile. I do not need to carry ghost doors with me when I am building a new house.

One more question, because I do not like surprises.

How do I make my voicemail less useful to scammers?

Set a PIN if your carrier still supports voicemail from any phone. Turn off options that let you access voicemail without a code. In your greeting, do not say your full name. Keep it short and plain. Example: "You have reached this number. Please leave a message."

I recorded the blandest greeting in the history of telephones and felt safer for being a little boring.

At four my email pinged with a password reset request for my internet account. I had not asked for one. I did not click. I typed the provider's URL myself in a new tab, logged in clean, saw no change, and set a new password anyway. Then I asked ChatGPT the question you ask when a thing will not stop nibbling at your calm.

How do I tell if a password reset email is phishing on my phone where I cannot hover links?

Check the sender's address carefully. Use the app or type the URL, never tap from the email. Look for odd grammar and generic greetings. Compare the email to a known good message from that provider. Turn on push alerts inside the account so the account tells you about changes directly.

I turned on push alerts and decided not to give the email any more of my time.

Ten minutes later the phone rang. "This is the fraud department with your bank," a voice said. "We detected an outgoing wire you did not authorize. We need to verify your identity by text code."

I did not sigh. I did not engage. I read from the script ChatGPT and Ms. Hall had helped me write.

"I do not verify by inbound call," I said. "I will call the number on the back of my card."

The line went dead before I finished the sentence. I typed the bank number into the phone myself and reached the real fraud department.

"There is no wire and no call from us," the woman said. "Thank you for checking. We will add a note and an extra step on wires."

I texted Peña. Bank spoof call. I called back using my card number. False. Adding notes with the bank. He replied, Logged. Good procedure.

Earlier, on the way out of the parking lot at the UPS Store I had tucked a simple test label to my suite number into my bag. I printed it and stuck it to a small box of kitchen gadgets I can live without for a week. I will see if it lands where it is supposed to land.

I fed Rusty and set him up with the toy mouse that has survived six moves and zero actual mouse behavior. Then I opened ChatGPT one more time.

I have a door tag with a QR code that is not from a company I know. Police have a copy. Anything else I should do?

Do not scan. Photograph front and back, keep the original in a bag. Pull stills from your camera. File a short report so you get a case number if you do not have one. Consider a small sign: "All deliveries to UPS suite address across town." It stops honest drivers from knocking and removes excuses for strangers.

A sign. That made sense. I printed a small one and taped it inside the glass where only a person who really walked up could see it. I added a second line in smaller print. No cash. No checks. No same day pickups without prior arrangement. It felt ridiculous and also like a fence that belonged where I put it.

Then I went back to Zillow, because hope is a habit I am allowing to become muscle. I checked my saved homes in Marion County and added notes. One had a pool that looked like it knew how to hold quiet. Another had a kitchen that forgave messes. I put stars by the ones that felt like they could hold a piano and a Friday night without complaint. I made a new saved search for rentals within thirty minutes of Ocala Regional because that seemed like a hospital you would want to know how to reach on a day you do not want to think about hospitals. I set the filter for properties with a fence because Rusty has opinions about the size of his kingdom.

The phone buzzed with a last text from the carrier. Port request denied. Account now flagged. I felt the small lift of relief that comes when competent systems do their job.

I wrote in the notebook to close the day. Port out PIN set. Port attempt blocked. UPS mailbox confirmed and tuned. Data broker opt outs started. Router locked. Password manager live. Clipboard man logged. Sign posted. Test package sent. Tomorrow: pick up the police report copy, print the camera stills for Peña, move two more vendors to the suite address, and start the rental checklist with Ms. Hall. Keep the circle small.

I blew out the candle Whitney poured and watched the smoke curl like a quiet line. Rusty blinked slowly and took his place on the couch like a small orange judge. The house felt held by the boring work I had done. I let that feeling count as rest.

The phone buzzed one more time as I turned off the lamp. Unknown accessory detected near you. The alert sat on the screen like a pebble in the shoe of a long walk.

I opened ChatGPT again with a hand that did not shake.

My phone says an unknown accessory is moving with me. What do I do right now?

Tap the alert to view the device details and play a sound. If it is an AirTag or similar, use Directions to locate it. If it is inside a bag or under a car, do not remove it on a dark street. Go to a safe, well lit place first, or a police station lot. Document what you find. Photograph the serial number. You can disable most trackers by removing the battery. If you feel unsafe, call non-emergency and ask for an officer to meet you in a public place.

I stood very still in the doorway with the porch light off and the house quiet behind me. The screen glowed. Rusty lifted his head and watched me like a judge who is also a friend. I took a breath and chose the next right step. I tapped the alert and walked toward the brighter part of my kitchen where the counters are clean and the decisions are simple.

Rumors & Shadows

I woke to a quiet that pretends to be kind. The house had its morning manners. Floorboards knew when to keep secrets. I started coffee and let the kettle talk while the light learned the room. Shower. Jeans. Hair back. List on the counter with a pen that writes the first time.

The alert from last night sat in my head like a pebble you cannot ignore. Unknown accessory detected. The crawl on my phone had said it twice before the sound even registered. Then the crawl became a flashlight beam under the bumper. A black magnet case where no case belongs. Peña at my curb with a steady light and steady voice. Evidence bag. Chain of custody. The device is gone to a room that eats signals and returns numbers with names.

I wrote the case number at the top of a fresh page and drew a box around it so it could not climb away. Date. Time. Two lines underneath: Car parked. Do not leave the block without eyes. Routes change today.

Rusty hopped to the counter and placed one paw on the notebook like he was swearing in. "You and me," I said. He blinked his approval and watched the kettle finish its small song.

Before I did anything else, I printed stills from my cameras for Peña. Three angles, timestamps in the corner. The dark sedan that does not belong, two passes, one pause. I slid them into a clear sleeve and put the sleeve in the folder with the USPS receipt and the QR door tag. The china cabinet drawer closed with the polite sound that tells me a plan has been fed.

I stopped at the police station on my way to work to pick up the formal report copy and drop the stills. Peña met me in the lobby, no rush, just the kind of presence that pays attention.

"We ran the serial on the tracker," he said. "It has not hit in other reports. We are holding it as evidence. If you get another alert, let me know immediately. Don't go hunting in the dark."

"Copy," I said.

He handed me a printout and a small card. "That is your updated report. This card has our non-emergency line and the case reference. If a news crew or anyone else pushes you for a comment, hand them the card and say all inquiries go through the department."

"Thank you," I said. Small words keep doing their work.

He glanced toward the door. "One more thing. Our community liaison is tracking online chatter about the Powerball winner. A rumor thread popped up overnight in a local Facebook group. It is getting clicks. No names. A few guesses about places. QT. UPS Store. Forney. You fit in on all of that so take the long route wherever you are going from now on."

"I will," I said. My mouth went dry for a breath and then came back.

I had to sit in the car for a minute. I pulled the visor down and looked at myself like a stranger. No hero. No victim. Just a woman with coffee and a plan. I drove the long route and counted the number of times I checked the mirror. I stopped at a different pump at a different station and paid at the pump without walking in. I didn't buy any tea. The habit tugged at my sleeve like a child. I kept both hands on the wheel.

At MetroCare the lot was full the way it is on Mondays and also on days that are not Mondays. I parked near the light pole and walked in at a pace that said I knew where I was going. Maya met me at my seat with a look that meant something had happened.

"You saw the group, right?" she said, barely moving her lips.

"What group?" I said, setting my bag down like it was just a bag.

She opened her phone under the desk and tilted the screen. Kaufman County Chat. The top post was a blurry photo of a white envelope with the USPS eagle. The caption read, *Heard the winner might be a woman who works in Forney, drives a red Kia Soul, shops at the QT in Terrell, and rents near downtown Wills Point. My cousin knows someone at the store.* The comments were a pile of theories and usernames that like to make noise.

Every hair on my arm noticed the air. My car is not the only red Kia Soul in East Texas. My life is not the only life that stops for tea. Rumors throw spaghetti until something sticks. I told my face to keep the same shape.

"People are bored," I said. "They said that when folks were looking for the dog that got out last week too. Do you think I would be here if it was me?"

Maya searched my eyes for a few seconds and then nodded like she had found enough. "If anyone asks you, you do not know what Facebook is," she said. "I will put out a bowl of candy so folks keep their mouths busy."

We logged in. The morning opened its claws. Payment portal glitch, followed by a script change for the first hour greeting, followed by an outage that ate voicemails. I took calls and pictured a lane of wire between my ear and a person who just wanted to be heard. That helped. The room felt a little thinner than usual. When a news van rolled by on the road outside, two people stood up at their stations to look and pretended they needed paper from the printer.

At ten fifteen an email landed from Tom with the subject All Hands in Break Room. He does this when his hands feel too empty and he needs a crowd to ask for the thing he should have sent in a memo.

We went. People lined the walls. Kendra stood near the microwave and looked at her shoes. Tom stood by the whiteboard with a stack of papers he did not hand out.

"Couple things," he said, and his voice already made my back tighten. "Scripts are changing this week. Effective now. We are eliminating the second identity question. That is a leadership decision. Also, attendance remains a priority. Coverage is tight. If you need time off, use the proper channels. We are not a cafeteria. You do not get to pick a schedule like you pick a sandwich."

He was not talking to the room. He was talking to me. People snuck glances the way people do when they want to know how to read the day. I kept my hands on my coffee and my eyes on a dent in the whiteboard frame.

He kept going. "Also, I do not want to hear anyone repeating rumors from social media. We are not children. If you have time to gossip, you have time to take another call."

Maya shifted near me. "He is worried about his own rumors," she whispered. I kept my mouth still.

The meeting ended the way these meetings end. A few questions, no real answers, everyone back to their row with a little less patience. As we filed out, Kendra brushed my arm by accident or by accident on purpose. Her eyes were glassy. She has made a choice and choices have side effects.

Back at my station I felt the hive turn. Two DMs from coworkers who like to know things. One from a number I did not have in my phone. *We know you are the one. Meet me or we will tell.* No name. No punctuation. The area code matched Dallas.

I did not respond. I took a screenshot and sent it to Ms. Hall with one line. New number. Threat flavor. No response. Ms. Hall replied.. Good. Do not engage. Block. Keep the screen.

The next call I took was a man who had received a disconnect notice in error and cried when I fixed it. The sound reset me. People and their bills are not the enemy in this story. People are people. The thing in the dark is the thing we will handle with lists and light.

At lunch I chose to leave the building. Fresh air felt like medicine. I walked to the far side of the lot, took a lap, and came back as a blue SUV with a magnetic sign that said News Now coasted along the curb. The passenger rolled down the window and lifted a hand in a way that tries to look friendly and often is not.

"Are you Rachel?" she said.

"Heading to lunch, sorry," I said. True enough, and a good shield. I walked to the side door and used my badge. The door closed behind me and the world got quieter by several degrees.

Maya met me in the break room with the kind of grin that stands in for a curse. "They are camped," she said. "I told Pam at the front to route all inquiries to the main number and she put the FAQ on the desk. We are a utility company today."

I ate a small apple like it was a plan. I put the core in the trash and washed my hands and went back to the floor.

The UPS Store in Forney called just after two. "Rachel, this is Tommy. Someone tried to pick up a package for you. Wrong ID, wrong story. We did not release it. We flagged your box to hold until you arrive and we will only release to you or the name you added this morning. We have a camera."

"Thank you," I said. "Please hold everything for me. I will be there after work."

Tommy paused. "There is also a man in a blue cap who has been sitting in the lot for thirty minutes. Not illegal. Not customer behavior either. I already called the non-emergency line."

"Thank you again," I said. Gratitude keeps company with fear and gives it less room to stretch.

I messaged Ms. Hall. UPS caught an attempt. Will pick up in person. Cameras rolling.

She replied. Good. Bring nothing sensitive to the counter. Watch your tail on the way home. If you feel watched, three right turns and into a lit lot. We prepared for this.

Suddenly the fire alarm went off. The kind that starts small and then becomes a demand. We filed out down the stairs, two by two, the way we have practiced. Outside the sun hit hard and hot. I keep a jacket at my chair because they keep the air so low inside you forget the shape of heat. The jacket did not come out the door with me.

We stood in the row where we always stand. Tom counted heads in a way that told me he was counting compliance more than safety. The news van drifted closer to the line like a shark that has learned the edges of a pool.

I tracked my car with my eyes. It sat under the light pole where I had left it. The blue cap man I don't know was standing two cars over, too casual, hands in pockets, eyes moving. Three right turns and a lot. That is for cars. I needed a version for feet.

I pulled my phone out and took a photo of the row behind me like I was taking a photo of the sky. The camera caught half his face. He looked away. I pretended I was choosing a filter. I was choosing an exit.

The Forney Fire Department showed up with their big engine. Out jumped a couple of men and the other girls almost started drooling. What's so special about them? I thought to myself.

When they let us back in, I told Maya in a voice that did not tremble. "I am going to the UPS Store now and then home. If I do not text you by six, call me."

"You got it," she said. "You want me to follow in my car and peel off if it gets weird."

"No," I said. "If anything gets interesting, I will go to the station."

On my way out I handed Pam at the front desk the card Peña had given me. "If the press comes back, this is the number for all inquiries," I said. She tapped the card like it was a badge.

I drove the long route to the UPS Store. Mirror checks at natural points. Three songs that have known me since I was fifteen and remind my body what calm feels like. I snarled through the entire shopping center before parking on the side of the store. The lot looked like itself. Tommy waved me in before I finished the hello.

He slid two small boxes across the counter. "Held for you ma'am. The man in the cap left when the police car rolled through. We printed his face from our camera. Here."

The still was grainy and still enough. Same cap. Same boring sneakers. I put the photo in the folder without letting my fingers touch the print.

"I added a note on your account to call you if anyone lingers," he said. "We can also hold everything in the back and not put any slips in the box if you prefer."

"Please do that," I said. "Also, do you sell those tiny key safes that look like garage openers?"

"We do," he said, pulling one from under the counter. "Combination is set by you."

I bought it and tucked the receipt into a second folder that now travels with me when the first folder rides at home.

By the time I got back to the highway my shoulders ached from pretending not to be made of bones. Traffic was itself. Trucks. Pickups. A school bus obeying rules I respect. Another red Kia Soul merged two cars ahead of me. I let it be what it is. A color. A model. Not a signature.

At home I made the pass inside the house that is now a habit. Back door latch. Slider sticks in place. Motion light. Front door. Camera blink. Everything where I left it. Rusty trotted behind me like a gossip until I put kibble in the bowl. He has a way of eating that lets me know he trusts the evening.

I sat at the table and opened the laptop. The rumor post had grown branches. Someone claimed the winner had been seen at a bank in Terrell. Someone else claimed it was a man in his twenties because their cousin knows a cousin who knows a bank teller. Ms. Hall texted very timingly. Do not watch.

I turned the page in the notebook to a clean space and wrote the next steps in a square hand that tries not to lean. Move the ticket to a safe deposit box under the trust. Private branch. Closed door. The sentence made my stomach drop and then steady. The Bible has held it before. The vault has held it since. The trust will hold it best. That plan stays between me and Ms. Hall.

I called her. We kept it slow.

"I would like to place the document under the trust," I said. "Quiet branch. Private room. Tomorrow. "

"Yes, that sounds like a good idea," she said. "I will arrange a room where the manager understands what a closed door means. We will use the trust name. You will sign the box card as trustee. Bring ID. Do not bring a bag you cannot afford to have searched. Meet me in the parking lot. We will walk in together."

"Copy," I said.

At six thirty my phone buzzed with a text from my mother. *Did you see they interviewed the QT manager? He said they cannot say who bought it. Your father says it was a woman because the Lord told him women deserve a turn. Come down this weekend.*

I typed one line. Soon. Busy week. Love you. She sent a heart. My father sent a GIF of a rocket and I laughed because the man learned GIFs last year and has been trying to keep up with the century ever since.

I put a pot of water on and stared out the window like the street had answers. A silver car rolled past slow and then picked up speed like it remembered itself. The porch light timer clicked. The world kept doing what the world does.

At seven, the doorbell app pinged. A person in a bright yellow vest stood very close to the lens, head tilted down like they were reading a book on the doormat. He put a door tag on the glass and walked away at a pace I do not trust. I waited thirty seconds, opened the door, and used a paper towel to collect the tag. The same format as before. Same QR. Same crooked attempt at my name.

I put it in a bag without breathing on it and texted Peña. Another tag. Same style. Same time in the evening. He wrote back. We will swing by. Leave it in the bag.

I poured hot water over tea because I needed a different flavor in my mouth. I sat at the table with the notebook and the folder and the new key safe and wrote a line that was less a line and more a promise. I will walk into the bank with a steady hand and a steady heart and I will walk out with the same.

The knock at the door was light and specific. Peña and officer Carter stood with the kind of posture that keeps neighbors calm.

"Bag," I said, and handed it over.

Carter sealed it with a strip of tape and wrote the date with neat block letters. Peña looked at the window trim. "Do you mind if we walk the yard with your permission?"

"Please do," I said. I watched from the porch. They took a full circle, slow, lights low. Peña stopped at the fence and crouched. He picked up a tiny disk of plastic from the dirt with gloved fingers.

"From a cheap tracker case," he said. "Probably the hinge. He might have practiced."

The hair on my arms stood again and then settled. He bagged the disk and made a note. We spoke only about perimeters, timing, and the non-emergency line. The rest stayed in my notebook.

They left with a wave that felt like a promise. I locked the door and stood with my back against it for ten full seconds. Rusty head butted my shin and said his line in the only language he has. I fed him a small treat. He accepted it like a monarch receiving tribute.

Dinner was a sandwich I ate because eating makes thinking work. I washed the plate. I practiced with my bank bag. Folder only. ID. One pen. No jewelry that can snag. Hair up. Shoes that do not slip. A jacket with pockets deep enough to keep hands from broadcasting nerves. I laid it all out like an altar to competence.

Before bed I opened ChatGPT and asked the question that had been purging in the back of my mind. *What do I do if the news crew tries to follow me in a car tomorrow. I want practical moves that do not escalate anything.*

The answer was simple and useful. Change your route naturally. Make three right turns that bring you back to the same street. If they are still there, drive to a police station lot or a grocery store lot with cameras and people. Stay in your car. Call the non-emergency number. Do not drive to your home. Do not confront. Park where the cameras see you and wait for the officer.

I wrote it in the notebook like a spell. Three rights. Safe lot. Cameras. Call.

I went room to room and touched the places that hold the day. Stove off. Lamp off. Door locked. Camera charged. Folder under the jacket, inside a tote that has had six lives and can have one more. Rusty jumped on the bed and walked in a circle like a man deciding where to pitch a tent. He chose the place near my knees. He always does.

Sleep came slower than I like. When it arrived, it came in two pieces. The first was a shallow drift that let headlights draw patterns on the wall. The second was a drop so deep I dreamed of blue water under live oaks and a fence line that has already forgiven me for leaving late.

The sound that woke me was not the door or the window or the phone. It was like the quietness after a car engine stopped. I lay there and listened. A cricket. The hum of the fridge. Then footsteps on the sidewalk and a pause.

I turned the screen of my phone face up and watched for the doorbell alert. It did not light. The footsteps moved on. My body shook the way a body shakes when it does not need to and cannot yet stop. I put the phone down and breathed into my hands the way my grandmother taught me when I was five and thought the light at the end of the hall was a ghost.

It took time for sleep to come back. Morning would come and I would walk into a bank and put a piece of paper in a steel drawer with a key that says the next part of my life will start on purpose. The rumor mill would keep grinding. Tom would find a new rule to throw across a room. The man with the cap would learn that his face is not a mask. I would keep my circle small and my steps measured. I would keep choosing.

The last thing I saw before my eyes closed was the small line at the bottom of the page, underlined so I could not miss it in the morning.

I leave because I choose, not because I am chased.

The Decoy

Weekday light leaked around the blinds and told on me. Coffee. Shower. The jacket with the inside pocket that fits a folder and a steady hand. I set my existing vault key on the table for one breath the way you lay a palm on a Bible. Then I put it in my left pocket where I could feel it without looking. The notebook went in the tote. Nothing else.

I drove the long route. Past Whisked Away Bake House where the morning smells like sugar. Past the church sign that changes on Tuesdays and today said to let your yes be yes. A mother steadied a backpack into the crosswalk with patience that belongs in a museum. Normal is medicine if you do not take too much.

Ms. Hall was already in the lot, three rows over, sunglasses on, hair pinned in a way that does not invite questions. Mr. Whitlow pulled in from the other side in a rental that could belong to any accountant. We walked in together like three strangers who had learned the same polite rhythm.

The branch manager met us at the door. Her tag said E. Molina. Her eyes said she keeps a list in her head that nobody else can see.

"Good morning," she said. "You have a personal box here already, Ms. Mercer. Would you like to access that first, then complete the trust box paperwork, or sign first."

"Personal box first, then trust," Ms. Hall said. "Private room, please."

Ms. Molina led us to a small room with a door that knew its job. No windows. A table. Two pens that worked. She asked for my key, took it with a nod, and left us. A minute later she returned with my current box in a metal sleeve, set it on the table, and stepped out again without trying to see the day.

I opened the sleeve and slid the drawer onto the felt. Inside, the plain folder with the sticky note from the first day at this branch sat where I had left it. I lifted the folder, opened the inner sleeve, and there it was. The ticket, wrapped in my grandmother's Sunday cloth. I did not say the numbers out loud. I let them live in my head like a prayer.

Ms. Hall looked once and nodded, slow and careful. Mr. Whitlow looked away for one respectful second.

"Now we move it," Ms. Hall said.

I closed the folder and kept both hands on it while Ms. Hall pressed the call button. Ms. Molina returned and set out the trust forms. Neutral name. Trustee line with my name. Secondary access line left blank for now. We signed where the cards asked us to sign. The ink dried without smearing. Ms. Molina spun the vault wheel and guided us to a mid level slot that does not require reaching.

She slid the new trust box out and set it on the table. Then she left again and closed the door. The room held its quiet like a favor.

I opened the folder. I folded the cloth back with two fingers. I lifted the ticket and set it into the steel. The sound was nothing. The weight was everything. We closed the lid. I turned the key. Ms. Hall nodded once more, the way a person does at a finished sentence.

Ms. Molina returned with the signature card. I signed the trust box card as trustee. She recorded the number, turned the outer lock, and handed me the new key. We kept my original personal box open on purpose with only the plain folder inside, now empty. Paper trail undisturbed. No drama.

Back in the small room, Ms. Hall gathered the executed forms. Mr. Whitlow slid the trust copy into his slim portfolio. I put the new key in my left pocket beside the old one and touched it once to teach my hands what to find.

The key sat in my pocket like a small iron promise.

Ms. Hall folded her hands and glanced at my phone. "Before we go further, I am calling your employer."

She dialed on speaker and introduced herself to Tornado Tom with the kind of courtesy that carries steel inside it. "Mr. Rigsby, I represent Ms. Mercer. Effective immediately, she is on protected safety leave tied to an active police matter and a standing protective order. Leave her personal matters alone. Any questions go through me. If you retaliate or attempt to compel disclosures, HR will receive my written notice and the Terrell and Wills Point Police incident numbers."

Even from three feet away I could hear his breath flare. "She cannot just not show up."

"She can," Ms. Hall said, calm as a courtroom. "She has PTO on file, and she has counsel. For the next seventy two hours she is unavailable except by email for essential process questions. Do not call her. Do not text her. Do not discuss her with coworkers. This is a safety directive. I will follow up with HR in writing."

A long pause, the sound a man makes when volume stops working. "Fine," he said. "But this is highly irregular."

"So is being stalked," Ms. Hall said, and ended the call. She opened her computer and sent an email with the same language to HR and cc'd me. The copy sat in my inbox like a doorbell camera. It would record who touched it.

"Now," she said, turning back to the table, "the other thing."

Peña knocked and stepped in like the air was his friend. I felt my stomach jump. This was not his jurisdiction. A bank in Terrell is not a Wills Point front porch.

"Officer Peña," I said before I could stop myself. "Why are you here?"

With him was a man in plain clothes whose badge sat in a wallet that closed with a snap. "Sergeant Laird," he said, "Dallas FBI field office, working in coordination with Wills Point PD." His voice had the gravel of a road that does not mind being driven every day.

I looked from one to the other and felt the question crawl up my throat. How did they know? How much did they know? If he says the word I do not say, this room becomes a rumor.

Ms. Hall touched the back of my hand, a small anchor. "The circle is very small," she said. "You are safe."

Peña kept his voice even. "I am here for continuity. You are my resident. I am not reading bank papers. I am perimeter and hand-off. That is all."

Laird sat, palms open on the table. "We do not use the word you are worried about," he said. "Not in email. Not on radio. Not in reports. In our files it is a high value document held by a private trust. Your name is redacted anywhere it does not absolutely have to appear. The trust name is used only inside attorney communication. Nothing about a lottery exists in RMS." He glanced at Ms. Hall. "Attorney-client privilege covers the rest. We sign for that line. We stay on our side of it."

I heard my own voice come out smaller than I like. "Will this leak?"

"If it leaks, it will not come from here," Peña said. "My report codes use burglary, surveillance, and suspicious persons. Not the other thing. My chief and I signed a confidentiality acknowledgment tied to this specific case number. Any officer who breaks it is off the case and in front of Internal. We do not play with a resident's safety."

Ms. Hall nodded once. "I briefed Sergeant Laird with your consent on the safety plan only. They need to know. No details beyond what keeps you breathing and calm."

Some part of me let go of the chair. I could feel the floor again.

"We will keep it simple," Laird said, returning to the map. "My extra officers today are also from the Dallas FBI office. Special Agent Tran is running comms. We are coordinating with the local PD, but this operation is federal led. We believe you have at least two actors. Blue cap. The telecom port artist. They could be the same or they could be cousins. Either way, they look tied to a larger network we are already tracking for thefts and fraud across North Texas. We are not doing this because of a ticket. We are doing it because we think they are practicing on you and others for bigger hits."

Ms. Hall added one rule that sounded like a lock clicking. "No one uses Ms. Mercer's name on the radio. You say trustee or client. If the word comes up, the word comes from me in a closed room."

Laird tapped the card he had brought. "You have a quiet panic fob. If you squeeze for three seconds and can speak, the keyword is the pet name we just chose. If you cannot speak, the fob gives us your location and case code. That signal goes only to my desk and Agent Tran. No shared channels."

Peña gave me a short nod I have come to trust. "We carry our part. You carry yours. Small and steady."

I chose one that made me smile and he wrote it on a card with my case number and tucked it back into his wallet. He clipped a palm camera inside my tote. "It sees what you see and streams to us," he said. "Do not try to make a movie. Just live in front of it."

Ms. Hall opened her briefcase and removed a bank envelope that looked real enough to stand up in court. Inside was a thick pad of paper cut to the size of hundreds and wrapped in a band. On top, a photocopy of a ticket that only a trained eye would doubt.

"We run a controlled bait," Laird said. "FBI led. Our timing. Our cars. You do not play cowboy. You do not improvise. We put decoys in motion and see who follows which one."

"We are not hunting," Ms. Hall said. "We are watching who hunts."

We spent the next hour setting bones. Timing. Routes. Stops. Three windows that look like errands, not theater. The rumor thread claims I like QT and have a UPS box in Forney. Let it think so. We will use its guesses against it.

Window one. I drive to QT at 4:10, park under a camera, and sit with both hands on the wheel, head down, phone in my lap. No tea. No walk in. Unmarked FBI car three rows over.

Window two. A female agent with my hair color walks into the UPS Store at 4:35 with the tote and the envelope and asks for a box size that does not exist. Tommy says no. She leaves. Tote visible. Another unmarked watches the lot.

Window three. Laird walks the Ben Gill Park path at 5 and does the shoe tie set down. The path camera records whoever records him.

We covered cover stories like a recipe. Work line: insurance matters at the bank. If pressed: private matter. If someone tries to draw me into a guessing game: no engagement. Ms. Hall would be reachable and would answer questions that do not exist with generalities. Mr. Whitlow would be the man with a folder and a calendar and no time for circuses.

"Before you go out," Ms. Hall said, "eat. Even a little. You can't pilot adrenaline on an empty stomach." She handed me a wrapped granola bar. We stood there in the private room and ate like two people in a hallway at a high school after a fire drill.

We split for an hour so the FBI could stage their cars. Ms. Hall and I walked the strip of shade behind the bank where crepe myrtles try to be a wall. "You are allowed to be afraid," she said.

"I am," I said. "I am also tired of being hunted."

"Then we hunt for patterns," she said, "and give them time to do their job."

Mr. Whitlow joined us with the look of a man who has put all the papers in their right places. "Remember the real you," he said quietly. "The important thing is sitting in a steel drawer that does not care about rumors. The rest is noise we will file."

We reconvened in the room. Laird tapped a map. "We stagger by twenty minutes. We do not want the same crew chasing all three. Rachel, you go first. QT at 4:10. If the lot looks wrong, keep driving. Your windshield cam is live." He held my eyes. "Remember you are not the show. You are a commercial break. Be boring."

"I can do boring," I said. "I have trained for years."

We left together, separately. Ms. Hall first. Mr. Whitlow second. I waited five minutes before stepping out. I texted Peña that I was wheels up.

Sitting in the car, I asked the quietness how a lottery line pulled me into a room with federal maps. The answer was simple and not kind. My paper woke a nest that was already there. The ticket is a spark. The network is the fire. I am not a detective. I am a middle aged woman who fixes passwords, drives a red Kia, and feeds a talkative red cat. Fear rode shotgun but kept its seat-belt on. Small and steady, I told myself. Do the boring thing well and leave the day quieter than you found it.

The QT lot looked like itself. Trucks. Teens. A man with a ladder on a van. A woman in scrubs with a coffee the size of a small trophy. I chose a spot under a camera and put my hands at ten and two like I was trying to pass the test. The panic fob sat under my phone like a pebble I did not want to lose.

Forty seconds in, an older man knocked lightly on my window and held up a piece of paper that said Jump start? I shook my head no and pointed to the store. He shrugged in a way that said he understood and moved on to a pickup where a younger man pulled out cables. The ordinary kept showing up to remind me how to label the day.

Two minutes in, a blue cap walked out with a soda and scanned the lot in a way a thirsty man does not. He looked at my car and then passed it like he had trained his eyes not to land on a thing he wanted. He set the soda on his roof and texted with two fingers. His car was a gray Altima with a front plate bracket but no plate. A dent on the rear bumper like a thumb print. I did not turn my head. I counted the dents in my dashboard vent and let the windshield reflection tell me the rest.

A boy in a letter jacket tapped a trash can twice like a drummer who forgot the sticks. A couple argued lightly at pump seven about chips. The blue cap took a slow loop behind my row, passed my bumper, looked at my tires like tires were the story, returned to his car, and did not leave. He didn't drink the soda. He waited like he was learning patience in public.

I texted one word. Cap. Laird replied. We see him. Stay.

A man in a safety vest asked a woman if she could spare a quarter. She handed him two and he thanked her like she had saved him from drowning. The world kept being itself. At 4:13 the blue cap finally drank. I let minute three tick and rolled out the back exit. He did not follow. The unmarked did, a car length behind a car that had nothing to do with us. I drove two rights and then one left, checked the mirror at natural points, and took the spur toward Forney where the air felt wider.

I parked under an oak on a side street and breathed. Hands flat on my thighs. Then I texted "clear" and turned toward the next piece of the day that did not belong to me.

Window two was Forney. On the radio Laird's voice was a steady line.

"Female decoy at counter. Two men by copier. One man with a blue cap in the lot."

Tommy played his part like he had been born for a small stage. He pointed to a size chart. Shook his head at the nonexistent box. Smiled in a customer service way that says he could do this forever. My double left with the tote in plain view on her shoulder and walked across the lot with patience. The unmarked filmed the people who film other people. The camera watched a hand raise a phone and pretend to check a weather app that never moved.

A silver sedan idled in a spot near the tree line. The driver had his seat back far enough to count as a nap. He didn't nap. The plate read a state that was not Texas. Tran called out the partial to someone who speaks in numbers and lives in a room with air that never changes temperature.

"Not stolen," Tran said. "Registered to a different household than the Altima. Both addresses are near the same strip of apartments."

The decoy got in her car, backed out, and left by the north exit. The sedan waited fifteen beats and then went the other way. Laird told the unmarked to let it be. "We catalog," he said. "We do not chase ghosts."

Window three was the park. Laird walked the path like a man who had good blood pressure and wanted to keep it. He set the tote down for ten seconds, tied a shoe without looking at it, and picked the tote up. A biker adjusted his cap and checked his watch five times in sixty seconds. A woman in a visor pretended to talk on a phone without moving her thumb. A boy on a scooter filmed everything because that is what boys on scooters do. The path camera saw them. Their cameras saw him. The quiet lies people tell their faces do not hold up under playback.

A small drone buzzed above the trees for eight seconds and then slid away. Tran marked the time stamp, sighed, and looked annoyed at a sky that thought it could behave any way it wanted. "Too high for a plate. Not high enough to be clever," he said. "Every big box store sells these. We will pull any signals we can."

By five thirty the operation stood down. We did not debrief on the radio. We met in Ms. Hall's office with the door closed and the blinds steady. No approach. Three sightings that mattered. Two plates tied to cars that do not belong on my block. No crime today. Plenty of curiosity.

Laird rested both hands on the table. "They are not stupid," he said. "And they are not only after you or a ticket. This crew looks tied to a larger network moving thefts and fraud through North Texas. Today was about pattern, not headlines. We will repeat when they think we got bored."

Tran opened a laptop and played the clips on the screen. QT from my windshield. The Forney lot with the men by the copier window pretending to need copies. The park path with the bike and the visor that never made a call. We watched faces try to be something they were not.

Peña let the silence sit, then tapped the folder. "We do not chase this tonight," he said. "We catalog. We add to your file. Tomorrow we run the pattern again. The Dallas FBI team keeps whispering pressure on their channels while we work the streets."

Then the part that made the hair rise on my arms. A controlled leak, placed by the FBI's online ops team. At noon tomorrow, a whisper will slide into that county thread on Facebook. Not slander. Not a lie. Just a confident sentence about Buc-Ee's at five. The goal is not to play journalist. It is to pull watchers to a lot with more cameras than a casino.

Ms. Hall had annotated the plan with three lines. "We are not doing this just because of a lottery ticket. We are doing it because federal investigators believe the same actors are probing multiple victims. We will draw fish into a net while keeping Rachel on the dock. The FBI leads. Rachel is never bait."

"Work," she added, turning to me. "Your story is the same. Insurance matters. Private details. You are on safety leave. If Tom calls, he will get me, and it won't be pretty."

Tom didn't wait to call. He sent an email to my personal address with a subject that could crack a tooth. Attendance and Corrective Action Meeting. Ms. Hall replied to him and HR within three minutes with a paragraph that had numbers in it. Case numbers. Statutes. The kind of language that makes grown men sit down. Tom sent back a single sentence. We will comply.

Maya pinged me again. You see the thread? They are naming streets now. I typed back, Do not send me rumors at work. Boundaries. Then I softened it. Thank you for caring. I am handling personal matters. I do not want to make an enemy of a person who keeps snacks in her bottom drawer and shares them on hard days.

Ms. Hall watched my thumbs. "You did fine," she said. "Civility and a fence."

We set the next window. Two days from now. Different jackets. Same discipline. Laird handed me an index card with two sentences. "Your official work story if anyone corners you," he said. "Insurance matters at the bank. You cannot discuss details. If pressed, it is private." I repeated it until it fit my mouth without wobbling. He nodded.

We broke to breathe. Ms. Hall took me to a diner two blocks over where the coffee is honest and the servers call everyone honey in a way that does not diminish anyone. We slid into a booth. I kept my back to the wall without making a scene. Ms. Hall ordered chicken and rice and the server brought us both extra napkins like comfort.

"You will need a formal note for HR," Ms. Hall said between bites. "I will write it tonight. It will reference the protective order and the on-going FBI investigation without telling them more than that. They can live on curiosity for once."

I smiled because I could not help it. "Thank you."

"Also," she said, "prepare a short line for Maya if she presses. Something kind. Something final."

"I have it," I said. "Personal matters. I appreciate your concern."

"Good," she said. "We do not feed fires that are already burning for their own reasons."

I paid the check because pride needs exercise like any other muscle. We walked back in the hot shade and pretended to be two people who had eaten lunch without talking about nets and whispers.

Finally back home I opened the door the way I always do now. Hand on knob. Listen. Step in with calm shoulders. A quick pass of the house. Back door latch. Slider stick. Motion light. Front latch. Porch camera blink. The small ordinary litany that makes it possible to sit down in a chair.

Rusty circled my ankles with a sound like a complaint and a compliment at the same time. I fed him and he forgave me for being a person with errands.

On the table the folder sat next to the notebook. I wrote the plan in simple lines a person could read while running. Text Peña when leaving, arriving, exiting. Park under cameras. Three minutes. Hands on wheel. No tea. Tote is a costume. Fob in pocket, word in head. Three rights. Safe lot. Call. I underlined the last word because I grew up in a house that believes in help.

The doorbell app pinged at four fifty. A person in a bright yellow vest stood close to the lens, head tilted down as if reading a novel on my doormat. He put a door tag on the glass and walked away at a pace I still don't trust. He turned before the sidewalk ended and looked back at the door like a man who wanted his own reflection to answer a question.

I waited thirty seconds, opened the door, and used a paper towel to collect the tag. Same format as before. Same QR. Same crooked attempt at my name. I put it in a bag without breathing on it and texted Peña. Another tag. Same style. Same time in the evening. He wrote back. We will swing by. Leave it in the bag.

Peña and Carter came with calm shoulders. Carter sealed the door tag in a bag and wrote the date in neat block letters like had done before, many times. Peña crouched by the hinge and nodded. "Practice," he said. "Somebody ran a dry run on your car last night or the night before. We will add it to the file."

"I hate that this teaches me new vocabulary," I said.

"You are not the only one learning," he said. "We keep files for a reason."

I told him about the plan for the controlled leak tomorrow. He already knew and added one more protection for my nerves. "Terrell PD will have a marked unit loafing at the far edge of Buc-Ee's lot. Folks behave better when there is a friend with a light bar nearby. This is a quite big operation now."

After they left I stood with my back against the door for ten full seconds and let my shoulders come down where shoulders live when they are not trying to touch ears. I fed Rusty a treat he had not earned because I needed to be the kind of person who gives good things on purpose.

At six thirty the phone rang from a number I did not know. I let it go to voicemail. The transcript arrived a minute later. You should be careful carrying cash. Lots of people are looking for lottery money. We can help keep you safe if you meet. No name. No place. No time. He wanted me to swim to the boat.

I saved it. I sent the audio to the thread. New voicemail. Vague help offer. No callback. Laird replied. Save everything. Thank you. Ms. Hall replied. Do not engage. Block if they keep calling.

Tom emailed again. We require a return date. Ms. Hall answered. You require nothing beyond the note on file. Ms. Mercer will advise when safe. I pictured Tom reading that sentence and sitting down hard in his chair.

Out of the blue Mrs. Keene texted with the tone of a woman who has been told not to but will anyway. I saw a man walk by twice. Same cap. Took a photo of my neighbor's flowers like he was a relative. She sent a photo. Side profile. Not quite our guy. Same habit with his hands. I thanked her and reminded her that if anything made her stomach feel wrong she should call me and then call the number on the card I had taped inside her pantry door.

I put water on for tea. I set my mug from Original Visuals on the counter because its weight tells me what decade I am in. I poured, stood by the window, and watched a boy throw a football toward nobody and then sprint to catch his own pass. The ordinary holds its own kind of courage.

I opened the laptop. The plan had another page. Laird had emailed the longer outline while we drove. I read the parts with my name.

Parking lot rehearsals. A fifteen minute block where Carter would be at the end of my street with the engine off and a sandwich. A second agent in the aisle at QT pretending to browse trail mix for six minutes longer than anyone needs. A cruiser parked by the Amazon pickup station to give the crew a clear reason to behave. A helicopter on stand by if a chase became necessary. That part made me grimace. Plans are not wishes. Plans are respect for the day you do not want.

Then the controlled leak details. The whisper would not claim anything. It would pose a question with confidence. *Anyone else saw that lady at Buc-Ee's around five with a bank envelope and a fancy tote? Looked like the winner to me.* The internet is not a court. It is a mirror that lies and tells the truth at the same time.

Ms. Hall had annotated the margins. Rachel is not bait. FBI leads. Witness only. She had an underlined witness.

I closed the laptop and put my forehead on my folded arms for one minute. The house hummed the way houses do. The plan felt like it had a spine.

I took the trash to the bin and rolled it to the curb. A car idled at the far end of the block with its lights off for three breaths longer than polite. The doorbell camera caught the shape. I didn't stand in the street and stare, even though that's what I wanted to do. I finished the roll and walked back up the drive with my keys in my hand and my shoulders in the place that keeps a person smaller than the night.

Inside, I set the fob on the nightstand. I tucked the vault key under the lamp base. I put the tote on the chair by the door, clipped and wired the way Tran had shown me. I set an alarm that would give me time to think in the morning and turned off the living room light.

Sleep arrived in stop motion. I woke to the sound of rain that did not become rain, and again to the sound of a cat defending the fence as if it carried a state border. My body is a barometer now. It tells me things I do not want to know at three in the morning.

Before the alarm could earn its keep, the phone pinged with a message Maya had forwarded. A user with a name like pond plant posted a confident sentence. *She will be at Buc-Ee's again. She always is. They never change their habits.* The comments multiplied like rabbits.

I did not respond. I brushed my teeth and told my face what it needed to hear. Be boring. Be kind. Be ready.

I stepped onto the porch. The sun was still arguing about whether it wanted to rise. The street was empty except for the newspaper wrapped in plastic two doors down.

There was a folded note under my wiper blade. My name in block letters that tried too hard. I did not touch it. I took a photo. I texted Peña. Note on windshield. Not moving it. He replied. On my way.

I waited on the porch where the camera could see me, hands wrapped around a mug that was not full. The note fluttered once in a small wind that came out of nowhere. It waited. I waited. The plan waited with me like a person.

While I waited, I looked at the houses on the block and thought about how long a life can live on a single street. Mrs. Keene and her porch roses. The boy who practiced trumpet at six on Saturdays until his mother spoke through the window with a tone that could move mountains. The couple that argued about a fence post and then fixed it together. I want to leave because I choose to leave. Not because anyone chased me off my own porch.

Headlights turned the corner and the city crest on the door calmed the part of my heart that holds a drum. Peña walked up my drive with a steady step and a small evidence bag. Carter followed with a camera and the look of a man who knows how to be quiet in a yard.

Peña slipped the note into the bag without reading it aloud. "We will dust it," he said. "We will photograph it and add it to the file. If it asks for a meeting, we will write a new plan on a new page. You will still not be bait."

I nodded. "I can be boring," I said again, because saying it makes it truer.

Rusty pressed his cheek to the glass inside the door and blinked like an old judge. Peña noticed him and smiled in the way a person smiles at a cat who has chosen a side.

They left after the camera had enough. The street went back to being a street. The porch light clicked off and then back on because the timer believed in itself more than clouds.

I stood for one more minute and listened to the neighborhood breathe. Somewhere a faucet dripped. Somewhere a toaster popped. The ordinary does not know how brave it is.

The decoy would not walk itself. We would have to escort it through a town that thinks it knows my steps. If danger wanted a dance, we would make it learn our choreography. Fear hummed in my teeth. I re-named it so I could keep moving.

Readiness.

The Hook Sets

Evening came in like a witness who had already taken an oath. The light turned the edges of everything honest, and then it went thin and gray, and then the neighborhood opened its palm to the dark. I moved through the house with a steady hand and a list I had already memorized. Doors. Latches. Camera angles. Battery checks. Rusty fed and flopped with that royal lack of apology only a cat can pull off. I washed the mug I had been carrying like a talisman all day, dried it, and set it mouth-down on the counter like a period at the end of a line.

Peña texted the group thread at six forty. We are in place. Tran at the van. Carter at the corner. Laird at the post. Two more across and down. We keep the lights low. We keep engines off.

Ms. Hall texted a minute later. I will monitor from my office with Mr. Whitlow and the liaison. Rachel, no porch sitting tonight. No trash runs. Curtains cracked in the front room, only two inches. If you step in front of that window, do it slowly and only once every ten minutes.

I typed back. 'Copy'. The word has become a room I know how to stand in.

We had three choices for the night and we took all three. Choice one, I would stay in my house, with the lights on a normal timer and the television muted. The volume would come from a white noise app, just enough to sell the picture through a window. Choice two, an agent would sit inside the guest room with a radio and a view of the back fence. Choice three, a simple decoy would stay visible in my car, not a bank envelope, just a tote that looked like it weighed something. The tote did not weigh anything that mattered. It had paper fliers from a grocery store, a sweater, and a spiral notebook with the first ten pages torn out to look busy.

Tran had wired a small motion sensor under my front steps that would ping his laptop when it felt a foot. Carter had placed a puck camera inside my car, hidden behind the rear seat headrest, watching the blue space between the seats. Laird placed a second sensor in the side yard where a hand might test the fence at midnight. The van sat three houses down and looked like an HVAC contractor who had worked late and had not yet found a reason to go home.

At seven the Kaufman County thread on Facebook climbed into another tree and began to throw fruit. Someone posted a still of a red Kia Soul, not mine, and claimed it had been seen at Buc-Ee's with a woman and a bank envelope. The caption said, *It is her, I am sure.* The comments multiplied and corrected and multiplied again. I watched it for sixty seconds and then listened to Ms. Hall inside my head. Do not watch. She is right. The internet wants to pull a person into a lake and pretend it is a conversation.

I stood by the sink and stared at a clean skillet like it might talk back. The white noise hissed. Rusty leaped onto the chair by the window and kneaded the cushion with the focus of a neurosurgeon. I made a cup of tea and didn't bring it into the front room. The front room needed to look like a front room, not a target practicing being a person.

At seven twenty one the side yard sensor pinged Tran in the van. He spoke low on the radio. "Blip at the east fence. Could be a possum. Could be a tester. Holding."

Peña, on the porch of his car with the door cracked, answered. "Copy. No movement on the street. Rachel, stay off the line of the front window."

The hiss of the white noise was a friend. The television glow painted a fake life on the wall. I stood in the hallway and felt my fingers go pins-and-needles and then come back. Breathing in on four. Out on six. The numbers ride like a bicycle if you have done it enough times.

At seven twenty seven the front steps sensor ticked and then ticked again. Tran's voice lost a half inch of smoothness. "Front steps, two pings. Not heavy."

The doorbell camera blinked. A face moved past the lens too close to focus, a cap brim down, a chin line I did not know. The figure did not ring. The figure did not knock. The figure bent, lifted the corner of the welcome mat, and then put it back down with care. He lifted the planter, then the other planter, then ran his fingers under the edge of the siding like a man who had watched too many videos about where people hide spare keys. He did not find a key. There is no key under my mat. There is no key in a fake rock. There is only a note inside my head, and it says, stop teaching thieves.

Carter spoke like a man who had moved his hand to a gear he did not plan to use yet. "Subject at the door. No knock. Testing. Standing by."

Peña answered. "Hold. Let the camera eat. We do not burn the night on a porch tap."

The figure stepped back and looked up at the corner of the house where the first camera used to be, before we moved it. He was a little shorter than I expected and a hair thicker, the way a man looks when he eats in his car. The cap was blue. The jacket was one of those generic windbreakers that come free at certain jobs. He tucked his hands into his pockets, turned his head right as if listening to a sound only he could hear, then walked down the steps and off the porch. The sensor went quiet.

The white noise hissed. I felt the house exhale.

At seven forty one the side yard sensor pinged again, this time in a quick double like a small animal and then a human ankle. Tran called it. "East fence, double. Camera three has motion."

I moved two steps deeper into the hallway. The agent in my guest room, a woman named Garrison who had the stillness of granite, lifted a hand to me without looking away from the window. I stopped where I was and stood like a person in a photograph.

Garrison whispered into her mic. "Visual on shadow at side gate. No climb yet. Holding."

Peña: "Copy. Unit at the corner, eyes left."

The shadow did not climb. It tested the gate latch, found it locked, and then disappeared for a full minute. My body wanted to fill the minute with predictions. I gave it numbers instead. In on four. Hold. Out on six. Repeat. The house clicked in the small way houses click when they are holding their breath with you.

At seven forty five the gate latch lifted. Tran again. "Gate. We have a gate. East side, inner yard."

Garrison lifted her hand a hair higher and then pointed at the floor. Stay. My legs became law. I did not move.

The figure slid through the gap and closed the gate behind him like a polite guest who does not want to be rude. He crossed the narrow strip of yard and pressed himself against the side of the house under the back windows. The kitchen window is too high to touch without a stool. The bedroom window is not. He tested the screen with a finger. The screen did not give. He pulled a tool from his jacket pocket, short and flat, and worked at the corner of the screen like he was peeling an orange he did not want anyone to smell. The tool slid. The screen popped with a soft sound. My throat made a similar sound and then refused to repeat it.

Garrison did not look at me. She spoke at a level that would not carry through a wall. "Subject at rear bedroom. Working screen. He is good at this. Carter move. Laird, hold."

Peña: "Copy. Rachel, inside line. You are doing perfect. Stay where you are."

The figure lifted the screen, leaned it against the siding, and set the tool between his teeth while he ran his fingers along the window track. He found the second lock, the one that lives like a secret between the two panes, and he flicked it with a thumbnail. Then he pushed the lower sash upward with the palm of his hand, slow and steady, and the window gave him the first inch like it was tired of boundaries.

Garrison stood then, a small rise without speed, and moved her palm-size radio to her shoulder. "On your call, Sergeant."

Laird came in like gravel poured into a bucket. "Hold one more beat. We want entry before contact. Then Carter takes the back, Peña takes the side, Garrison holds inside, Tran rolls the van to block the street. No weapons unless we see a weapon. We are fishing for a live one, not a trophy."

The lower sash moved another inch. The man paused, listened, and then pushed again. Garrison slid her hand to the holster at her hip, not a full draw, just a friend waiting in the next room.

The sash rose enough for a shoulder. The man ducked his head, angled his cap, and slid sideways into my house like a trick of light. One foot on the carpet. Then the other. He was inside.

Garrison: "Entry. Subject inside the residence."

Peña: "Execute."

Carter's shoes hit the grass outside with the sound of a plan turning into a fact. The back door shook under his hand and then opened because I had left it unlocked for him, just for this. Peña crossed the side yard at a low run a neighbor would call a jog. Laird moved fast around the front with a second agent, the kind of fast that does not splash.

The man took two steps in my bedroom and stopped. He was in the dark and did not know that my eyes knew my own home. He passed the dresser with the tray that holds the ring I wear to church. He paused at the mirror and adjusted his cap like vanity is a habit even when you should drop it. Then he turned left, into the hall. He walked toward the kitchen in the kind of half-crouch that makes a person look like a question mark.

I stayed where I was, two rooms away, body against the hallway wall, the white noise hissing like a patient. Garrison stood a half step in front of me, an arm extended, not touching, just there.

Carter came through the back in three strides and froze when the man froze. Two silhouettes facing each other across the line where linoleum meets carpet. Carter spoke first in the voice cops have learned from a thousand nights like this.

"Police. Hands where I can see them."

The man did not lift his hands. He pivoted on the ball of his foot toward the sink. Carter stepped left. The man faked right and then threw his shoulder toward the gap between the fridge and the wall. Carter closed the space and reached for his elbow. The man slipped and twisted with a move I did not expect from a body shaped like his. The fridge door swung. Rusty darted from the chair to the doorway like a streak of orange opinion.

"Freeze," Carter said. "Hands."

The man's right hand went inside his jacket. Carter's left hand went to his belt by muscle memory. The man pulled out a black shape and threw it at Carter's chest. Carter flinched. It was not a weapon. It was a phone. It hit Carter and fell to the floor, clattering under the table. The man used the flinch to dive for the door.

Peña reached the side entrance as the man lunged, and the doorway turned into a tangle. Shoulders. Elbows. A short hit of breath. Then the kind of contact that sounds like someone dropped a suitcase onto carpet from a low shelf. Laird came through the front with a sweep that I felt in my ribs. Garrison moved me backward two steps, firm and kind.

"Hands," Peña said again, the word now a shape in the room. "Hands. Now."

The man finally put both palms out on the floor. Carter slid the cuffs on with speed and no apology. The room breathed again all at once. The white noise hissed like it knew the cue. Rusty reappeared at the doorway tail-up, offended that a scene had occurred without his consent.

I stayed where I was until Garrison lowered her hand and nodded. Then I stepped forward into the light the ceiling had bothered to give us. The man on my kitchen floor looked up over his shoulder in a way that said he had expected a different woman. He was not Travis. He did not look like Travis from any angle. Blue cap. Generic windbreaker. A face that would not have stood out in any grocery line in Texas.

Peña asked the questions they asked first. "Weapons on you. Needles. Any reason I should not search your pockets."

The man shook his head without looking anyone in the face. His breath smelled like soda and nerves. Carter patted him down. Knife. Folder style. A plastic pry tool with a flat edge. Two rubber bands. Fifty in small bills. A key ring with two keys and a fob from a gym in Mesquite. A wallet with an expired temporary ID. No gun. Small relief, but relief.

Laird picked the phone up from under the table with a paper towel like it was a snake that could still bite. He set it on the counter and looked at me. "We will bag this. We will work on it carefully."

Carter pulled the cap off and set it on the table. Sweat had marked a salt line around the brim. He looked smaller without it, which is the strange miracle of hats.

Peña read him his rights in a voice that does not need to be loud to be clear. The man nodded at the right places and kept his eyes on the floor. "Name," Peña said.

"Evan," he said. "Evan Pike." The word sounded like something he had said often enough to believe it most days.

"Job," Peña said.

"Gig," Evan said. "Lots of gigs."

"Tonight," Peña said.

"Cleaning," Evan said. "I clean."

Which is not a lie if you count breaking a window and wiping fingerprints a kind of cleaning. Laird looked at Carter in the way a man looks across a dinner table to a colleague he has sat with before. Carter opened a small evidence bag and collected the pry tool and the rubber bands, then a second bag for the keys and the gym fob.

"Shoes," Laird said.

Evan looked at them like he had never seen them before and then wiggled his toes inside them as if to test if his feet were still there. They were a brand you buy at a discount store when you failed to plan. The sole pattern was a grid with three ovals set in a line. Tran's voice came soft from the van. "Copy. We have prints by the side fence with an oval grid. Photo ready."

They stood him up. He swayed a little. The kitchen looked strange with a cuffed man standing in it. The stove clock blinked eleven. Time behaves how time behaves when it stops and then resumes like a stubborn lawn mower.

"Sit," Peña said. Evan sat in my chair at the table. He looked at the place where Rusty had been kneading and maybe saw a small proof that people live where they also get arrested.

"Who sent you," Laird said. The sentence did not bend. It did not need to.

Evan looked at the ceiling. "Nobody," he said.

"Try again," Laird said. He said it like an instruction in a workbook for adults.

Evan's left knee bounced under the table. "Saw the thread on Facebook," he said. "Saw the car. That is it."

"We will get to your phone," Laird said. "We will get to your messages. I am giving you the gift of going first."

Evan swallowed. "I clean," he said again, like the sentence might be a life raft if he said it often enough.

Peña set a bottle of water on the table. Evan looked at it but didn'tt touch it. The room smelled like sweat and old coffee.

"Where do you clean," Peña asked.

"Stores," Evan said. "Night sweep. Janitorial. Whatever."

"Which stores," Peña said.

"QT sometimes," Evan said, and my chest did the small catch even though my head still knew I had moved the ticket. "UPS maybe once," he said. "Not sure which one. I will go where they send me."

"Who sends you," Laird said.

"Temp," Evan said. "StaffNine."

Laird wrote it down like he already had the number and the supervisor's favorite lunch spot. "And who gives you errands that are not cleaning."

Evan closed his eyes for a second. "A guy," he said. "Online. Cash app. I do not know his name."

"Handle," Tran said from the van, his voice now threaded through the room like wire. "We will take a handle if that is what you have."

Evan spoke without opening his eyes. "Oats," he said. "Sometimes Oats. Sometimes Mainline. The icon is a picture of a blue bird that is not the blue bird you think."

"Pay," Peña said.

"Small," Evan said. "Mostly small. Twenty for a plate. Fifty for a porch. Hundred if there is something to lift. More if somebody leaves a thing in a car and I get a picture."

"Pictures of what?" Laird said.

"Envelopes," Evan said. "Bank shit. Sorry. Bank stuff. Packages with a label that means gift cards. I do not touch the big stuff. I am not stupid."

Peña looked at me. I kept my face a piece of furniture.

"Who told you to come here," Laird said.

"Thread," Evan said. "The county one. And the other one that nobody talks about in public."

"What other one?" Tran said.

Evan hesitated. "KaufmanLine," he said, like a confession. "Not the big group. The small one. Oats says what to watch. People like me watch. We post. Somebody else decides. Then someone like me goes where they say and checks the mat and the planters and the usual. I do not break much. Not usually."

"You broke tonight," Peña said.

Evan looked at my window like he wanted to apologize to it with his eyes. "He said kitchen first. Bible second. Freezer third. I know the order. I did not make it up."

I looked at Garrison. She looked at me. The thought we shared did not need words. The burglary had put my grandmother's Bible on the floor. The note asking where the ticket was had sat on my table like a dare. This man had a script. Someone had handed it to him.

Laird held Evan's gaze until it could not pretend anymore. "Who is he?" Laird said. The pronoun had a face now, and it was not Evan's.

Evan shifted. "Oats," he said. "Maybe not Oats. Someone Oats knows. Sometimes I get a new number and it is the same guy. Sometimes it is Mainline. Sometimes Ledger. They change the name like hats."

Carter had been working Evan's phone into a bag with a Faraday sleeve while the talk moved. He nodded at Laird once. "Locked," he said. "Swipe pattern. We will take it in."

Tran's voice colored the air. "Already scraping his Cash App handle from old transactions. Pulling the alias Oats and Mainline through local feeds. We have a rumor broker in this stream, maybe two. Twice removed from the solvers who show up to do the touching. I see the outline of a pipeline."

Peña turned the bottle cap and set the water closer to Evan's hand. "Drink," he said. It was not out of kindness and it was not unkind. It was a way of moving the scene forward.

Evan drank and the water left a shiny trail down his chin. He looked young like that. Then he looked old again when he wiped his mouth with the back of his hand and swallowed hard.

"Why you?" Peña said. "Why tonight?"

Evan did an embarrassed half laugh that did not belong in my kitchen. "They said tonight she will be sloppy," he said. "They said she went to the bank and got cocky and carried stuff and went to Buc-Ee's with it. They said winners make a mistake after they make a plan."

"We fed that line," Laird said quietly to me, a sentence as simple as a shrug. "Good. It worked."

He looked back at Evan. "You are done talking here," he said. "We will take you in. You will have a lawyer. You will decide how you want your night to go. Think very carefully about whether Oats will send you soup in the county thread."

Evan stared at the far wall, the one with the picture of my parents on their porch with their hands around a mug that looks like a sunrise. He did not look like a man who gets soup from a person who uses a bird for an icon.

They stood him up again and walked him toward the door. He looked at Rusty with a face that had a little real life in it, like a man who once had a cat and a normal day. Then the moment closed. The door shut behind the trio like a book whose next chapter you cannot read yet.

Garrison exhaled the breath she had been paying attention to. "Good," she said. "Nobody bled in your kitchen today."

I sat down in the chair Evan had warmed. I did not mean to sit there. My knees chose it. The white noise hissed. The clock clicked. I looked at the ring on the tray and picked it up and put it on, an action I usually reserve for Sundays. It made my hand look like it belonged to someone who gets to decide what goes on it.

Tran came in from the van with the laptop and set it on the counter. He spoke in that quick layered way that people who live inside networks use when they know they might lose a signal. "Cash App alias Oats tied to five handles in the last three months. Oats1, OatsOne, Oatmeal, Oats_1978, and one with a carrot emoji because the word Oats was taken. Linked to a Proton address that forwards to a maildrop. The maildrop shares a recovery number with two other aliases, Mainline and Ledger. We have a Telegram channel fork with the name CedarFeed. Small. Invite only. They sell tips for twenty, plates for fifty, front door stills for one hundred, and share bounties when someone can lift. There is crossover with SIM swap chatter and gift card cracking."

He swiped to a still of a chat list. "See this. The bingo card of places to check. Bible. Freezer. Under sink. HVAC vent. Flour bin. Houseplants. People think they are original. They are not. Someone in this thread trains men like Evan and pays them in small hits and instructions that sound like grown up dares."

Ms. Hall arrived with Mr. Whitlow and a woman from the FBI liaison team whose name I did not catch because my ears were full. The liaison set a printed sheet on the counter. "We are already pulling the CedarFeed chat through a warrant we had standing from a separate case," she said. "KaufmanLine piggybacks inside a cluster of rumor pages. There is a single admin who calls herself Bay. She never posts photos. She only posts times and breadcrumbs. She is not local. She is an operator. The men who do the walking know her as that name and a schedule."

"Bay," I said, like a taste on my tongue I did not like.

Mr. Whitlow took in the kitchen like he was entering a courtroom assembled by a set decorator. He looked at the pried window. He looked at the screen leaned against the siding. He looked at my hands. "You did what you needed to," he said. "You did not show yourself. You did not break formation. That matters."

Ms. Hall placed a palm on the table near my notebook. "Drink water," she said. I drank.

Peña came back, face set to work. "We are transporting Evan to the county jail. Dallas FBI will ride a point on the phone and the Bay thread. We will keep the cruisers rolling by tonight and tomorrow. The tote stays in your car tonight with nothing in it. We do not move it until the clock changes."

"Others," I said. My voice came out normal. I didn't know it would.

"Not today," Peña said. "The blue cap could be three caps. Evan's cap is in our bag now. Someone else watched the park. Someone else watched the UPS lot. We will work on the plates and the faces. We are not done."

"Travis," I said, because the question will not leave my house unless I let it in and then point it to a seat.

Peña's eyes held mine. "This was not him," he said. "We are not seeing his car on any of this. We are not seeing his work on any of this. Your protective order holds. If he calls you, that is a violation. If he comes near you, that is a violation. Today's arrest is tied to a different animal."

I nodded. Relief and anger exist in the same stomach. They do not agree about what they want to eat.

Garrison took photos of the window, then the screen, then the pry marks in the wood. She used a scale card with black and white squares.

The card made the marks look like they existed in a museum exhibit called Things People Do When Money Makes Them Forget What Houses Are For.

Tran turned the laptop to show me another list. "We are seeing schedules," he said. "Not just rumors. Schedules. Tuesday nights are good because people put their bins out. Thursday mornings at parking lots are good because people do returns at the big box stores. Sunday afternoons are good because people nap after church. They are buying the ordinary and selling it back to the kind of men who never learned how to build their own. We will get them where they think we are not looking."

Ms. Hall reached for my hand and squeezed it once in a way that did not require me to squeeze back. Mr. Whitlow studied the tote in the car through the front window. He nodded at the angle like it passed an exam.

"Rachel," Ms. Hall said. "We extend safety leave through the end of the week. I will send the updated note to HR with a polite tone and a spine. Tom may rage. Let him rage at his inbox."

I smiled out of one corner of my mouth. "He will print it," I said. "He prints things he cannot make go away."

We were still standing in the room when Peña's radio whispered. "The unit on the east end saw a sedan slow roll twice. Plate unreadable in the rain. Driver obscured. Logging." The rain had started. I had not heard it begin. It tapped the roof in small nails and then got serious.

The liaison took a call and put it on speaker. A male voice spoke in the near distance. "We got a ping," he said. "Telegram sub-channel pushing a location that matches your block. A new post, two minutes old. Bay wrote, 'Window open on Willow Street. All you need is a gentle hand.' She did not say a house number. She does not have to. We are already on it."

"Who is leaking," Ms. Hall said, low and mean to the air.

"Could be one of the watchers who drove by and texted the admin," the liaison said. "They are not magicians. They are collectors. They crowd source crime and then harvest the easy parts."

"Turn the faucet off at the knob," Mr. Whitlow said. "Not on the drip."

"Working on it," the liaison said, and her voice had the strength of a person who has already broken three knobs this year and is not tired yet.

The house felt a little smaller. The white noise kept doing its small job. Garrison took the scale card photo of the pry tool and the rubber bands and the purse of cash. Peña checked the trash under the sink and the drawer with the utensils. Men like Evan throw a glove away when they get spooked and then forget where they put the bag.

No gloves. A torn corner of a latex wrapper. That is the kind of detail that makes a prosecutor smile later. Carter dropped it into a bag without touching it with anything that grew on a human.

The arrest was the part the story would want to end on if the story had not learned about the internet. The part that came next is the part that invites another chapter. Tran's laptop pinged with an update. He read it and his eyebrows changed shape.

"What?" Ms. Hall said.

"Evan's Cash App," Tran said. "He got a spike last month, three deposits of two hundred from an alias that looks like a woman but is probably not. The alias is tied to a phone number that belongs to a prepaid account in Pleasant Grove. That number is linked to a bundle of spoof calls that hit three banks last week. They spoofed the fraud department. They got two people to read back codes. We have one victim in Terrell on record. We have a second in Mesquite. We have a third that did not lose money because their kid told them not to say anything on the phone. The alias that paid Evan shares a recovery email with Bay's admin account. It is thin but it may be just enough."

The house went very quiet and then the rain made itself known again as the air freshener clicked and gave me a scent called Linen that had never met linen in its short life. Ms. Hall put a hand to her forehead and rubbed a place between her eyebrows that has carried other people's stress for twenty years.

"Bigger than a rumor page," she said.

"Pipeline," Tran said. "Rumor broker at the top, two lieutenants who feed different streams, a handful of solvers who do the walking and prying, and a shelf of cashers who take gift cards to three stores in three towns in two hours and turn them into things that never make it back into a bank. There is a thread to SIM swaps. There is a thread to mailbox keys. There is a thread to porch pirates with circuit boards who pop MUTCD locks on drop boxes. We have seen versions. This is our version."

"Who is Bay?" I asked. It felt like the first real question, which is strange after an arrest in a kitchen.

"We will find out," the liaison said. "We have warrants ready in another case. We will draft one for this tonight and hand it to a judge in the morning. The CedarFeed admin will feel the light. If we are lucky, Bay will panic and make a mistake like normal people do when their work gets named out loud."

A siren whispered somewhere far and did not come close. Peña looked at me. "You are not the only person they are after," he said. "That does not make your house cleaner. It makes the work bigger. Bigger is what these people know how to do."

"I am not the only person living on a street, driving a Kia Soul," I said. My voice had a little iron in it I did not have to add.

"You are not," Ms. Hall said. "You are the person we have and we will keep that circle tight."

We did not sleep for a long time. Garrison stayed until midnight and was replaced by a second agent whose name I caught and then lost like a piece of lint on a sweater. Peña left and came back once with coffee and a bag that held two breakfast tacos and an apology for how late it was. We ate at my table and did not talk much. Rusty climbed into the chair and pretended he had always lived there.

At one in the morning Tran sent a photo to the thread. Evan's phone, opened under a warrant and a pair of hands that know how to be patient. A list of chat handles scrolled up a screen. Oats. Mainline. Ledger. A fourth I had not heard yet, called Nest. Nest posted rules. One of the rules said, *No follow homes on Sundays. God sees you and He has a temper.* Tran had underlined it in red in the image like a teacher and then texted, 'Idiots'.

At two, the white noise app clicked and restarted, and the hiss changed pitch. The house felt like it had turned over in its sleep. I closed my eyes on the couch for what I thought would be ten minutes and woke to Garrison' replacement, a man named Jacobs, handing me a blanket with the careful hands of a stranger who does not know if you are the sort of person who likes being tucked in.

The rain came hard during the night and the sound put a lid on my thoughts. I dreamed in fragments. Doors without handles. Water that climbs upward. A blue cap sitting on a church pew. I woke to Peña standing by the window with his radio quiet and his shoulders more level than mine will ever be. He saw my eyes open and nodded in the human language that means, You are still here and I am glad.

At four thirty, the street woke the way it does when the first person who has to be somewhere gets in a truck. The headlights wrote lines across my ceiling. Rusty sat at the crack in the curtains like a sphinx and treated the lawn as if it needed his opinion. Jacobs wrote a note in a small pad for the agent who would relieve him at six.

At five, Ms. Hall texted me one sentence. You did well.

At five thirty, the liaison texted the group. Bay deleted two posts and changed her banner. We already have the old ones. She is spooked. Good.

At six ten, Tom emailed my personal account with a question mark. Just that. Ms. Hall replied with her note and a copy of the policy on protective orders and safety leave. HR replied with a sentence that said they had logged it. Tom didn't answer. He probably printed it and then put it in a file that he will not label with my name.

At six thirty, Peña took a call and sent a one line summary. Evan flipped on Oats. He wants a deal. He gave a second handle.

The second handle was someone named Poppy. The name made something inside my rib-cage loosen because it was silly. Then I saw the thread where Poppy told someone with a cowboy emoji to stop parking on Willow because it makes the neighbors suspicious. Poppy knows my street with a first name. Poppy is not silly. Poppy is a person who thinks of people as pieces on a board.

I changed clothes and put my hair in a braid and looked like a woman who had woken up after a hard night and was going to do dishes. I did the dishes, because pretending can be a form of prayer. Rusty sat on the counter like a foreman and flicked his tail when I missed a spot.

A knock. Two beats. Then a familiar voice, "Peña." I dried my hands and cracked the door with the chain set.

"Welfare check," he said. He stayed on the porch. "Quick update only. No documents in person."

I stepped out and pulled the door to my hip.

"We have your suspect held on state charges that fit the facts we have today," he said. "Burglary tools. Criminal trespass. Stalking elements under review. His phone is with forensics under a warrant. I cannot promise outcomes. I can promise the process is doing its work."

"Will he stay in?" I asked.

"For a minute," Peña said. "Then we see what the phone sings. You will get any public documents through Ms. Hall or via the records portal. Do not print anything that comes to you. Do not forward anything. If anyone calls you about this, route them to Ms. Hall."

He slid a small card across the threshold. Shift hours. Case number. Non-emergency line. "Extra patrols tonight," he said. "Text me if anything taps your instincts. That is all for now."

"Thank you," I said. Small words again. The ones that do the work.

He gave Rusty a nod through the glass like a man who respects a house cat with jurisdiction and left the step as quietly as he had come.

Inside, my phone buzzed. Subject: Secure update available from Ms. Hall. A short line in the body. *Redacted incident summary and preliminary excerpts uploaded to the client portal. View only. No downloads. We will brief you in person tomorrow. 9 am at my office.* A second message arrived from an unknown number ending in 2710. Special Agent Tran, Dallas FBI. *We just posted chat captures to the same portal. Do not respond to any messages that reference them. Do not share. We brief tomorrow with counsel.*

Ms. Hall called and added me to a short three way call with Agent Tran. No small talk. Just doors that open and close.

Tran's voice was even. "You do not need details that don't keep you safe. Here is what you do need. The chats confirm a rumor broker and at least two field actors watching you and others. Your name is not used. Your car color is. Your block is described poorly. There is a number string we like that ties to the tracker. We will walk you through redacted excerpts tomorrow. Please do not discuss any of it by text."

"I will not," I said.

Ms. Hall's tone was the kind that builds a fence. "Rachel, your only job tonight is to sleep and document anything unusual. You will not receive paper at the door. You will not sign anything without me. If you need comfort, write three lines in your notebook and put the pen down."

"Copy," I said.

We ended the call. I did what she said. Three lines. Patrols tonight. Briefing at nine. Do not feed the fear. Rusty head butted the notebook like he agreed.

After The Hook

The next morning came in an honest light. I sat at my kitchen table when Rusty jumped up like he pays the mortgage and planted both paws on my notebook. A tiny tiger on a cliff from a calendar nobody kept. I scratched his head exactly right and he forgave the entire world for twenty seconds.

I wanted to cry and did not. I did the thing that has been saving me all week. I made a list.

Next moves.

One, extend safety leave through Friday.

Two, decoy round two at Buc-Ee's after the whisper lands.

Three, box the books with my grandmother's notes for Florida.

Four, call the landlord and move the locksmith to today.

Five, text Mom a normal photo of Rusty and a sentence about the weather.

Six, practice the official work line until I can say it in my sleep.

Seven, be boring. Be kind. Be ready.

I took a quick photo of Rusty looking like a mayor and sent it to my mother with the line, 'Rain coming later. Rusty says hi'. Then I locked the door, checked it twice, and drove to Ms. Hall's office for the 9 am briefing.

The conference room was the kind with blinds that do not gossip. Ms. Hall had a small stack of redacted printouts with my name nowhere on them. View in the room, leave in the room. Mr. Whitlow set a legal pad in front of me like a calm anchor. Sergeant Laird stood by the map.

Special Agent Tran opened a laptop that showed a network diagram that looked like a subway for bad ideas. Officer Garrison joined by invitation, in person, because the meeting was on her beat and the room was not my house.

"Let's review," Tran said. "Pipeline, Bay at the top. Two feeders, Poppy and Nest, who moderate small groups like KaufmanLine and CedarFeed. Two or three rumor accounts that toss questions like bait and watch who bites. Then the solvers, men like Evan, who do the touching. After them, the cleaners, the cashers, the SIM voices, the delivery runners. Oats is a runner. Mainline is likely a cleaner. Ledger trains the new ones. Names change. Jobs do not. Dallas and Houston have years of this. Now we have your chapter."

"Our chapter ends," Ms. Hall said, "with a safe woman in a car heading east."

"Soon," I said. The word lived in the room and did not rust.

Laird glanced at his screen. "Update. The serial on the tracker from your car does not tie to Evan's phone. It ties to a device that has touched two other trackers since July in two other towns. That device pinged near Ben Gill Park two days ago. The owner is not in hand today."

"So Bay stays a name?" I said. "And the person who likes trackers stays a ghost."

"For now," Laird said. "For now but not forever."

Garrison stood in the doorway, one hand on the frame like a coach who likes the team she has. "We hook one," she said. "We do not stop until the line is empty."

"The hook set," I said. The words fit in my mouth like a prayer.

We closed the loop on rules. No paper leaves this table. My identity remains off the radio. If anyone outside this circle asks for a comment, all inquiries go to Ms. Hall. If the pipeline rattles the rumor pages again, FBI online ops will be listening, not arguing.

Ms. Hall touched my shoulder, a gentle order. "Eat something and lie down on the couch for twenty minutes. Then we move the day."

We broke the room. Laird and Tran headed back to the Dallas office to run the feeds. Garrison returned to her patrol. Mr. Whitlow stayed in the lobby to make calls. Ms. Hall walked me to the small sofa outside her door.

I did as told. The office couch was firm and honest. I did not sleep. I put my eyes under my hands and let my body practice the idea of calm.

My phone vibrated with the sound I use for the client portal. New view-only item from Ops, forwarded by Ms. Hall. I opened it. A fresh capture from CedarFeed. Bay had posted a notice:

We are cleaning house. If you came here from the county group, you will be removed. Only vetted friends stay. New invitations only through Nest and Poppy. No exceptions. No cops. You think we do not know. We do.

Arrogance on the surface. Fear underneath. Fear makes mistakes.

Ms. Hall stepped out with her tablet and nodded at the same screen. "Ops scraped it already. Delete is theater."

At noon the locksmith arrived at my place with a kit that could open a submarine and a hat that said his name was Jerry. Ms. Hall had me meet him there with Peña doing a drive by on his patrol route. Jerry worked in quiet competence. Two deadbolts and a keyed knob later, he handed me two new keys that felt like new pennies. He did not ask. I did not tell. He wished me a better afternoon than morning and left. Peña idled past once more, lifted two fingers from the wheel, and kept the street safe by being seen.

Mr. Whitlow drove me to his office and set me down with coffee and a form. We told the story of last night in a way a person who was not there can read without confusion. Garrison's note. Peña's commands. Laird's timing. The sensor pings. The entry. The command. The short chase. The cuffs. The chair. The cat. Plain language for the insurance and banking package. No drama. No adjectives that would salt the earth. I read it aloud. My voice did not break.

Laird called from a hallway that sounded like a high school. "We have a hit on Oats," he said. "Delivery runner for a strip mall phone store that does side work under the counter. Not brave. Not smart. Useful until he is not. We have Poppy's backup number and a meeting spot at a storage unit in Mesquite. You are not involved. We go as buyers who speak his language."

"Good," I said, in the tired way good can be meant by a person who has been awake for a night and a half.

Ms. Hall entered Whitlow's office looking as stunning as always. She carried her purse and a cup of coffee. She looked at me over the rim of her mug. "When do you want to give your notice?"

"After the claim," I said. "After the paper is a story in a vault and not a paper in a folder. After we set the Florida mail and boxes for real. After the FBI runs the second loop."

"Good," she said. "We will write a letter that gives them nothing to eat."

Peña texted a still. Evan's left hand. A small wave tattoo on the ring finger. Then a second still from a Buc-Ee's camera two weeks ago. Same tattoo. Different cap. Different weights. Caption: pipeline.

At five, the whisper went out again, as planned, but not from us. A different admin on a different page tossed a smug question about Buc-Ee's at dusk. The lot filled the way Buc-Ee's lots fill anyway. Camera record. That is their simple religion.

Shortly after, Tran sent three images. A woman with a visor at the park two nights ago. The same woman in a different visor at the UPS lot the week before. Then a manicured hand holding a phone with a pop socket that said Bay in a sweet little font. It was probably nothing. It was probably something. Tran wrote, Working. Do not engage.

While the internet did what the internet does, Maya texted a cupcake from Whisked Away and a heart. *You okay girl? The thread is nuts.* I typed, Thank you for caring. Personal matters. I am fine. Please don't send me screenshots. She sent a thumbs up and a cat with sunglasses because of course she did. People are not the pipeline. People are people.

I went home and the kitchen light made the day look gentle again. I fed Rusty. He sat with his paws together like a prayer and ate like a creature who trusts bowls will be filled.

We were pulling one edge of the net. We had a name that was not yet a face. We had a man in a blue cap who was not the only man in a blue cap. We had a device that tied to other devices and towns that had not asked to be in our story. It would take time. The fish were not clever. They were persistent. So are we.

I wrote the last line of the day on a clean page and closed the cover like a door. I leave because I choose, not because I am chased. The words felt heavier and more true.

Somewhere, Poppy had a number. Bay had a folder. Nest had rules like a Sunday school that fell in love with control instead of grace. Somewhere, the person who planted the tracker on my car was still a ghost and had not made the mistake that gives a face.

Not forever, Peña had said. Not forever is enough for me to sleep. I turned the white noise down. The house settled around me like a friend I have known since I was five. I chose the couch because beds hold too many new thoughts. Rusty climbed up and laid his whiskers on my arm like a string on a finger. I did not need the string. I know what to remember.

Be boring. Be kind. Be ready.

And listen for the sound of a line that has been cast and now holds. The hook is set. We are not done. Not yet.

Claim Day

The house felt steadier than it had in a week. The white noise was off. The porch camera light was green. Rusty stretched across my shins with a groan that sounded like an old door and then thumped to the floor to begin his important walk to the food bowl. I lay there for one more breath and listened to the quiet. It was a weekday, the kind where my headset would normally be waiting like a collar. Instead, my phone glowed with a list that belonged to a different life.

Laird had texted at six. Units will orbit during your travel windows. Nothing flashy. You will not see us unless you need us.

Ms. Hall at seven o'clock. Trust claim at ten. Meet me at the bank at eight thirty. We retrieve the ticket together. Mr. Whitlow will bring the binder and the CPA letter. We travel in separate cars. No stops.

Mr. Whitlow at seven ten. Private banker on standby at noon. CPA will join us at the claim center after verification. We will keep your part simple. Sign where flagged. Breathe. Eat something.

I set the phone face down and looked at the ceiling. A slow warmth moved through me like tea does. A thought entered, simple and honest. I am going to claim this. It did not sound like a trumpet. It sounded like a bowl set on a table.

Coffee. Shower. The jacket with the inside pocket and a zipper that does not catch. The tote that is a costume, cleared of yesterday's decoy camera and outfitted with only what matters. ID. Trust binder summary. Ms. Hall's card. A pen that my hand likes. I left my personal phone in the kitchen and took the small trust phone Ms. Hall had set up with a number that does not share blood with anything I own.

Rusty circled my feet, then sat on the mat and adopted his Judge of Breakfast posture. I filled the bowl, topped the water, wiped the lip of the saucer because small acts let the bigger acts make sense. I put a single treat on the mat and watched him choose. He chose the treat first. He is a cat who knows celebration when he sees it even if he will never call it that.

I locked the door, checked the back slider stick, checked the window latches I could reach without dragging a chair, and stepped onto the porch in time to see the neighborhood yawn. A pickup coughed. A woman in leggings with a leash wrapped around her palm hustled a reluctant dog toward a promised future with bacon. The sky had the clean face it gets before the heat takes over.

Maya texted at seven twelve. Are you good today? Did you sleep? That thread is still wild. People have nothing better to do.

I typed back. Handling personal matters. Appreciate your concern. Please do not forward me screenshots. Then I added a second line because kindness is a fence. See you soon. I stared at the word 'soon'. It gave me nothing back. I let it go.

The drive to the bank felt like a rehearsal for leaving. Two rights. A straight. A check in the mirror at natural points. The light at the bakery, still off. The sign at the diner, still changing its letters one by one. The lot had the same number of birds on the wire as it did yesterday, which felt like a blessing you should not say out loud.

Ms. Hall was already there, professional outfit, hair pinned, sunglasses, a legal pad that had more muscle than paper. Mr. Whitlow pulled in from the far entrance. We didn't walk in like a group. We drifted, then aligned at the door.

Ms. Molina met us with a smile that included three forms and a key card. "Good Morning," she said to me like the word was a bridge. "We have the small room open. Vault access is ready."

The room had no windows and a table that welcomed binders like a long porch welcomes guests. Ms. Hall set her case down and clicked the latches with a sound that always makes me feel like I am about to enter a chapter where someone knows what they are doing. Mr. Whitlow laid out the trust binder and the letter from the CPA, a page of numbers that had confidence without swagger.

We signed the vault log and walked behind Ms. Molina to the wheel that looked like it belonged on the front of a ship. The vault whispered its heavy hello. The box slid out and into the private room like a suitcase that had decided to be helpful for once.

I set the felt mat on the table. Ms. Hall nodded. I unzipped the inner sleeve of the folder and removed the soft cloth that had been my grandmother's ring house. The ticket lay in it like a polite secret. I lifted the cloth by its corners, set the paper on the mat, and looked at the numbers the way you look at a face in the mirror before you say something true to it.

Mr. Whitlow looked away for a second because he is a man who remembers to give the sacred a half inch of air. Ms. Hall rested a finger on the margin of the trust letter like a priest with a liturgy. I picked the ticket up in both hands and slid it into the bank envelope Ms. Molina had labeled for us with the trust name. I wrote the date on the flap and my initials on the seam. Ms. Hall wrote her initials under mine. We closed the flap.

"Ready?" Ms. Hall said. It was not a question.

"Ready," I said, and felt the shape of the word in my mouth.

We walked it back to the main vault room together, not as if it were made of air and paper, which it is, but as if it were a small animal. Ms. Molina opened the inner gate and let us pass into the corridor where the boxes look down like a congregation that has decided to bless you without telling you why. She set us in a second private alcove by the back door of the vault and handed me a small clipboard with a chain. "This is for your list," she said. "You can write today's visitor names for your records."

I wrote them. Molina. Hall. Mr. Whitlow. Me. I drew a short line where I could add more later and left the pen hanging from its chain like a tiny anchor. We left the vault. The bank door swung shut behind us with the gentle confidence that comes from doing a thing for a very long time.

In the small room again, Ms. Hall placed her phone face down and looked at me. "One more thing before we move," she said. "Your work."

"Tornado Tom," I said, and I nearly smiled because the name felt like a weather report you turn down if the sirens are quiet.

She pressed a button on her phone and the blue light blinked. Conference call. Her voice took on that tone that has steel inside it and still somehow sounds like a gift. "Good morning, Mr. Rigsby. Rachel is on safety leave for the remainder of the week. That is not a request. HR has the documentation. If you call her or text her, I will forward the messages to the court that issued her protective order. If you discuss her with employees, I will issue a formal notice to your counsel. If you have essential process questions, email me."

His voice came through the small speaker with that splashy anger that made my back tighten. "This is unacceptable."

"This is lawful," Ms. Hall said. "Unacceptable is a man who stalks a woman in her own yard. Unacceptable is a company that ignores a court's directive. We will not be adding your name to that list."

He found a new gear. Quiet. "Fine."

"Thank you," Ms. Hall said, and ended the call. She took her phone and emailed HR a copy of the policy with my case numbers in bold. Then she slipped her phone into the case and looked at me like a sister who does not mistake firmness for cruelty. "You breathe now. Then we go."

We went.

The Texas Lottery claim center did not look like I had imagined. I had pictured a game show with windows. The reality was concrete floors buffed to a dull shine, a reception desk with a printer that had a sense of humor, and a sign that asked for patience in a font that had seen better design. A guard with a polite face scanned our bags. Ms. Hall introduced herself and slid a letter across the counter that had more weight than leather.

"Trust claim," she said. "Appointment at ten for a large win. We request a private room. No photography. The trustee will sign."

The receptionist glanced at the letter, then at me, then at the envelope with the trust name. She pressed a button with her foot under the desk. A door buzzed. A woman in a blue cardigan appeared, same polite face as the guard, but with a desk badge that said Coordinator. She shook Ms. Hall's hand, then Mr. Whitlow's, then mine, and gave me a look that had the kind of softness you usually find in churches or school nurses.

"We will use Room Three," she said. "You will like it. It has a quiet air conditioner and no leaks." She smiled at the joke like she had used it successfully before. "Your counsel can accompany you. We will verify the ticket in the room. We will bring the forms to you. No cameras. No press."

The room felt like the bank room with less dignity and more fluorescent honesty. The table had hundreds of forms. The chairs had seen things. The wall had a framed poster about unclaimed prizes that made my stomach do a small and unhelpful turn. I sat on the side of the table with my back to the wall. Ms. Hall sat next to me. Mr. Whitlow sat near the corner, a guardian with a spreadsheet in his blood.

The coordinator set a small scanner on the table and plugged it into a tablet. "When you are ready," she said, and looked pointedly at the envelope. I slid it across the table to Ms. Hall. She opened it. The ticket lay there, soft and loud. The coordinator took it in both hands, glanced at the back to see my signature in the place where signatures live, and slid it into the scanner with a motion that told me she has done this very thing and also wiped tears with the same hands.

The tablet chimed. She looked at the screen, then back at us. She did not grin. She did not blink more than the regular number of times. She nodded once, as if to herself, and then said, "Verified. Winning ticket.

Amount to be finalized by the Multi-State Association. Cash option selected here or annuity. Texas allows a trust claim for anonymity at this level, which you already know." She looked at me again. "Congratulations."

The word landed in the room and did not bounce. It sat. It took up the space of a brisket pan. Ms. Hall squeezed my wrist once, quick and strong. Mr. Whitlow inhaled in a way that made papers sound like music.

She printed a preliminary receipt and slid it toward me. Three lines changed the temperature in my hands.

> Advertised jackpot: $1,800,000,000.
> Cash option: $850,000,000.
> Federal withholding today, 24%: $204,000,000.

She circled the provisional wire amount with a quiet pen. $646,000,000. Ms. Hall wrote in the margin the piece no receipt will say out loud. Total federal at 37 percent means $314,500,000. Do the subtraction and you still keep about $535,500,000 after all filings. I looked at the figure until the commas made sense. I am rich. Not in a headline. In a ledger that does not blink. And us in this room are the only ones knowing the amount. The butterflies started flying around in my stomach uncontrollably.

The coordinator placed the ticket in a clear sleeve and sealed the edge with a dotted bit of tape that she smoothed with her thumb. Then she slid the sleeve into a larger envelope and wrote a code that meant nothing to me and a lot to the person who had to carry it to the next building. A man with a badge took it and left with the posture of a person who moves delicate things for a living.

Forms arrived. They came in on a clipboard that looked too small for their content. Ms. Hall walked me through them. Claim by trust. Trustee information. Address for correspondence that is not a home and not a place you can stand in front of with a camera. Contact method. No phone calls. Email only to the trust address. We declined the press packet. We declined a photo. We declined everything that wanted a spotlight.

The coordinator explained the part that the internet never gets right. "Federal withholding at payment, twenty four percent. Additional tax responsibility when you file. Texas has no state income tax. You will receive a payer statement. The Multi-State office verifies all numbers and wires to your trust account after bank verification. We do not accept phone instructions for banking. Your counsel will set the wire with us today in writing. We will place a test deposit of forty dollars to validate the ABA and account number. The wire will follow after the Multi-State office finishes the cross checks. Timeline typically ten to fourteen business days. Sometimes faster."

Mr. Whitlow slid his sheet forward with the ABA and account number for the trust operating account. "Dual control on our side," he said. "Callback to my office and to Ms. Hall's. No phone changes permitted. We will also open a temporary sweep at the custodian for parking into the Treasury-only money market until the CPA allocates." He turned to me. "That is our short-term aprons and gloves."

The coordinator nodded like she had heard this song and liked the version. She wrote on her own pad. "Test deposit, then wire. Two callbacks required. No exceptions."

A man in a gray suit popped his head in the door. He had the look of a person whose email folders have their own email folders. "CPA?" he asked.

"Here," Ms. Hall said, and stood. The man shook hands, then set a small leather folio on the table. Inside were a few pages with boxes drawn in big friendly shapes. "We will keep this boring," he said, and looked at me until he saw that the word boring made me want to live another thirty years.

He pointed to the first box. "Short-term parking. We do not chase yield with money that can still get misdelivered. Treasury bills only. Laddered. Four weeks. Eight weeks. Thirteen. It buys us time to be wise and time for the FBI to finish their hunt. We park the bulk at the custodian in a Treasury-only money market that settles the same day and never touches commercial paper. You will still be very rich while you wait."

Very rich. The words did not crash. They made a small bell sound in my chest that did not stop ringing as quickly as I expected.

Second box. "Operating. We keep a small working balance in a separate trust checking account for basics that must be paid. Nothing with a card until we finish your controls. No debit. No credit on this entity yet. Two approvals for every wire. Physical tokens for the third factor. We will give you a key that looks like a flash drive. You will put it in the computer each time you approve a wire, and you will not carry it in your regular purse."

Third box. "Acquisition. Florida. We will set up a separate entity that buys property. We will fund it from the Treasury parking so that the purchase does not need us to pull from the operating account. We will run the title clean. We will avoid any sudden glam that sets off gossip. We will choose a closing date that is a Tuesday or a Wednesday because Fridays attract attention."

Fourth box. "Obligations. Taxes first. You will owe more than the withheld twenty four percent. We will prepare estimated payments based on the cash option. You chose the cash option." He looked at Ms. Hall.

"We chose it," she said.

"Good," he said. "Annuity is for people who want to argue with a calendar. We like calendars for different reasons. We will coordinate with Mr. Whitlow to set aside a safe pool for quarterlies. Your first estimate will feel like a yacht. You will still own the ocean."

Fifth box. "Charitable. Not today. We seed the idea now. A donor advised fund can be created later this month or next. You can choose to use it like a fire hose or a drip line. We do not name it anything cute. We give it a name that sounds like a file cabinet. You can be generous without becoming a billboard."

He stopped talking. He waited. He let the air get unspecial. I realized I had been holding my breath in a shallow way and corrected it. In for four. Hold. Out for six. Numbers are an old friend that does not ask for a favor.

"Questions?" he said.

"I have a cat," I said, because sometimes your mouth surprises you when your heart is thinking. "His name is Rusty. He will be fine with Florida. The richest cat in town I guess."

The CPA smiled with exactly the right amount of teeth. "We will add a small budget line for a screened lanai and a vet that does not try to sell you vitamins."

I looked at Ms. Hall. "I want a pool," I said, and then I did not breathe for a second. I looked at Mr. Whitlow and he nodded like a metronome. "You will get a pool," he said. "We will have an insurance company that knows how to spell water."

We signed more forms. The anti fraud acknowledgments. The sheet that said the claim will be processed at an office that lives in a city I do not live in. The sheet said I decline to answer questions for the press and that the press will receive a version of the story that uses the word trust and none of my words.

The coordinator brought in bottled water and a small plate of cookies shaped like stars. I took one because it felt rude not to. It tasted like vanilla and sugar and a little bit of a birthday party I did not realize I wanted.

Then the part where I left the room. There is always a part like that on days that will cut their outline into your life. I told Ms. Hall I needed the restroom. She looked at me with a question in her eyebrows and stood to walk with me even though I do not need an escort to find a sign that has a stick figure on it. She knows what bathrooms are for on days like this.

The mirror did not do anything dramatic. It was a mirror. My face was my face. My hands were my hands. I turned the water on, let it run, then turned it off because I have ethics even on claim day. The paper towel dispenser hiccuped and then offered two. I took one and pressed it to my cheek where a single tear had thought it might try to see the world. The tear did not need a speech. It just wanted to exist, then be over.

"I am rich," I said out loud, very softly, because sometimes you need to hear a line read by the actor you chose for your own role. The sentence did not change the air pressure. It changed mine. A slow warmth started at my sternum and moved outward like a hand laying down a blanket on a tired person.

I came back to the room and sat. Ms. Hall glanced at my face and did not say anything. She slid a small tissue packet across the table with a motion that would not be seen by a person who did not owe a lot of people discretion.

The coordinator returned with a folder. "Receipt for the claim," she said. "Temporary acknowledgment while Multi-State verifies. The ticket will not be returned to you. It goes to a bank we can both respect. We will contact counsel after the test deposit lands. We will set the wire date in writing. You will not have to step into a lobby again."

"Thank you," I said. I meant the words for her and for the idea of a process that had made a path for a person like me.

Mr. Whitlow's phone buzzed. He looked at it, then at the coordinator. "Test deposit sent," he said. "Forty dollars. We will confirm from the bank on a known number. We will not call you. You will call us on the number on this card." He slid her a printed sheet with the names, numbers, and the code word that Laird had told us to choose. It was a word that had once belonged to something funny, now repurposed as a door.

We stood. Hands were shaken. The room did that strange thing rooms do after a ritual, where the air seems to look around for its keys. We walked back through the lobby. The guard nodded. The door buzzed. The heat outside had matured while we were inside and now wanted to be taken seriously.

Ms. Hall would not let me drive alone until we reached the second way-point, the bank where the trust accounts lived. We went there together, parked in different rows, and walked in with a casual choreography we had developed over the last few days. The private banker had a room ready. He had a tie that did not call attention to itself and a smile that made me think of accountants in black and white movies.

He ran his side of the test. "The forty landed," he said, looking at his screen like a priest reading a good verse. "We will call your CPA and your counsel on the numbers on this sheet. No substitutes. No exceptions. We will refuse any phone instructions that do not match the code phrase. We will perform a second call to a third number if anything bothers my gut."

"Good," Mr. Whitlow said. "Your gut is invited to all meetings."

We set signatures. Trustee. Counsel. Advisor. The private banker slid two small keys across the table, each on a ring with a tag that looked like something a librarian would attach to the keys to a room that holds old maps.

"These are your hardware tokens," he said. "You plug them in when you send a wire for approval. You cannot approve without the token. Neither can anyone else. The token does not care about persuasion. The token is an old man who likes rules."

I nodded. My brain had begun to make a list of old men who like rules as a way to make the world less slippery. It helped.

We left the bank. The sun stared. We drove again, three cars, one simple pattern. Laird texted once while we were between intersections. You look boring in the best way. I laughed, alone in my car. It startled me to hear the sound.

Lunch was at a small place that had a neon sign in the window that had probably been neon since the seventies. Ms. Hall ordered iced tea and a chicken salad that came with half a strawberry on the side like a garnish from a storybook. Mr. Whitlow had coffee and a club sandwich cut into triangles that made me think of family reunions. I ordered grilled cheese and tomato soup that tasted like it remembered everything my grandmother ever taught me about kindness.

We did not toast. We chewed. We looked at each other with the relief of people who have just shepherded a fragile thing across a busy street without dropping it.

Ms. Hall set her fork down and asked in a low voice, "How are you?" She did not add words like really or honestly. She is not a person who pokes the obvious.

"I feel like I don't have to hold the ticket in my hand anymore," I said. "I feel like somebody else is holding it and that person is in a room with a lock."

Mr. Whitlow took a sip of coffee and smiled into the cup. "That is the correct feeling," he said.

The CPA joined us for ten minutes, long enough to hand me a folder with a summary page in the front that reduced the whole morning to five lines. Claim accepted. Test deposit confirmed. Wire plan set. Parking instructions attached. Tax withholding acknowledged.

He tapped the last line. "Breathe," he said. "Don't buy anything today. Nor anything tomorrow. Let the line between today and tomorrow exist without an invoice."

"I can do that," I said and smiled. I thought of a house with a screened lanai and a rectangle of blue water and knew that patience was part of the purchase price.

We did not speak loudly. Two women at the next table were discussing a church bake sale and whether Mrs. Norris should be trusted with the sheet cakes if the event was outside. The world went on. That was good. It gives a person cover for breathing.

While Ms. Hall paid the bill, my phone buzzed. Maya again. You will not believe this. Someone just said the winner was seen at the claim office in Dallas. Is that even where they do it? She added a manual eye roll. She likes to type her emojis like she is telling a friend a secret.

I read the line twice. It landed wrong. It landed like a person who guesses and guesses until the guesses get close to true. I thought about her first text in the morning. I thought about the forwarded screenshots from last night. I thought about the way people in that thread like to ask a question and then answer it as if holding both sides of a broken fence. My stomach did a small turn that had nothing to do with soup.

I typed back. People will say anything. Personal matters here. Please stop sending rumors. Then I set the phone face down and let the question sit in a corner. I did not invite it to the table. I did not ask it to leave. I let it be a thing that might grow or might die on its own.

Mr. Whitlow was looking at me. He had the kind of face that knows when a thought takes up more space than necessary. "You will notice more now," he said. "It is a side effect of a larger life."

I nodded. I did not say the name that had entered my mouth without permission. Maya. I would not pronounce suspicion into form. Not yet.

The afternoon had the long soft edges of a day that has had enough drama. We went to Ms. Hall's office and sat in her conference room with the door closed while her assistant brought in a bowl of peppermints that tasted the way waiting rooms tasted when I was seven. Mr. Whitlow opened a laptop and walked me through the parking plan again, not because I had not understood it but because he knows that repetition turns nerves into practice.

"Tranches," he said. "I do not normally use that word for humans but it helps when talking about money. One tranche is ultra safe. One tranche in the ladder. One tranche earmarked for property acquisition when the time comes, still parked in Treasuries. No checks for anything that involves a promise you do not fully understand".

"Two approvals for every wire," he continued. "No wire instructions by phone. Written only, through the trust email. Out of band callbacks on numbers that are physically printed on this card. Tokens present. Security phrase used. No one will ever talk to you about moving money without talking to me and Ms. Hall at the same time."

The CPA joined by video, his face in a rectangle that made his forehead look like it was making life choices. He reviewed the tax edges in a way that made the sentences stay in their lanes. We will assume top brackets. We will overpay estimates and take a refund if one is owed rather than cut it too close. We will hold your hand through two Aprils and you will forget what tax fear tastes like.

Ms. Hall added a sheet to the pile. "Protective order reminder. Enforcement protocol. If Tom bothers you, I will answer. If Travis breathes near your porch, Peña will answer. If anyone from the rumor mill tries a phone scam, you let it ring and send me the transcript."

"Copy," I said, because the word had become a small religion inside me.

The private banker called Ms. Hall's line on the number on the card and read the code phrase. She read back the second phrase. They laughed like people who enjoy rules. He confirmed the test deposit rested where it was supposed to rest. He confirmed the wire file would be set as pending until the Multi-State office authorized the release. He confirmed that his gut had eaten a good lunch and remained at work.

Ms. Hall printed the claim receipt and made three copies. One for the binder at her office. One for Mr. Whitlow. One for my folder at home. She slid mine into a clear sleeve and wrote the date on the tab in a neat hand that made me think of nuns. She handed it to me without ceremony. The ceremony had already had its say.

Outside in the parking lot, the air felt like a fresh baked cookie you had to hold in a paper towel. Laird's car sat in the shade with its door barely ajar. He lifted a hand and then closed the door and drove away. He does not make entrances for applause. He makes exits that feel like promises.

"Do you want company on the drive home," Ms. Hall asked.

"I want to drive alone for twenty minutes and listen to a song that makes no sense to anyone else," I said. "Then I want to call my mother and tell her that God is good in a general way and that I love her and that I will visit soon."

"Good plan," she said. "Text when you land."

I drove. The road did not have more or fewer bumps than it had yesterday. The same billboards tried to sell me the same versions of ease. I turned the radio to static and then to a station that played a country song about leaving and staying at the same time. The voice on the song was a woman who did not need my help.

Halfway home, I said it again to the inside of my car. "I am rich." It sounded less like a piece of trivia this time and more like the first line of a prayer. I did not say a second line. I let the first line sit.

At the light near the park a boy in a hoodie crossed the intersection with his hood up even though the heat was doing its best to make him choose otherwise. He looked at his phone and smiled at something small. The world was doing that, everywhere, all day, for people who would never sit in a room with a ticket that changed their blood pressure.

Home. The porch was itself. The mat was where I left it. The planter remained an honest citizen. The lock turned and the latch settled. Rusty trotted down the hall with a look on his face that said I had left him for a year and he had written me a letter about it.

I put the binder in the cabinet. Not the drawer. The cabinet with the plain dishes. It won't be the home for it forever, but today I wanted it to sit near the bowls that hold soup and the plates that hold grilled cheese. Money belongs to rooms where people eat. That is a thing I believe.

I texted Ms. Hall three words. 'Home. Thank you'. She sent back a heart that had a lawyer's restraint and a friend's weight.

I sat on the couch and opened my notebook to a clean page. The words came out of me like a faucet that has been waiting for the handle. I am a millionaire, I wrote. Then I wrote it again. The second time I added a period. The period made the sentence behave.

I made a list of things that would not change because numbers had changed.

I will still say please and thank you. I will still stop at red lights. I will still tip well when people carry heavy plates to my table and my gratitude needs a backyard to run in. I will still say yes to the cat when he wants to sit on my arm even if I am reading. I will still call my mother on Sunday.

I made a list of things that would change.

I will not work for Tornado Tom. I will not answer the rumor page. I will not buy a house the size of grief. I will not tell people who do not need to know my business. I will not diminish joy in order to avoid envy. I will not apologize for leaving.

The phone buzzed. My mother. The ringtone I use for her sounds like a kitchen. I answered and she breathed into the line like she had been running because she loves me. "Hi, baby," she said. "Your father saw a hawk on the fence this morning and he has been talking about it for an hour."

"I like that hawk," I said. "I like your voice more."

"You sound good," she said.

"I am good," I said. It was the truth. "Busy. Personal matters. Good."

"We will not ask," she said, even as she was asking. "We just want to see your face soon."

"Soon," I said, and this time the word gave me something. "I love you. Tell Dad to take a picture next time and send it to me."

"I will," she said, and we said the goodbye that is a script in our family. It has never gotten old.

The sun moved. The light in the living room changed from polite to gold and then to the color that looks like butter in a photograph you can smell. I opened my laptop and went to Zillow and Realtor.com and looked at houses in Marion County and surrounding areas with pools and trees that know the word shade. A farm with ten acres and a porch that wraps like an arm. A place with a barn that does not need to be a barn but could be. A rectangle of blue water that looked like a recipe for resilience. I set the price slider like a person who has permission. It felt like a new kind of honesty.

For a moment I did the math Mr. Whitlow had shown me in a neat column. Cash option this. Taxes that. Parking this. Acquisition that. I will be rich for the rest of my life if I do not try to be a volcano. I will be comfortable and generous without becoming a spectacle. I will be free.

A car rolled past the house. It did not slow. The porch camera blinked. The app sent me a screenshot as if reminding me that normal is a gift you should not treat like an old shirt. I thanked the app the way a person thanks a dog that only barks when the right thing happens.

Maya texted one more time near six. They say the winner was a woman with a tote and that she brushed past somebody in the lobby and said no comment. This town is eating itself. Dinner this weekend if you are free. I will buy you a cookie from Whisked Away.

There was a word in that sentence. Lobby. I let it slide past me. I watched it leave the room. I smiled at the cookie. I typed back. Thank you for the invite. I have plans. Be safe. Then I put the phone on the table and walked away from it like a person who has bought her own quiet.

I stood in the kitchen and took a glass from the shelf. I filled it with water. I added two ice cubes, which I almost never do. I held the glass with both hands and felt the cold travel through my fingers. The cold felt like proof that I live inside a body that can know what water feels like on a day when numbers tried to take over.

I walked Rusty to the back door for his evening inspection of the yard. He did a perimeter check from the safety of the threshold because he is brave in a very specific way. I told him about the pool again. He blinked like a small judge and said that he would allow it.

I took the claim receipt out of the sleeve and looked at the font and the numbers and the date. No trumpet. No spotlight. No headline. A piece of paper that knew its job. I slid it back into the sleeve and put the sleeve into the cabinet next to the cereal bowls. Breakfast and claim receipts. That is a category that makes sense to me.

Night came in with the steady feet of a person who knows where the furniture is. I turned on the porch light. I left the lamp in the living room at its dimmest setting. I set my alarm for a reasonable hour. I wrote a short line in my notebook with a pen that will outlive a lot of nonsense.

Be boring. Be kind. Be ready. I added one more for tonight. Be grateful.

Rusty climbed up and made the circle that leads to sleep. I pulled a blanket over my knees and let my eyes close on a room that had room for more than fear. I saw a pool in Florida, blue like a promise. I saw a screened porch with a fan that hums. I saw a quiet lane not far from a road that will take me to the ocean when I decide the day needs salt. I saw my parents on that porch, their hands around mugs that steam in a summer rain.

The wire will come. The FBI will keep pulling on the thread they caught last night until the sweater is something you would not wear in public. Tom will print an email that he will not put my name on. Maya will either be a friend who is too curious or a footnote in a story that does not belong to her. I will choose where to place my bed. I will choose where to turn my porch light on and where to sit when the sun leans toward evening.

I am rich. It is not the whole story. It is enough of the story tonight to let my body rest.

In the other room the cabinet door clicked as it settled. In this room the cat breathed in the slow way cats breathe when they have chosen their person. Outside the neighborhood told itself the small truths it tells every night. I fell asleep inside one of them. The truth is that you can hold something precious without putting it on display, and it will still be yours in the morning.

Quiet Exit

Morning did not knock. It let itself in and stood in the kitchen like it had a right. The house felt like a tent after a storm. Poles are still upright. Canvas still taut. A little damp at the seams, but standing because we had tied it down on purpose. I lay there and watched the slice of light on the wall move from gray to the first color that belongs to a day.

I knew what today was for. It was not for errands. It was not for pretending. It was for stepping out of a room that had stopped being mine.

Rusty stretched, then flopped on my ankle with the authority of a cat who understands jurisdiction. I paid the toll. Scratch behind the ear. He forgave and went to his bowl.

My phone had three messages waiting. Ms. Hall at six. The resignation draft is in your email. Keep it short. No reasons. We will hand it to HR and take a receipt.

Agent Laird at six oh five. Dallas FBI units will sit near your work window. Quiet. If Tom chooses confrontation, call me.

Mr. Whitlow at six ten. Private banker confirmed test deposit. Wire file is staged to release when Multi-State finishes the cross checks.

I read Ms. Hall's draft in the kitchen light, the kind that makes paper look serious. It was simple.

To Whom It May Concern,

Please accept this letter as my resignation, effective immediately. I appreciate the opportunity to have worked at MetroCare. I will be available by email for transition questions through counsel. Please send all final pay information to the address on file.

Respectfully,

Rachel Mercer

No apologies. No stories. A line that closes a door without slamming it.

I showered and wore the jacket with the inside pocket that fits a folded letter and a small envelope with a key card. I put the vault key back in its plain tin on the shelf and told it I would not be taking it with me. I fed Rusty and packed the tote with almost nothing. Phone. Ms. Hall's note about HR. The printed resignation on good paper. A whistle of resolve that I did not need but carried anyway.

At seven thirty my mother texted a photo of a hawk. It sat on the fence like a judge who enjoys his work. Dad says this is the same one from yesterday, she wrote. He wants to know if you are eating enough.

Tell him I am eating, I wrote back. Tell him the hawk is handsome. I love you.

I put the notebook in my tote and wrote three lines before I left the driveway. Be courteous. Be brief. Be gone. Then I drove.

The MetroCare parking lot looked like it always does. A few cars early, a shift of smoke near the loading dock where someone who should not be smoking was smoking. The door with the badge reader had a scrape near the bottom where carts kiss paint. Inside, the lobby smelled like coffee that had been made by an optimist.

Maya was at her desk. She lifted a hand like the friend she has always tried to be. "You okay?" she mouthed. I returned the half smile that lives in my face when I do not want to tell the truth or a lie.

"HR," I said quietly, and lifted the folder like a passport.

Tom's door was open. The wall of screens showed their usual grid of cameras. The little squares made people move like they were being watched in a different century. Tom was not in his office. The chair sat like a threat without a throat.

HR was two doors down. The HR manager, a woman who has collected every badge a training company can invent, looked up when Ms. Hall stepped in with me. Ms. Hall had beat me by three minutes. She held a leather folder and the kind of face that turns confrontation into procedure.

"Good morning, Mr. Rigsby," Ms. Hall said as Tom appeared behind us in the hall, but she kept her eyes on HR. "We are here to hand in a resignation letter. Effective immediately. We would like a date-stamped receipt."

The HR manager blinked three times, then found the part of her that understands policy. "Of course," she said. "We can do that." She pulled out a little stamper that made a sound like a toy for adults and set the mark on the copy Ms. Hall had brought for me. Date. Time. A small rectangle that turned air into a record.

"I will notify Mr. Rigsby," HR said.

"You may notify him," Ms. Hall said. "Ms. Mercer will return her key card and badge to you, now." She turned to me. "Rachel."

I set the card on the desk. It did not clap. It did not make a speech. It existed. HR slid it into a small bag with a bar code on it, the kind they use for employee equipment. She wrote my name on the label and then crossed it out and wrote my employee number instead. Procedure respects numbers more than names.

"Final pay?" Ms. Hall said.

"Processed within the next cycle," HR said. "We will mail the statement."

"When you do," Ms. Hall said, "you will send it to this address." She handed over a sheet with the UPS mailbox. The HR manager read it and nodded. She is the sort of person who nods when the information is correct and not because a person asked politely.

Tom appeared in the doorway like a weather front. "What is this?" Not a question. A temperature drop.

"Good morning, Mr. Rigsby," Ms. Hall said again, still not turning to him. "We are concluding a voluntary resignation. Effective immediately."

"This is not how it is done," he said. His voice had found the setting between lecture and threat.

"This is how it is done today," Ms. Hall said, and signed the receipt line like she was signing a birthday card for someone she liked. "Ms. Mercer is on protected leave. She is not available for your commentary."

He took two steps into the room and set his hands on the back of a chair that was not empty. The HR manager looked at his knuckles and then at his face and then at the handbook on her desk like she wished it had a taser.

"Two weeks," Tom said. "Minimum."

"No," Ms. Hall said. "Minimum safety. Minimum dignity. You have cameras and policies and a woman who is doing what she needs to do to remain unharmed. If you wish to discuss dignity, we can invite your counsel to the conversation."

He looked at me then, for the first time since he had pushed into the doorway. "You are abandoning your team," he said. "Maya is already handling more than she should because of your absences. You are making a mess and leaving it for other people."

I felt the sentence touch the place in me that wants to make everything tidy before I leave a room. I let it touch and I did not let it settle. "I am resigning," I said. "Effective today." I kept my voice inside the lines.

He opened his mouth. Ms. Hall's phone buzzed and she looked at the screen and smiled in a way that never uses teeth. "Agent Laird," she said to the air. "Good timing." She did not put the call on speaker. She did not need to. Tom knows the shape of a name that comes with paperwork.

He took a step back. "Fine," he said, which is the word he uses when he has lost a thing he cannot keep by talking. He left in a line of air that tried to be a door slam and could not be because the hinges on HR doors have been trained to be calm.

The HR manager printed a short confirmation. It had two lines and the kind of signature where people write their name as if they were trying to cross a street fast. She handed it to me. "Best wishes," she said, and she meant it in the way a person with a sensible haircut means things.

We walked out together. Maya stood up from her desk like a person who thinks they should stand when a moment is happening.

"You okay?" she said again, out loud this time.

"I am fine," I said. "I am moving on." I tried to give her my eyes, the way you give a person a clean plate. "Thank you for everything you have done for me here."

Her face changed in a way that did not know where to go. Relief. Worry. Curiosity that wanted to be respectful. She lowered her voice. "Are you sure you should not stay until the end of the week? Tom is going to flip."

"Tom flipped," I said. "He flipped upstairs. It did not change gravity."

A small sound came from Tom's office. The sound a chair makes when a man sits down hard.

I left my headset on Maya's desk because symbolism is sometimes worth the trouble. Maya looked at it like it should have had a speech to give and was failing us by being plastic.

"Lunch sometime?" she said.

"Maybe," I said. "I will be busy for a while with personal matters." I used the line I had learned to use because lines can be guardrails if you let them.

Outside, the air felt different on my face. The lot looked like the lot. The sky did not know I had just removed myself from a mailing list and a calendar. Ms. Hall and I did not talk until we reached our cars.

"You were precise," she said. "Precision is kindness."

"Thank you," I said.

"Now one more kindness," she said. "Let me make the next call."

"To whom," I said, though I knew.

"Maya," she said. "You told Laird your feelings. He wants to ask her a few questions, gently. She will be treated with care. But they need to see her phone."

I closed my eyes for a second. "Do it," I said. "I do not want to be right. I do not want to be wrong, either. I want the river to go where it should."

The interview did not happen under a light in a room that smells like bleach. It happened at a table in the break room with a pot of coffee that had been brewed twenty minutes ago. Laird and Special Agent Garrison from the Dallas FBI came in like people who have sat in a thousand break rooms and know no two are alike. They introduced themselves to Maya and asked if she had ten minutes.

"We are following up on an arrest," Laird said. "Someone entered Ms. Mercer's home the other night. We think a local rumor channel helped steer that person."

Maya nodded like she had heard the rumor channel and also its cousins and grandparents. "Everyone reads those," she said. "You cannot get away from them even if you try."

"We know," Garrison said. "We would like to look at your messages to see if anyone contacted you about Ms. Mercer or sent you requests for information."

Maya looked at her phone. "I do not know what I have," she said. "I forward silly things sometimes."

"That is not a crime," Garrison said. "We are interested in the men who pay for silly things and try to turn them into money."

She handed over the phone. Her hand shook the way a person's hand shakes when they have not eaten and also when they are not sure where their circle ends anymore. Garrison set the phone on the table and asked for her pass-code while Laird wrote the number on a small white card that clipped to his belt.

They scrolled. They did not make faces. They did not make sounds. They looked like people reading instructions for a chair in a language they do not speak but can guess at.

"Here," Garrison said, and turned the screen. A DM thread. A handle that makes any stomach move. Nest. The profile icon was a bird drawn by a person who remembers childhood but not joy.

The messages were not dramatic. They were friendly. Hey neighbor. You have such a great eye. We love your community updates. If you ever see the red Soul on your side of town can you ping me, lol, we are trying to keep the neighborhood safe from scammers.

Then another. Gas card for a tip. Not kidding. We help each other here.

Maya had responded with a sticker at first. Then with a sentence. Saw a red Soul yesterday at QT, might not be hers though. A picture of a parking lot where cars were cars.

Later. Does she still work at MetroCare. No punctuation. That was the line that matters.

Maya had typed, Yes. Please do not make me part of any mess. Tom will kill me if drama lands on the floor.

Nest replied with a heart and a gift card emoji. Community first.

A week later there was a new message. Hey, seen her at Buc-Ee's at five. She does a loop before she goes home.

Maya had written, Sometimes.

Laird scrolled. Another DM. Poppy. Poppy used more emojis. Poppy liked jokes. Poppy asked if my porch camera was the new model or the older one. Poppy made a comment about how cute Rusty was in a photo I had posted two months ago, which means Poppy looked at my public face and liked my cat enough to weaponize him.

Maya covered her mouth with her hand. "I thought they were just neighborhood busybodies," she said. "I thought they were just nosy like me."

"They are nosy with a business model," Laird said. His voice did not punish. It explained a fact. "It is a racket. You are not alone."

Garrison asked for permission to copy the threads. Maya nodded. A tech from the van pulled the messages without digging through the parts of a life that do not belong in a case file. Maya's eyes watered. She did not cry. She chewed a corner of a napkin.

"I am sorry," she said. "I did not know. I was bored. I was trying to be helpful and funny."

"Thank you," Garrison said. "We may ask for a formal statement later. Today we needed to confirm the pattern. We did."

They walked out through the lobby into the late light. Ms. Hall and I were at the far end of the lot near the live oak, waiting for a word before we left. Laird gave it to us in one minute that respected both time and nerves.

"Your hunch was right," he said to me. "Nest and Poppy leaned on her. Small tips for small cards. She did not understand what she was feeding. She cooperated and consented to a copy. We will handle the rest. Good instincts. Keep trusting them and keep your distance."

Ms. Hall nodded once. "Upload only, view only," she said.

"Portal tonight," Laird said. "No paper. You two go home."

Ms. Hall followed behind me to the UPS store in her own car because it was a weekday and I wanted to check the box that keeps my mail from being a public performance. She would peel off after, and I would head home solo.

Tommy looked up when I walked in and raised his eyebrows in a way that conveyed that I should look in the direction of the coffee shop two doors down. "They were in here earlier," he said quietly as he handed me two packages and a stack of mail. "Clipboard guy with a woman who never buys anything unless she is buying opinions. I did not like their questions. I like yours."

"What did they ask?" Ms. Hall said, looking like a person browsing bubble mailers.

"Asked if the lady with the red Soul comes in on Tuesdays," he said. "Asked if we receive certified mail for trusts. Asked if we accept oversized packages. I told them we accept packages that fit and conversations that do not."

"Good answer," I said.

Tommy added a small box to my haul, the size of a candle. "Someone paid for this yesterday and asked me to hold it," he said. "Said it was for a friend. It has your box number."

Ms. Hall and I looked at each other. She nodded once. We took it to the car and opened it on the trunk with a key, not our hands. Inside was a phone. Cheap. New. No branding. Under it, a single Post-it. Keep this charged. Watch for instructions. No signature. No emojis. It buzzed once in my hand, a small insect trying to be an orchestra.

"Bag it," Ms. Hall said, and I did. We called Agent Laird. He and Garrison met us in the lot with a Faraday bag that looked like a lunch sack for spies.

"Thank you," Laird said, and Garrison took the phone like a person accepting a sleeping snake. "They want to talk to you. We will let them talk to us instead." After that, Ms. Hall waved, turned back toward her office, and I pointed my car home.

I drove home on streets that looked like streets. The porch was as I had left it. The mat behaved. The planter had not joined a union in my absence. Inside, I set my handful of mail on the table, only mine; I had already handed Ms. Hall's and Mr. Whitlow's pieces to them in the lot, and flipped past a flyer for a car wash I do not need because I am washing my car in other ways these days.

I called my landlord. He answered with his last name, as always. I told him I needed to end the lease early. Safety concerns. Protective order. Police case. A relocation that would be sudden and kind to me.

"I would like to help," he said. "You have been a good tenant. Give me thirty days to find a replacement. I will release you if I cannot. I do not want to keep you in a place that does not feel like yours anymore."

"Thank you," I said, and I let the word carry weight across the wire.

"Changing the locks was a good idea," he said. "Keep the receipt. I will reimburse half."

"Keep it," I said. "You have been fair. I will leave it better than I found it."

"That is what everyone says," he said. "Only some do it."

"I will," I said. He believed me. I could hear it in the way his breath made the phone line light instead of heavy.

Then I opened the notebook to a fresh page and started the logistics that make a life move without breaking. Two PODS containers, booked online for delivery next week, with pickup the week after. Storage at their facility for at least two months while I rent a furnished place in or around Marion County, Florida, month to month, quiet street, screened lanai if I can swing it. I sent a message to East Texas Moving to load the containers so I do not have to watch friends lift what they should not lift. I added a checklist: bubble wrap, dish packs, wardrobe boxes, label color system, photo inventory. Forwarding address set to the UPS box so nothing lands on a porch that is not mine. Utilities to cancel on a rolling schedule. Rusty's vet records scanned and saved to the trust drive with a note to find a new vet near Ocala. Car title and insurance paperwork flagged for later, when Florida becomes more than a search bar. The plan looked like it might work the first time if I let it.

I taped a small envelope to Mrs. Keene's door with a note that said thank you in the handwriting my grandmother taught me. Inside was a gift card to Lula Mae's Bistro in Terrell and another to the hardware store in Wills Point because Mrs. Keene is the kind of woman who buys nails and lunch on the same day. I did not knock. I let the note do the knocking for me.

Back inside I sat at the table and made a list with bigger ink.

Resignation done. HR receipt in the folder. Maya interviewed. Landlord notified. UPS box clean, except for the unwanted phone that was now making new friends in a Faraday bag. Call parents tonight with a story that is true enough to keep the love where it belongs.

As I capped the pen on that list, Ms. Hall looped me into a call from the private banker. Wire verification from Multi-State is queued for to-morrow morning, he said. He sounded like a man who likes clocks. He explained the callbacks again. Then he said a thing that made my shoulders find their natural place. "We received a spoofed call twenty minutes ago claiming to be your CPA asking us to change the ABA. We declined and called the number on file. Thank you for the token protocol. It works."

"Thank you for calling back," Ms. Hall said. "Thank you for not being stupid."

"I like my job," he said. "I like keeping it."

The evening wanted to bring a quiet dinner. It brought a knock on the door instead. Not loud. Not soft. A rhythm that said delivery or neighbor or federal agent. I looked out the window. Agent Laird. I opened the door.

"Walk," he said.

We walked to the end of the driveway. The air cooled my face. The sky had the pink at the edge that people take photos of and then do not look at again because they cannot bear to injure it with likes.

"We pulled the first metadata off the phone from your box," Laird said. "The SIM never touched a tower. It woke once when you opened it and tried to handshake with nearby Bluetooth devices for a name. Tran faked a name for it and it nibbled. It wants a secret to live on. We will not feed it."

"Bay?" I said, naming the unseen admin who sits above Poppy and Nest.

"Maybe," he said. "Or a cousin. The better news is Maya's messages gave us a map we can show a judge. Nest is an admin. Poppy is a moderator. Oats and Mainline are runners. Ledger is the trainer. We have them swapping the same three recovery numbers behind five different email addresses. We have a storage unit rental in Mesquite that ties two of the phones together. We will knock when the sun is not looking."

"How will you handle Maya?" I said.

"Gently," he said. "She is a witness. She may also be a victim. She will not be a defendant unless she tries to be."

"Thank you," I said, and I meant it in a way that could stretch across a field.

He shifted his weight. "One more thing," he said. "Your resignation. Mr. Rigsby called the non-emergency line after we left the building and tried to file a wellness check on you because you were acting erratically at work and he feared for your safety. We declined to be his errand boys. We called Ms. Hall instead. She laughed in a way that I have not heard in weeks."

"Tom is Tom," I said. There is a reason for his nickname Tornado Tom.

"Tom is a man who will now receive no more of your hours," Laird said. "Good for the hours."

We stood there and pretended we were two people looking at a tree we had always meant to identify. Then he left and I set the alarm and turned on the lamp that makes the room feel like someone loves it.

Suddenly, the doorbell camera pinged. A package sat on the mat that had not been there a second ago. No feet. No hand. Dropped from a height. The kind of drop that comes from a drone when a person wants to stop having to share a sidewalk with your doorbell.

I did not open the door. I texted Officer Peña. Package drop. No person on camera. He replied with one word. Hold.

He arrived so fast I imagined he had been around the corner practicing arrival. He did not step onto the mat. He looked at the package through the lens of his phone, then through his eyes, then through something that looked like it might sniff for more than dogs sniff for.

"Wire," he said quietly. "There is a wire under the tape. Could be nothing. Could be something. Could be a tracker. Could be a microphone. Could be a method for sending you a thing you did not order and then telling a story about it online."

Peña got Carter on the phone. He was nowhere near Wills Point, and Carter's advice was simple: treat it like it matters and call the bomb squad. Peña notified the Van Zandt County bomb squad, set a perimeter with a second unit, and asked me to get Rusty and wait outside the perimeter.

Two black vans pulled up to my house. A tech in heavy gear and then a small robot took the lead. They lifted the parcel into a containment tote for x-ray and later analysis. Nobody touched the tape. Nobody played the hero.

They cleared the porch after half an hour, I sat on the couch and let the room settle around me. Rusty jumped up and made the small sound that means he has decided to be content. I looked at the folder with the receipts. I looked at the stack of boxes labeled in my private code. I looked at the empty space on the table where a headset used to live.

I wrote the last lines of the day in the notebook.

- Left.
- Lived.
- Do not open packages on the porch.

Somewhere, a blue cap sat on a table in a county facility. Somewhere, a phone in a Faraday bag dreamed of towers. Somewhere, men with handles for names made a plan for a storage unit. Somewhere, a woman with a visor looked into a mirror and rehearsed a version of herself that says community a lot.

Here, a woman with a cat put the receipts in a folder and set the folder in a cabinet near the cereal bowls and turned off the lamp and went to bed. The chapter did not end with the drone. It ended with the sound a person makes when they decide they have done enough for one day and can let sleep try its small rescue.

Just before I closed my eyes, the phone on the counter buzzed once with a text from an unknown number that paired the words everyone in this town shares when they do not know what else to do.

Soon.

I let it sit. I let it be a word that belongs to me, not to people who believe the future is a net they can throw on a stranger's porch. I turned my face to the pillow and found the part of the night where rooms are allowed to be quiet.

Tomorrow would be the day the wire file waited for a green light and the day the FBI knocked on a door at a storage unit that still smelled like cardboard. It would be a day Mrs. Keene watered roses and a hawk watched a fence and a man printed an email he will not file correctly. It would be a day I would drive without a headset in the passenger seat. It would be a day that belonged to itself.

Sleep came like a visitor who had decided to stay.

Florida Drive

Morning brought the kind of bright that keeps its voice low. The porch camera light was steady. The inbox was quiet. The calendar had one word written in my hand with a square around it. Move.

The PODS truck arrived five minutes early and idled at the curb like a patient animal. Two white containers slid into the driveway with a grace that felt at odds with the clank and groan of the lift. East Texas Moving rolled up right behind it, box truck door flying, two men and a woman in matching shirts stepping down with that cheerful competence that belongs to people who do hard things before breakfast.

"Morning, Ms. Mercer," their lead said. He had the biceps of a man who trusts straps more than heroics. "Walk us through zones and labels."

I showed them the color code my late night brain had invented. Blue for kitchen, green for books, red for memories, yellow for clothes, white for the things I would not put into a box no matter who asked. We set the runners, taped the corners, and the house began that soft transformation good movers know. Cardboard propped, doors pinned open, a hallway that turns into a sensible river.

They introduced themselves without making a production of it. Clay on the lift. Tasha in the kitchen. Marco in the garage. Tasha shook out a roll of paper like a flag, then wrapped my mother's pie plate as if it were a contract. "Corners take hits," she said. "We pad corners and the universe behaves."

By nine, the first container was half full and the living room looked like it had never had a couch.

"Faster than I figured," I said.

Clay smiled without showing teeth. "Most folks are," he said. "You did the prep. Prep makes speed."

I wrapped the last stack of plates in big sheets, exactly the way the internet taught me, then let Tasha tap the corners to her standard. She nodded once. Approval from a professional is a small solar panel. It charges a lot.

Marco made a list out loud while he loaded the garage shelves. "Tools, holiday, camping, memory." He stopped at a shoe box and looked at me. I opened it and saw letters in my grandmother's hand. We moved the box to the white label stack. Some things do not ride with tools.

At nine thirty my phone rang. The private banker on the number on the card, code phrase clean, voice warm. "Verification cleared," he said. "Wire released. Parking complete at the custodian per CPA instruction. Treasury-only money market, then the ladder goes out tomorrow. You are fully funded and fully boring. Congratulations."

There is a heat that moves across the scalp when the world tilts one more click into a new position. I felt that heat and did not try to stop it.

"Thank you," I said. "Please stay boring."

"Every day," he said, and hung up so the conversation would not get fancy.

I stood in the middle of the kitchen and let the sentence make its circle. The money is there. It is parked where it cannot be tempted. It will do its job while I do mine.

Tasha slid a drawer out of the buffet and raised an eyebrow at the tangle of cords every modern life knits. "Trash, donate, mystery," she said. We made piles and the house exhaled. Clay strapped the first container and sealed it. The second swallowed the bedroom like a polite beast. The crew breathed steady, hands sure, the kind of people you do not have to supervise. They loaded the garage with a tenderness that felt like theater and church.

A text from the PODS dispatcher buzzed. Pickup can be moved to this afternoon if you prefer. Reply YES EARLY. I looked at the house, at the crew that was about to outrun my anxiety, and typed back. YES EARLY.

Clay checked his clipboard and nodded. "You will be free by two, ma'am." He is probably not a man who says ma'am to everyone, but he said it to me like a fence.

I called Ms. Hall to tell her the containers would leave early. She smiled through the line. "Good. Less porch time is better. What is your travel plan?"

"Farewell loop in Wills Point and Terrell," I said. "Then home to load Rusty, then head east. I will drive through the night if the rain stays quiet."

"I will tell Laird your route," she said. "He can make boredom happen in the background."

I called my landlord to confirm the walk through. He would swing by after the PODS left, check the lawn, check the walls, shake my hand in the doorway. "Do not worry about nail holes," he said. "Leave me the can of paint and the color name. I will brag to the next tenant that you were tidy."

He asked where to send the deposit. I told him the UPS box. He laughed and said it was the first time a mailbox looked like a bodyguard.

The second container closed at one forty. The crew signed the inventory, I signed their timesheet, and they folded the blankets in a way that made me want to learn something about folding.

"Thank you," I said.

"Drink water," Tasha said, and pressed a cold bottle into my hand. Her tone made the advice feel like a receipt.

I watched the lift take both containers back onto the truck. The yard looked like a yard again, and the house looked like a page with most of the words erased. I grabbed my tote, checked the windows, set the alarm, and stepped into the bright sun with the feeling that the air was new but polite about it.

Goodbye to Wills Point needed no witnesses. I started at Ship & Print, because small towns put pieces of themselves on shelves and call it retail. The bell over the door was the sort that rings as if it lives in a poem. Inside, the owner Kathy waved and pointed toward the vendor cubbies along the wall.

"New candles from Be The Light Wax Trade," she said. "Whitney dropped a batch off yesterday. Original Visuals sent a few mugs too. She said they are the ones with the old Terrell water tower drawn a little wonky on purpose."

I ran a hand over a label and let a tester whisper cedar into the air. A rack of local honey gleamed. There were cards with pressed flowers, a display of key fobs that said things like Be Kind and Feed The Cat. A table held stickers for kids and a stack of church cookbooks that looked like they knew secrets about butter. I picked a candle that smelled like orange and clean linen, a set of thank you cards, and one of the mugs with the wonky tower.

At the counter I paid cash because it felt like the correct way to say goodbye to shelves that have been kind to me.

"Headed out for a while," I told Kathy.

"We will keep your spot in the line if you come back," she said. It sounded like a blessing with inventory management built in.

Back in the car I let Moore Street in Terrell roll through my mind, then pointed the Soul west for a few minutes, then south, then west again. Between Wills Point and Terrell there is a stretch of thinking, long enough to let the two towns turn into separate rooms in the same house. Past pastures. Past the Elmo feed store that smells like hay and hope. Past mailboxes that hold more news than they should.

Terrell met me with brick and sky. The Heart of Avon window was staged like a sermon about light. I went in this time and told the owner Erin her colors could cure a day. She laughed and said she would bottle the cure if she could. We traded two sentences about rain and mascara and then I kissed the air and left.

Akins Insurance Agency sat bright with big windows that let every hour in. No blinds. Nothing to hide. I parked and walked in because some goodbyes deserve eye contact. The lobby smelled like paper and shampoo, a smell I will always trust.

"Rachel," Casi, the owner said, smiling with her whole face.

"I wanted to thank you," I said. "For answering phones when the wind blows. For those monthly networking nights you hosted. I am not even an entrepreneur and I still had a blast. I met people. I remembered that towns work because women decide they do."

They laughed like bells. Someone slipped a cookie from a tray into a napkin and pressed it into my hand the way aunts do. We signed a school fundraiser card, I left a donation that would still feel generous if I were not rich, and I hugged the woman who should have been my aunt in another life. Outside, the windows threw back a version of me that looked ready to go.

Terrell Coffee Co gave me a cup that steamed like punctuation. I sat for three minutes at the corner table that had seen every version of my face. A man at the counter ordered something complicated and smiled at the barista like she was the only weather that mattered. I left a tip that would be kind even if I were not secretly a person with a Treasury ladder.

Whisked Away Bake House had a tray of chocolate chip cookies that looked like they had practiced for this day. I bought two and ate one while it was still warmer than physics requires. The other went into the bag for later. Sugar and butter have a job. They do it.

Lunch at Lula Mae's Bistro felt exactly right for a day when the bank had said the quiet version of congratulations. I sat alone, back to the wall, the way Ms. Hall would prefer. The server brought water without asking, and when I ordered steakbites with fries and Bearnaise, she smiled the smile of a person who understands a ritual even if she does not know its origin.

The plate arrived like a memory. The first bite took me straight to a kitchen on a Saturday with my mother at the stove and my father at the table telling a story about a hawk or a carburetor. My eyes stung in that way that has nothing to do with onions. I ate slowly. I put a fry into the little lake of sauce and let salt and fat and tarragon do the heavy lifting my heart could not do for itself.

When I signed the check, the pen felt heavier than a pen. I thanked the server by name and left a tip that made her blink and then try not to look back at me. I prefer that kind of gratitude. Quiet. Private. Strong.

Hickory Roots BBQ sat where it always sits, smelling like weather and smoke and holidays. I ordered ribs and potato salad to go because I had a long road inside my day and wanted the kind of food that knows how to sit in a passenger seat without complaint. The man at the counter put extra napkins into the bag without asking. He has seen the future of many shirts.

The sun had leaned just past its bravest place when I walked back to the car. In the corner of the lot, a silver Tahoe idled with a dent in the rear quarter panel. My stomach did a small and specific flip. That same dent had been at the UPS store two days ago. It had been near the bank this morning. A dent is a signature a person does not choose.

I sat in the car and did not turn the key. I unlocked my phone and opened the Bluetooth list. Devices pinged. My car. My earbuds. Two things with numbers for names that could belong to the restaurant or to the man who sells screen protectors three doors down. Then a third line appeared. AirTag_7F9. The letters did the opposite of what steakbites had done.

I did not panic. Panic is a stranger I do not invite in. I called Laird. He answered on the second ring.

"I have a Tahoe with a dent and a new AirTag," I said.

"Copy," he said. "I am three hours out. Special Agent Garrison is closer. Thirty minutes. She is on the way. Tran can stop by if traffic be-haves. Do not leave the lot. Step out of the car slowly, lock it, and walk inside Pop's Chicken. Sit at a window. Order iced tea you do not have to drink."

I did exactly what he said. The server brought tea with lemon. I touched the glass to say thank you and left it to sweat on the table. The Tahoe idled. A man in a cap looked down at his phone and then up at the lot and then down again. He did not look at me. He looked at the world like it owed him clarity and had been withholding it.

Garrison arrived in a dark sedan that could have been a rental. She parked two rows over and walked in with the casual attention of a person buying a sandwich before a long drive. She is small and alert, the sort of woman whose ponytail tells you she has work to do and would like the day to stay out of her way. She is out of the Dallas office. She is not a Terrell person. Today she chose Terrell because that is where the problem chose to stand.

She set a badge on the table edge where only I could see it and spoke like we were two friends deciding between soups. "This is your bumper as of ten this morning," she said quietly, holding up a photo on her phone. "No tracker. We will look again."

A second agent came in five minutes later. I had never seen him before but I could tell he was with Garrison. He didn't look toward me. He ordered coffee and sat two tables back facing the lot. A third man I did not know either took a spot near the door. If they were actors, they had rehearsed being furniture.

Garrison' phone buzzed. Under the plate. Magnetic. Then a photo. A small gray coin wedged near the license plate light. A different brand from before. Smart people learn from failure. Smart cowards do too. She wrote on a small pad and tore the page off. A number. A place. "Drive to the Terrell Police Department on Highway 34," she said softly. "Use the route I text. I will coordinate from here. If the Tahoe follows, we will let a decoy collect him. You will park in visitors and walk inside. Tell the desk you are here for a federal contact. Hands visible. Eyes forward. Look like a woman running errands."

"Copy," I said.

I paid for the tea and left a tip like the tea had been a full dinner. I walked to the car, buckled in, and eased out of the lot with my breathing in its lanes. The Tahoe didn't move at first. It moved when I hit the second light. A text from Garrison. He is behind you. I have it.

I turned into the Terrell PD lot, parked in a visitor spot, and went inside. The lobby smelled like powdered cleaner and tired coffee. The desk sergeant looked up.

"I am here to check in with a federal contact," I said. "They asked me to wait inside."

He picked up the phone, dialed, listened, and nodded. "Have a seat. An agent is on the line."

A side room opened. A plain phone sat on a small table with a notepad and a pen that worked. The line clicked.

"Tran," the voice said. Not in person. Calm on a wire. "You did fine. Garrison just pulled the Tahoe for an equipment violation. We have the plate and the driver's ID. That is all we have right now. No labels yet. You will wait there while she runs the stop."

"Understood," I said. I watched the clock do its honest job.

Seven minutes. The line clicked again.

"Update. Warning issued. The driver is texting a number we already know from the rumor channels, but we do not have a full read yet. Your job is simple. Leave by the south exit in five minutes. Take the side streets home. No direct route. If you feel watched, come back to this lobby and call the desk. Do not engage anyone."

"Can I go home after that?" I asked.

"Yes," Tran said. "Load the cat. Pack what you planned. Keep your movements ordinary. We will keep eyes on the wrong car so the right car gets quiet."

The door opened a crack. The desk sergeant leaned in. "You are clear to roll when you are ready, ma'am."

I thanked him for a lobby that smelled like work and walked out into the air that felt like someone had closed a door on my behalf and done it kindly.

At home I pulled into the driveway and let the quiet be loud. I walked in and Rusty made the noise that means he knows a crate is coming out. I put him in his travel crate with a blanket that smells like the old house and the new promise. He complained for one verse, then accepted that he was a passenger and not the driver.

I checked the windows, stove, back door stick, and the cabinet with the binder. I set a note on the counter for the landlord with the spare garage remote and a packet of lightbulbs because I am the kind of woman who cannot leave a man without a lightbulb. I laid the Ship & Print mug on top of the white label box marked kitchen to remind myself that goodbyes can be useful.

Mr. Beasley knocked as promised. We did a slow walk through. He pointed at a scuff and told me not to worry. He looked at the roses and said Mrs. Keene has a gift with water. He handed me an envelope with the deposit, less the last utilities, and told me to text him if the mailbox gods fail. We shook hands twice. Some exits prefer two handshakes.

I looked around the living room for the last time. The empty made sense. The walls said thank you without words. I turned the porch light off because it was not my porch light to leave on anymore.

I locked the door. I stood still for three beats. I touched the door with my fingertips and thanked it for holding it. I gave Mr. Beasley the key and then I got in the car.

The radio found a song that fit the moment without calling attention to itself. The sky kept its blue. I merged onto the highway that has held my tires so many times it knows my alignment by heart.

Highway 64 from Wills Point is a familiar first chapter. Canton first, where First Monday lives even when it sleeps. I pulled off near the flea market grounds for fuel stop number one. The pump clicked, the card reader blinked, a man in a hat nodded without turning it into a conversation. I checked Rusty. He blinked slowly like the patient animal he is. I topped off windshield fluid because bugs have their own schedules and do not care about your plans.

Back on the road the lanes opened. Lindale slid by with quiet pines. Tyler stayed politely to the south. Longview rose with the kind of earnestness that builds yards and welds bridges. I kept a sensible speed. I kept my thoughts where my hands were.

Marshall was next, red brick and memory, then the state line arrived with a small thrill that never gets old. Louisiana held out its hand and I took it.

Shreveport was stop number two. I used the clean station on the east side where the lights are bright enough to count by. Rusty drank water like a polite guest. I ate half a rib standing next to the car and laughed because there was no one to scold me. A trucker said the rib smelled like someone loved me. I told him a man at Hickory Roots in Terrell knows how to hand a stranger a good evening.

I drove. Ruston and Monroe passed, then Rayville and a wide sky. The river at Vicksburg shimmered like a medal earned by a long race that no one watched.

Clouds stacked ahead of Jackson like chairs at the end of a church supper. The first heavy drops were polite. The second wave forgot how to be polite. Spray from the semis built a gray wall and the wipers did their best impression of a small choir trying to sing a big song. My shoulders crept up. I told them to go back home. I eased back five miles an hour and left a space no one could mistake for an invitation.

A pickup threw a sheet of water across my windshield and for one breath the world went white. I did not touch the brake. I counted to three and the world returned, damp and chastened. I took the next exit and parked under the awning of a closed tire shop until the worst of the temper moved east. Rusty meowed once like he had an opinion about weather. I agreed with him and fed him a single treat for being alive.

Jackson was stop number three and a coffee pour that respected my future. I walked Rusty in his carrier to the edge of the sidewalk, let him sniff air that did not belong to a house, then tucked him back in with a promise I intend to keep about screened lanais and morning birds.

At Meridian I angled south on I-59 toward Hattiesburg. Pine stands gathered like choir members who know the alto line and are proud of it. The tires hummed the key of travel. I did not sing. I listened.

Hattiesburg was stop number four and a bathroom so clean I wanted to send a thank you card. I bought a bottle of water for me and a small one for the cat. A woman at the register called me honey without needing to own me. Outside, a young couple argued softly about a map on a phone. I told them I-10 would be easier if they liked bridges. They thanked me like I had given them a recipe.

Night likes to pretend it is important. I treated it like a mile marker.

Mobile, Alabama opened ahead with lights and the smell of water. I rolled onto I-10 and east felt like a word I could say without apology. I saw the beaver sign for a Buc-Ee's down the way and laughed. I didn't need a wall of jerky tonight. I needed a road and a cat who believed in me.

Pensacola greeted me with a sign that knows how to wave without being corny. I stopped for a stretch that included a look up at stars that did not know my name and loved me anyway. Back on the road, I let the cruise control do what it was made to do.

Near Tallahassee I pulled into a bright station for a quick restroom stop and a check of the tires. The air gauge hissed its tiny truth and I topped one by two pounds. I looked at Rusty and told him he was brave. He accepted the compliment with a chin lift.

As Lake City approached, my phone buzzed with a Dallas number. I let it ring once so my breath could find its lane, then answered the speaker with the safe phrase.

"Ms. Mercer," the voice said. Not a sergeant. Not a clipboard. "Special Agent Garrison. Courtesy update. The county bomb squad completed a first look at the package recovered from your porch. The interior had a consumer microphone and a SIM that never registered, plus a note with a vendor code we are tracking out of Mesquite. That code lines up with a purchase order number on a locker at a storage facility. We are coordinating with Wills Point PD and will keep your counsel in the loop. Nothing further needed from you tonight. Sleep if you can."

A lead. Not a net. A thread. I pressed the hands-free button twice and let the words stroke my nervous system the right direction. "Thank you," I said. "Please keep the boring parts loud."

"That is the plan," Garrison said, and the line went quiet in a way I trusted.

I rolled through Lake City and turned south on I-75. Florida felt like a word I could spell with my shoulders. I hit the hands-free button and called my parents.

"Hey, you two," I said. "I need to tell you something big."

My mother's voice softened. "Are you safe?"

"I am," I said. "But I have been sitting with a decision for a while. I am taking a break from MetroCare and a short-term contract in Florida. I found a furnished place for a few months so I can rest, write, and get my feet under me. It is something I need to do."

Silence. Then my father cleared his throat. "Why didn't you tell us sooner?"

"Because I was not sure yet," I said. "I didn't want to worry you or invite opinions before I had the basics set. I needed to make the choice on my own two feet. I have housing lined up, mail handled, and a plan. I will send the address as soon as I am settled."

Mom exhaled like she had been holding air for both of us. "Do what gives you peace," she said. "We are proud of you. Call me when you park and I will pray over the kitchen phone like I do."

Dad went practical. "Watch for troopers near Gainesville. Keep water in the car. Quarters for tolls, even if the world thinks it is fancy now."

"I will," I said. "And I will come back to Houston soon for a weekend. We will do steaks and baseball and I will bring Rusty to judge you both."

"Deal," he said, and I could hear his smile.

"I will call when I park for real," I added. "Love you."

"Love you," they said together.

I ended the call. The road opened in front of me like it had been waiting. Tradition sleeps in small advice.

Dawn finally made its case. The trees found edges again. I could feel rust on the underside of fear flaking off in small pieces that did not need a trash can. I drove the last miles like a person arriving and not escaping.

At a quiet neighborhood on a quiet street near Ocala, I found a furnished rental that had said yes to me without asking for more story than I had in my pocket. I parked under a tree that could learn to be a friend. I carried Rusty in and let him explore the baseboards while I stood in the center of the living room and listened to the house breathe.

I set my tote on the counter and took out the notebook. I wrote one line.

Hello.

I opened the bag from Hickory Roots and ate the last rib cold because some meals are communion whether they are hot or not. I looked out at the small patio beyond the sliding door. It didn't yet have a pool. It had a sky that looked willing.

I sat on the couch and closed my eyes. Not to sleep. To mark the day when the map in my head became a road under my tires and a key in my hand.

No trumpet. No headline. A car that did what it was told, a cat who forgave the trip, a ledger that will not blink, and a woman who will learn how to be a neighbor all over again.

Florida, I am here. Keep my secret like a good porch keeps a package from the rain. I will keep my word to myself. I will build the rest from the inside out.

Stay In Touch

Thank you for reading. I would love to hear from you.

Website
www.CeciliaWichmann.com

Email
contact@ceciliawichmann.com

Entrepreneur socials
Facebook, Instagram, TikTok, Threads: **@CeciliaWSpeaks**

Music socials
Facebook, Instagram, TikTok, Threads: **@TheCeciliaWichmann**

Wichmann & Co, LLC
Website: www.WichmannAndCo.com
Email: hello@wichmannandco.com
Social: **@WichmannAndCo**

www.ingramcontent.com/pod-product-compliance
Lightning Source LLC
Chambersburg PA
CBHW071107100726

47908CB00008B/2291